Titles by Jaci Burton

RIDING WILD

RIDING TEMPTATION

RIDING ON INSTINCT

RIDING THE NIGHT

WILD, WICKED, & WANTON

BOUND, BRANDED, & BRAZEN

THE PERFECT PLAY

CHANGING THE GAME

TAKING A SHOT

Anthologies

UNLACED

(with Jasmine Haynes, Joey W. Hill, and Denise Rossetti)

EXCLUSIVE

(with Eden Bradley and Lisa Renee Jones)

LACED WITH DESIRE

(with Jasmine Haynes, Joey W. Hill, and Denise Rossetti)

NAUTI AND WILD

(with Lora Leigh)

continued . . .

BOUND, BRANDED, & BRAZEN

"Burton is a master at sexual tension!"   —*RT Book Reviews*

"As always Jaci Burton delivers a hot read."   —*Fresh Fiction*

"Not just a sexy, get-the-body-humming read, but also one that melds the sensual with the all-important building of intimacy and relational dynamics between partners."   —*Romance: B(u)y the Book*

RIDING ON INSTINCT

"Kudos and beyond for Ms. Burton's best book yet! I cannot wait to see what comes next!"   —*Fallen Angels Reviews*

"Everything about *Riding on Instinct* is picture-perfect and I stayed up half the night, unable to put it down until finishing the very last word."   —*Romance Junkies*

"Another smokin'-hot Wild Riders story you will love reading."
            —*Fresh Fiction*

RIDING TEMPTATION

"Full of intrigue, sexual tension, and exhilarating release. Definitely a must-read."   —*Fresh Fiction*

"*Riding Temptation* has it all—action, suspense, romance, and sensuality all wrapped up in a story that will keep you on the edge of your seat and have you clamoring for the next story in the Wild Riders series!"
            —*Wild On Books*

"Kudos to Ms. Burton for creating this exciting new series!"
            —*Romance Junkies*

RIDING WILD

"A wild ride is exactly what you will get with this steamy romantic caper. This sexy and sizzling-hot story will leave you breathless and wanting more."   —*Fresh Fiction*

"A nonstop thrill ride from the first page to the last! Grab a copy of *Riding Wild* and take your own ride on the wild side of life!"
—*Romance Junkies*

"What an exciting and wonderful book!"   —*The Romance Studio*

"*Riding Wild* is a must-read for anyone who loves sexy romances filled with plenty of action and suspense."   —*Kwips and Kritiques*

WILD, WICKED, & WANTON

"*Wild, Wicked, & Wanton* starts off with a bang and never lets up!"
—*Just Erotic Reviews*

"This is the best erotic novel I have ever read! I absolutely loved it!"
—*Fresh Fiction*

"Jaci Burton's *Wild, Wicked, & Wanton* is an invitation to every woman's wildest fantasies. And it's an invitation that can't be ignored."
—*Romance Junkies*

continued . . .

TAKING
a
SHOT

JACI BURTON

HEAT | NEW YORK

THE BERKLEY PUBLISHING GROUP
Published by the Penguin Group
Penguin Group (USA) Inc.
375 Hudson Street, New York, New York 10014, USA

Penguin Group (Canada), 90 Eglinton Avenue East, Suite 700, Toronto, Ontario M4P 2Y3,
Canada (a division of Pearson Penguin Canada Inc.) • Penguin Books Ltd., 80 Strand, London
WC2R 0RL, England • Penguin Group Ireland, 25 St. Stephen's Green, Dublin 2, Ireland (a
division of Penguin Books Ltd.) • Penguin Group (Australia), 250 Camberwell Road, Camberwell,
Victoria 3124, Australia (a division of Pearson Australia Group Pty. Ltd.) • Penguin Books India
Pvt. Ltd., 11 Community Centre, Panchsheel Park, New Delhi—110 017, India • Penguin Group
(NZ), 67 Apollo Drive, Rosedale, Auckland 0632, New Zealand (a division of Pearson New
Zealand Ltd.) • Penguin Books (South Africa) (Pty.) Ltd., 24 Sturdee Avenue, Rosebank,
Johannesburg 2196, South Africa

Penguin Books Ltd., Registered Offices: 80 Strand, London WC2R 0RL, England

This book is an original publication of The Berkley Publishing Group.

PUBLISHING HISTORY
Heat trade paperback edition / March 2012

Library of Congress Cataloging-in-Publication Data

Burton, Jaci.
Taking a shot / Jaci Burton. — Heat trade pbk. ed.
p. cm.
ISBN 978-0-425-24552-1
1. Young women—Family relationships—Fiction. 2. Bars (Drinking establishments)—Fiction.
3. Hockey players—Fiction. 4. Creative ability—Fiction. 5. Self-realization—Fiction. I. Title.
PS3602.U776T35   2012   2011040584
813'.6—dc22

PRINTED IN THE UNITED STATES OF AMERICA

10 9 8 7 6 5 4 3 2 1

*This book is dedicated to all the amazing readers
who've so wholeheartedly embraced my Play-by-Play series.
Thank you for loving hot sports guys as much as I do.*

ONE

JENNA RILEY WANTED NOTHING TO DO WITH SPORTS.

Which was ironic considering she owned and operated her family's sports bar. Doubly ironic considering one brother was an NFL quarterback and the other brother was a major league baseball player. And triply ironic considering her entire family loved sports of all kinds.

Personally, she was fed up with baseball, hockey, football, NASCAR, basketball, tennis, or anything having to do with a ball or a fast car—unless she was the one behind the wheel driving it. Her distaste for anything sports related likely had something to do with having sports of all kinds shoved down her throat her entire life. And now she lived with it twenty-four hours a day, hearing about it every damn night at work. The bar was constantly filled with sports.

She was in the wrong line of work. She should quit her job and be a roadie for a rock band. Now that's something she could get behind in a major way. She snickered at the thought. Like she could ever be free from the chains of familial responsibility. Ever since her father semi-retired from the bar, Riley's had become her responsibility, which meant, like it or not, sports had become her life. Big-screen televisions broadcast every event, blaring out the voices of obnoxious announcers calling plays behind her, in front of her and to the side of her. Excited fans filled the bar after every game, so not only did she have to listen to the games on television, she also had to bear witness to the patrons' recaps after.

And if that wasn't bad enough, there were the sports networks rehashing player stats and player drafts and all the game replays with analyst commentary.

For someone who hated sports, she had a head full of statistics on every player who had ever played any sport.

Which meant everyone at Riley's loved her.

"Hey, Jenna."

She glanced up from wiping down the bar. Steve Mahoney, one of her regulars, signaled for another beer. She grabbed a bottle, popped off the top, slid it over to him, and added it to his tab.

"You see the game tonight?"

She smiled and nodded. "Of course." As if she had a choice.

"Two goals for Anderson. The Ice scored a winner by picking him up last year, didn't they?"

"Yeah, he's great."

Dick Mayhew got into the action, sliding onto an available bar-stool someone had vacated. He lifted one finger and Jenna grabbed a beer for him.

"He and Eddie make a hell of a team," Dick said. "I think they're unbeatable."

Steve nodded. "I think we have a serious shot at the cup this year. What do you think, Jenna?"

Jenna thought she'd like to extricate herself from this conversation and refill some of her customers' drinks down at the other end of the bar. Instead, she did what she always did when talk of sports came up. She grinned and leaned her elbows against the bar and did her best PR. "I think you're right. Anderson is quick on his skates and he's magic with his shots. It's like he knows right where to put them. I've never seen anyone who can shoot a puck like he can. He has no fear going to the boards. He's as tough as they come. And we already know Eddie is a proven winner at right wing. That's why the Ice have held on to him as long as they have. Together they make a hell of a duo. With Victor at left wing, they're an unbeatable trio. Their combined stats on goals are off the charts."

"Not to mention power plays. When one is down, the other two pick up the slack," Steve said, and he and Dick launched into their own conversation, which freed up Jenna to grab a few drinks for her other customers and see to the bar orders from the waitresses who served the clients throughout Riley's.

Riley's always packed in people like sardines after a game, which meant Jenna lost all track of time. She'd been here since before noon and it was now midnight. Her feet hurt, she smelled like food and alcohol, and she was ready to go home, fall into bed, and sleep for twenty-four hours.

Too bad she had to be here tomorrow and start all over again.

It was mid-week. Maybe people would start clearing out soon. After all, it was a work night.

But the sounds of raucous cheers made her cringe. She took a quick glance at the door and her worst fears were realized when she saw a half dozen of the St. Louis Ice hockey players stroll through the front door.

Crap. Now no one would leave until closing time, which meant almost three more hours for her and her team. And the players were probably hungry. She headed into the kitchen.

"Players just walked in," she said to Malcolm, her head cook.

Malcolm, who had the patience of a saint and always took things in stride, just nodded. "I'll get out the steaks."

She laughed, shook her head, and went back to the bar. She refilled a few drinks and decided to let her waitresses handle the players. She'd go over there and say hello when she had a free minute. Right now she was slammed filling drink orders. Something about players coming in hopped up her customers' excitement level and made everyone thirsty.

It was good for business, though. She loved having the players frequent Riley's. She had Mick and Gavin—and Elizabeth—to thank for that.

"You look busy."

She lifted her head and stared into the steel gray eyes of Tyler Anderson. He wore his raven hair a little long and shaggy, just the way she liked . . .

No. She did not like this guy. He was a jock, a hockey player, and she most definitely did not like sports players. Especially not Ty.

"Yeah, Ty. I'm a little busy here. What can I do for you?"

"Thought you could use some help. Why don't you have two bartenders?"

"Because I can handle it by myself. Is Lydia taking care of your table?"

"She is. We're fine. Steaks are ordered."

She planted her palms against the side of the bar, sucking in a quick breath. "Then what do you need?"

He came around the open end of the bar. "Nothing. I came here to help you."

Her eyes widened. "What? Get out of here. You can't be back here."

"Sure I can. You need help."

"No, I don't." She shoved at him, but she might as well try to move a car. "Go away."

The crowd thickened around the bar as soon as Ty made himself at home back there. He filled drink orders while Jenna stared dumbfounded. He popped the tops off bottles of beer like a pro, poured hard liquor, fixed mixed drinks, and operated like he knew what the hell he was doing behind a bar. He then took the customer's money or credit card and handled her cash register, too.

What. The. Hell.

He slid a glance her way. "You have customers at the other end of the bar."

She finally gave up and took care of her patrons while Ty drummed up more business.

"Hey, Ty, your steak is ready," Malcolm said a half hour later.

"Just leave it behind the bar. I'll eat it here."

"You got it."

Jenna rolled her eyes and watched as Ty ate his steak standing up while he visited with the guys at the bar, then went back to serving drinks.

By two thirty she called for last round and everyone began to make their way out the door. Jenna started cleaning up while the last of her patrons left. She called taxis for those who needed them, helped the waitresses bus tables, and cleared her bar registers.

She let the waitresses go, locked the front door, and headed into the kitchen. The kitchen had been cleaned up, the other cooks and the busboys had left, and only Malcolm remained—with Ty—the two of them talking about football.

"What are you still doing here?" she asked, looking at Ty.

"Sorry. Got involved talking postseason with Malcolm."

"Who is now leaving," Malcolm said with a yawn. "Want me to walk you out, Jenna?"

"No, thanks. I've got a few things left to do."

Malcolm narrowed his dark brown eyes on her. "Go home. Don't stay here all night doing paperwork."

She laughed. "I don't intend to."

She locked the door behind him, then turned to tell Tyler to go, but he wasn't in the kitchen. She found him in the bar pouring a whiskey.

"Hey. Last call was an hour ago."

He smiled at her, tipped the glass to his lips, and downed the drink in one swallow, then put money on the top of the bar. She grabbed the money and slipped it into her pocket.

"Pocketing the profits, I see."

"No, smart-ass. I already closed out the register. I'll add it in tomorrow."

He shook his head and leaned against the bar. "This is how you talk to your customers?"

"You stopped being a customer when you came behind my bar and served up drinks."

"You needed help."

"No, I didn't."

He folded his arms. "Are you always this bitchy, or just to me?"

"Just to you. Now get your ass out of here so I can finish closing up."

He didn't seem insulted, just cracked a smile instead, showing off perfectly straight white teeth. Weren't hockey players supposed to be missing teeth because of all their fights on the ice? Why did he have to be so gorgeous? The damn man made her panties wet and had a habit of showing up here fairly regularly, which did make her bitchy because he hit all her hot buttons and she hadn't had sex in a really long time.

She needed to get laid soon. Real soon. By someone who didn't play sports.

She hit the master light switch, bathing the bar in darkness.

"Scared of the dark?"

She jumped, not realizing he was right behind her until his breath swept across the back of her neck. She'd turned the heat down so now she was freezing, but his body was warm. She resisted the urge to move in close to him. She bent down to grab her purse and sweater, brushing her butt against his crotch. He felt solid. Hard. Yummy.

Damn. She straightened, her eyes adjusting to the lack of light. "No."

"No, what?" he asked.

"I'm not afraid of the dark."

He turned her around to face him. The light from the full moon cast him in grayish shadow. She could see his face, though, as he cocked a grin. "Too bad."

"Why?"

"Then you might have to lean on me to protect you."

She took a step back. "Why the hardcore press here, Ty?"

"Come on, Jenna. You're not a kid. You know why. I've been coming to the bar a lot, hanging around. I like you."

"I don't like you."

He laughed. "Liar. I see the way you look at me."

"You are so full of yourself, Anderson. Go pick up another girl. I'm not the least bit interested in you." She brushed past him and headed to the door, waiting for him to meet her there so she could set the alarm.

He did, his coat in hand. She had her fingers on the keypad ready to turn on the alarm.

"Wait a second," he said.

"Did you forget something?"

"Yeah." He hauled her into his arms before she could take her next breath, and his mouth came down on hers.

For a fraction of a second she thought about objecting and pushing him away, but hell, it had been a really long time since she'd been kissed. It was February, cold as the polar ice cap outside, and Tyler's lips were warm. His body was hot and as he folded her against him, she felt that heat seep into her.

She dropped her purse and coat and went with it, letting his lips claim hers.

It was just as she'd imagined it would be, and okay, she'd thought about this a lot. His mouth was firm and demanding, a hint of whiskey on his lips. He didn't kiss like a sissy, thank God. He wasn't hesitant at all. He just took the kiss, sliding his tongue inside her mouth to wrap around hers.

She tingled all over, her toes curled, her panties got wet, and her sex pulsed with a roaring need. If he put his hands down her pants, in two or three strokes she could come. The kiss was that good.

He reached up and cupped her breast, and she moaned against his lips, pressing her breast into his hand. She wanted more, wanted it all, and wanted it right now. Her mind was filled with images of him lowering her to the floor in the back of the bar, or bending her over the pool table.

But that would be going against everything she wanted. And didn't want.

She wasn't going to let him have it. Not this guy. Not ever this guy. She pressed her hands to his chest and broke the kiss.

"Stop. We can't do this."

He stepped back, his eyes dark with passion.

"Why not?"

She fought for breath, for her bearings and some semblance of sanity.

"Because I don't want to." She licked her lips, bent down, and grabbed her coat and purse. She turned away from him and with shaky hands she set the alarm, walked outside, and locked the front door, Ty right behind her.

She started to walk away but he grabbed her wrist, burning her with a look that melted her to the cold cement sidewalk.

And then he smiled at her. "Good night, Jenna."

She pivoted and walked to her car, conscious of him standing there watching her. He waited, hands in his coat pockets while she got in and drove away.

Bastard. Her body was on fire from his kiss and she was going to have to take care of herself when she got home tonight.

She was never going to let him kiss her again.

TY WAITED UNTIL JENNA PULLED OUT OF THE PARKING lot and onto the street before he climbed into his car to head back to his place.

He had known Jenna for almost a year now, had met her through his agent, Elizabeth, and Jenna's brother Gavin.

Jenna wasn't at all his type. Oh, she was beautiful, all right, but she was skinny with small breasts. He liked his women full and lush with big tits.

He liked his women with long hair he could run his fingers through. Jenna had short, spiky black hair that had weird purple tips at the end, which was kind of wild and funky.

Jenna had multiple piercings in her left ear and that tiny little diamond on her nose. It always made him wonder what other parts of her body were pierced. And those tattoos he'd only gotten glimpses of intrigued him. He wanted time to explore them, to study them, to strip her down and see where else she was tattooed.

But her eyes were what really drew him to her. They were an amazing sapphire blue that were so expressive and so vulnerable, even though she liked to play the tough chick.

Okay, so maybe she was a little different. And maybe he was drawn to how utterly different she was.

So he played with her, irritated her, and baited her because he knew he could get a rise out of her.

Not interested? Bullshit. That kiss had told him just how interested she really was. He'd bet if he'd gotten his hands into her panties she'd have been wet.

Just the thought of getting into her panties made his cock throb. He could still taste her on his lips—peppermint and some kind of cherry-flavored lip gloss. He licked his lips, wanted more.

Yeah, he wanted a lot more of Jenna.

And just like in hockey, when the goal was in sight, he never gave up.

TWO

TY FLEW DOWN THE ICE, SKATING PAST THE DEFENDER.
Victor Putinov slid the puck across to him and he took a shot.

Missed. He skirted around the net and fought the defender for
the puck, slamming up against the boards, their sticks in combat for
the prize. The shouts from the home crowd were deafening, spur-
ring him on to scramble.

He lost the fight and skated his ass off after that black disc. When
he was on the ice it was the only thing that mattered to him.

Eddie Wolkowski went after it, skidding to a halt against the
center for Toronto. Ty wanted to beat these guys badly. He liked all
the guys on his former team, but hey, business was business and it
was time to get down to it.

Parker took a shot against Roger "Ice-man" Rantzen, the Ice's
goalie. Roger blocked it and Wolkowski took it and sent it shooting
toward the center. The left wing picked it up and Ty took the charge

across the line, skating in tandem with Toronto's center. It was a race to see who could get there faster.

Ty was a damn good skater and had the stamina to beat his opponent. When the left wing passed the puck to Ty, he took it and passed it to Victor, who fought off the Toronto defenseman, giving Ty time to get into position.

Victor slanted the puck back to Ty. He saw the opening and took a hard shot.

Ty loved when the lamp lit up. The crowd was on its feet and the roar inside the arena never failed to give him chills. He lifted his stick in the air and pumped it up high, then went over to his teammates to celebrate.

They won the game three to one. It had been close. Toronto was a tough opponent.

After the game, he showered and dressed.

"How about a steak at Riley's to celebrate?" Eddie asked.

Ty knew that Eddie had a major crush on Renee, one of the waitresses at Riley's, and that's why he kept suggesting they hit the bar.

And since he liked to irritate the hell out of Jenna, he was up for it. "Sure."

Eddie grinned. At twenty-eight, Eddie was the Ice's golden boy, with his dark blond hair and Nordic features. He was huge at six-five, nearly imposing, but had the freckled face and wide grin of a teenager. He was as good-natured as anyone Ty had ever known. A fierce killer on the ice, Eddie was as gentle as a kitten off it. He was a mix of contradictions, which made it hard for him to get women.

Except for Renee. She'd taken to Eddie right away, and Ty had the feeling Eddie's crush was reciprocated—big time.

They went to the bar with a few of the other guys who said they wanted to unwind with some pool.

As soon as he walked in the door he caught Jenna's eye. She frowned. He grinned.

Game time. Only this was a different kind of game than the one he'd played earlier on the ice.

SECOND VERSE, SAME AS THE FIRST. EVERY NIGHT RAN together until Jenna didn't know what day it was. With hockey season going on and so many rabid fans in attendance at the bar, Jenna ran her legs off serving drinks, and her waitresses were just as busy filling orders.

The logical part of her knew business was good, and in this economy that was an awesome thing. The bar was packed, her customers were happy, and Riley's was making money. She had no business being dissatisfied with her life. If this wasn't what she wanted to do, too bad. She was helping out the family, they had a successful business, and it kept stress off her father, who had suffered a heart attack and subsequent surgery last year. On those rare occasions when he came to the bar he was happy and smiling, and all he had to do was enjoy his friends. She was relieved he was still around after last year's scare.

No complaints, right? Even if Riley's was still primarily her responsibility and the family counted on her to keep it running. It could be a whole lot worse.

"If the Ice keep winning, I'm going to lose ten pounds," one of the witnesses said. "They keep packing in here. And it gets even more crowded when they show up after the home games."

Sure enough, they were here again. More important, Ty was with them.

There were loads of bars near the arena, many that catered to hockey fans. Why did he have to choose hers?

Renee, one of her top waitresses, leaned against the bar and gave her a drink order.

Jenna would be lost without her. Renee was bubbly and pretty in that Barbie doll kind of way—curvy and blonde and petite and all the guys loved her. She had infectious laughter, but she never encouraged any of them, though Jenna was certain Renee had a thing for one of the Ice players. She hadn't acted on it, but there was something about the looks she and Wolkowski exchanged.

It was cute. She'd have to find out what was going on with the two of them.

Jenna grabbed the list and started making drinks. "Your boyfriend is here."

Renee did a quick glance. "I know. I took their drink order. And Eddie's not my boyfriend."

But Renee's cheeks were pink. And she couldn't hide her smile. "Seeing him?"

She shook her head, her curls bouncing. "He hasn't asked me."

"Men are stupid. He's staring at you."

Renee lifted her head to meet Jenna's gaze. "He is?"

"Yeah." She loaded up the drinks on Renee's tray. "So ask him out."

"Nope. If he wants me, he can do the asking."

"You're such a traditional girl."

"Aren't I?" Renee winked and sauntered off.

After Renee left, Jenna had a few moments to breathe. She just couldn't get a freakin' break. Ty's gaze met hers as he pulled off his jacket and headed to a pool table. Every ounce of estrogen in her body surged with joy as his lean, muscled frame settled over one of the tables, pool cue in hand.

Her damn estrogen could just calm the hell down. He might have kissed her, and she might have tingled for hours over it, but that was as far as it was ever going to go. He was sports and that meant no.

He leaned a hip against the pool table and accepted the beer Renee gave him, his body ripped and hard all over as he relaxed and laughed with his friends.

Just the sound of his voice made her nipples harden.

Did you hear that, body? No. No, no, no.

Deciding to ignore him, she went into the kitchen and told Malcolm to start the steak orders, then busied herself with her customers. She would not be interested in Tyler, even if her libido was.

But watching him play pool was more than she could take. She wasn't nearly busy enough. It was late, the crowds had thinned, and it was mostly him and his player buddies, and if she had to wipe down another glass until it sparkled to avoid looking at his ass she was going to hurl said glass against the nearest wall.

Escape wasn't an option since she was still in charge of the bar, and the pool table was off to the left—in her line of sight whenever she had to grab a beer.

She tried not to ogle, but Ty had a great butt. He was good at pool, too. Of course. Jocks were good at everything, which was why their egos often went unchecked, something she found utterly intolerable about sports figures.

Which was why she never intended to date, have sex with, or otherwise get involved with one. She made a concerted effort not to watch him, instead glancing at the clock and the minutes ticking down to closing time. She decided to do hard liquor inventory to keep her mind engaged on something other than Ty.

"Can I get a beer, Jenna?"

She hadn't realized time had passed until Ty pulled up a stool at the bar. She glanced over at the pool table. His friends were nowhere to be found. In fact, the bar was nearly deserted and it was closing time.

Renee waved to her on her way out the door with Malcolm right on her heels.

She was alone in the bar again. With Ty. How had she let that happen?

"Bar's closed."

He skirted around the bar and helped himself. She crossed her arms and glared at him.

"You don't own this place, you know."

He popped off the top and took a long swallow, then let out a grateful sigh. "Pool makes me thirsty, thanks. And no, I don't own this place, but your parents do and they like me."

"Finish your beer so I can get out of here."

He went around and took his seat on the stool again. "What is it about me that you don't like?"

She wiped down the top of the bar, ignoring his question.

"My looks?"

God no. He was panty-dropping good looking. Not that she would ever admit that to him.

"My personality."

Utterly annoying. And charming.

"My manners."

Perfect. He always held the door for women and the elderly. He was respectful, not too loud, and never drank too much. For every beer or whiskey he drank, he followed it up with a large glass of ice water. Some athletes wanted all the attention drawn on themselves. Ty liked to blend into the background, preferring to mix with her clientele, not be a showcase because he was a star on the Ice.

"So tell me, Jenna. What is it about me that bugs you?"

She tossed the rag into the bin and palmed the edge of the bar. "I don't date sports players."

He quirked a brow. "Yeah? Why's that?"

She held her arms out to her sides. "Look at all this, Ty. I'm surrounded by it all day, nearly every day. And then there's Mick and Gavin and all their friends who passed through the house. I've had sports ad nauseum all my life."

He tilted the bottle up to his lips and drank, then handed the empty to her. She tossed it.

"I see. You've had your fill of guys like me."

"Now you're beginning to see the light."

"So I'm damned because of my profession. Out of the running before I've even had a chance."

She nodded. "Yup. You're wasting your time on me. Might as well go find another girl to charm."

He came behind the bar. "What if I don't want another girl? What if I want you?"

Uh-oh. Her body was pinging like a Geiger counter and Ty was radioactive. The closer he got, the hotter she became. She took a step back. "I don't want you."

He stopped, his lips curving in a knowing smile. "You keep saying that, but I don't think I believe you."

"Arrogant men are not appealing."

"I'm not being arrogant. I'm just good at reading signals."

"You are so full of shit." She bent down, grabbed her bag, and held it in front of her like a life preserver. "What signals?"

"You're breathing fast. Your cheeks are flushed. Your pupils are dilated."

"I'm exhausted and out of breath from running around trying to close down this place. And it's hot in here."

He laughed. "It's not hot in here. And you've been standing still."

He had her there. "Go away, Ty. I need to close up." She fumbled in her bag for her keys.

"Go out with me."

She jerked her head up. "What? No. Hell no."

"It wouldn't be so bad. I promise."

"I'd rather have a root canal."

He didn't seem insulted. What would it take to get him angry, to hurt his feelings? To get him the hell out of this bar?

"I promise you that going out with me is way more fun than dental surgery."

"I'm . . . seeing someone."

One perfectly formed brow rose. "You're seeing someone."

"Yes."

"Who?"

"You don't know him."

"How do you know I don't know him if you don't tell me who he is?"

"He's not involved in sports."

"I know a lot of people not in sports, Jenna."

She was digging this hole deeper and deeper. "He's not from around here. And I have to go."

"Got a date?"

"Yes." She pushed on him until he finally budged and headed for the door. She punched in the code and hurried outside, tossing on her jacket to ward off the frigid temps.

Of course he just had to walk her to her car. Damn him for being a gentleman. He'd be a lot easier to not think about if he were a prick.

"A little late for a date, isn't it?" he asked when she got to her car.

"None of your business, Ty."

"So, it's a booty call."

She gasped. "It is not a booty call. It's a date."

"He taking you out to dinner at three a.m.?"

She clamped her lips tightly together.

"The movies, maybe?"

"You're an asshole." She pivoted and got into her car.

"Good night, Jenna."

He stepped back when she peeled out of the lot, and just like the last time, he stood there watching until she drove away.

Damn him for making her think about him, for making her want him.

She'd show him. She'd get herself a guy.

Maybe if she found someone else to go out with—and ultimately have sex with—Ty wouldn't be front and center on her mind.

THREE

TY HADN'T INTENDED TO SHOW UP AT THE RILEYS'
house, but Gavin had invited him.

Sunday dinner was apparently a big deal to the Rileys. Ty had no
family here, but he and Gavin had become friends over the past
months, playing basketball whenever they both managed free days.
That wasn't often though, since Gavin was prepping for the beginning
of the baseball season and Ty was on the road playing hockey. But
every now and then they managed to hang out together, like today,
though the family had held up dinner waiting for Gavin and Elizabeth
to show up.

He'd actually gotten to know Gavin through his agent, Elizabeth
Darnell, who was now Gavin's fiancée. Gavin hadn't liked Ty at all
when he'd first met him, because Ty had flirted with Liz to try to
make Gavin jealous. Apparently it worked since the two of them
were engaged and planning to get married.

But first it was Gavin's older brother Mick's wedding coming up

in a couple weeks if he remembered right. And judging from the
frenzied talking going on between Liz and Tara, Mick's fiancée,
along with Gavin and Mick's mother—it seemed like the wedding
planning was in full force.

Ty was glad he wasn't taking part in it. Weddings were so not his
thing.

He hung out in the living room, drinking beer and talking with
Gavin, Mick, and their dad, along with Nathan, Tara's teenaged son.

This was a nice family. There was a warmth and closeness to this
family that he hadn't felt with his own. Mick told Ty that he and
Tara had decided to make the permanent move to St. Louis, including relocating Tara's business so Nathan could go to school here.
Family was important to them, and even though Mick still played
for San Francisco, it was easier for him to travel, and more important
for Tara and Nathan to be near Mick's family since they had all
become so close.

He understood that. A tight family was a family that stayed together. He wished it had worked out for his parents, but that was a
different situation.

"You're looking good on the ice, Ty."

"Thank you, sir." Ty smiled at Gavin's father, Jimmy Riley.
Jimmy had heart surgery several months back, and ever since he'd
been robust and healthy, had lost weight, and laughed more than
anyone Ty knew. It was like getting a second chance had showed him
how great life was.

"Don't call me sir. Makes me feel old."

"You are old, old man." Mick, who sat on the sofa next to his dad,
nudged him in the ribs.

Tyler wondered if Mick's dad's surgery was a motivating factor in
the whole relocation thing. Almost losing someone you love could
make you alter a lot of life decisions.

"You think I'm old, boy? Ha. Not too old that I can't kick your ass in a game of Horse."

Tara entered the room, crossed her arms, and rolled her eyes. "Here we go."

"I'm young enough to take both of you with one hand tied behind my back," Nathan chimed in.

Jimmy tilted his head back and laughed. "You're teaching that boy well, I see," he said to Mick.

Mick grinned. "Doing my best to make a smart-ass out of him."

"Mick. Language," Tara warned.

"And a quarter for the cuss jar, Dad," Nathan said.

Tyler sat back and soaked it all in. The warmth, the obvious love they all felt for each other. This was what it was like when people genuinely cared for each other. No tension, no walking on eggshells, no pretending things were all right and everyone was happy when they weren't. Because everyone in this house *was* happy.

"Dinner will be served as soon as Jenna gets here," Kathleen said as she entered the room. "She's just waiting for her relief to show up at the bar."

Tyler had wondered if Jenna was going to be here. Now he knew.

She breezed in about twenty minutes later, tossed her purse on the table in the entryway, and flung herself onto the sofa next to her mother. Her mom kissed her cheek.

"Rough day?"

Jenna shrugged and propped her feet on the table. "Nah. Casey was late, as usual, but it wasn't a busy day, so no big deal."

Jenna greeted everyone, and her gaze landed on Tyler. She arched a brow. "What are you doing here?"

"Waiting to eat the great dinner your mother prepared. And Gavin invited me."

Jenna shot Gavin a glare. Ty smirked.

"We played basketball earlier today, so I invited Ty to dinner. You have a problem with that?"

"Why would I care who comes to dinner?" She shrugged and pushed off the couch. "I'm going to get a drink. Anyone want one?"

She left the room and her mother rose, too. "I'll go check the roast and put the potatoes on now that Jenna's here."

"I'll come help you, Mom," Tara said.

"Me, too." Liz got up to follow, and Ty figured that was a signal for girl talk to commence, either about him or about the wedding. Or maybe both.

"What's going on with you and Jenna?" Gavin asked.

"Nothing. I tried to get her to go out with me. She said no."

Mick snorted. "She hates sports and any guy who plays them. Except her brothers, of course."

"Dude. She barely tolerates us and we're family."

Mick nodded at Gavin. "True."

Ty tilted the bottle of beer to his lips and took a long swallow, then nodded. "Yeah. She made it pretty clear I didn't stand a chance."

"Do you like her?"

Ty shifted his gaze to Nathan. "Yeah, I like her."

"Then go for it."

"Kind of like beating my head against a brick wall, kid."

Nathan dragged his gaze away from the soccer game that was on to focus his full attention on Ty. "So? Dad always tells me not to give up on something I want."

Ty didn't plan to give up, but he wasn't going to have this conversation with a teenager and Jenna's brothers. "I'll give it some thought. Thanks for the pep talk."

"Anytime."

Mick grinned over Nathan's head at Ty. "He's right. She's stubborn, but we kind of like you."

"We do, though I don't know why," Gavin added with a wink. "And God knows she never goes out. Give it a shot."

"She said she was seeing someone."

"She's lying," Mick said. "Tara said she's not bringing anyone to the wedding. If she had a guy, she'd have a date. As far as I know she's going solo."

Interesting.

JENNA HID OUT IN THE KITCHEN WITH HER MOTHER until the last item had been dragged into the dining room. Then she had no choice but to join the family—and Ty—in there.

It seemed like every time she turned around, there he was. At the bar, and now at her parents' house. What was it going to take to get rid of this guy? It was bad enough he haunted her fantasies. Did he have to stalk her reality, too?

Of course, since everyone was paired up, and Nathan had such a fierce case of hero worship of Mick that he had to sit next to him, Tyler ended up being seated next to her. The physical attraction she felt for him was intense. She tried to focus on her food, but she had damn good peripheral vision, which meant even glancing at her plate meant she could see his hands—strong and large, with dark hairs that crept up his wrists. He'd pushed the sleeves of his Henley up so she couldn't help but notice his muscled forearms. So instead, she focused on her lap, which meant she'd occasionally steal glances at his thighs, and then her gaze would travel inward toward his—

Stop. She would not stare at his lap, would not imagine him pushing his chair back so she could climb on and rock against him.

For God's sake. She was in her parents' dining room. She would not have sexual fantasies about Ty.

Her cheeks burned with the visual and her head shot up, expecting to find her entire family staring at her.

They weren't. They were engaged in conversation, everyone ignoring her.

Everyone except Ty, of course, who glanced her way with a knowing quirk of his lips.

Bastard.

Maybe she should just have sex with him, get him out of her system, and then she'd never have to think about him again.

"Jenna."

Grateful for the distraction, she looked to Tara. "Yes?"

"We have dress fittings on Tuesday night at seven. Can you make it?"

She relaxed and smiled at her soon-to-be sister-in-law. "Wouldn't miss it. I've already got coverage at the bar that night, so I'm free for the evening."

Tara wiggled in her seat. "I know I shouldn't be this giddy, but with the wedding under two weeks away, I can't help it."

"We're all excited," Jenna's mother said. "It'll be here before you know it."

Then Tara did the unthinkable. "Tyler, will you be available to come to the wedding?"

No. *Please say no.* Maybe he'd have a game.

"What's the date?"

She told him and he paused, mentally calculating the date. "That's a Friday. There's no game that night, so yeah, I'm free."

Tara's eyes sparkled. "We'd love to have you come to the wedding. I know it's last minute, but if you're available, please say you'll be there."

"I don't want to intrude."

Jenna bit her lip.

"Don't be silly. It's not an intrusion. You're friends with Gavin and Mick, and Gavin says you don't have family here. Mick and I would love to have you at our wedding."

Mick cast a grin at Jenna before turning his gaze back to Tyler. "Sure. Come to the wedding. It's going to be a great party."

"Thanks. I'd love to come."

Jenna had a feeling she'd just been set up. By her entire family.

FOUR

ON TUESDAY SHE MET TARA AND ELIZABETH AT THE bridal shop, along with Maggie, one of Tara's best friends from her event planning business, who had flown in to spend the final week and a half with Tara before the wedding. Maggie had taken over the event planning business from Tara in San Francisco.

Maggie was Tara's maid of honor. Liz and Jenna were bridesmaids, and they were all enjoying the final dress fitting before the big day.

"I have to say you're being pretty cool about all this," Elizabeth said as she watched Tara being fitted for her dress. "I'm going to be a freakin' wreck when it's my turn."

Tara smiled as the bridal shop seamstresses put the finishing touches on what Jenna thought was a breathtaking gown.

"I love Mick, and I'm getting my happily ever after. Everything else is just icing on the cake. Besides, I'm an event planner. It's in my nature to stay calm under pressure."

Maggie snorted.

"What?"

"Just wait until it's *the* day. We've done weddings. You know how even the calmest of brides gets. I'm going to be prepared for anything, just in case, but I think you're a simmering volcano waiting to erupt."

Tara lifted her chin. "I am not going to erupt. My emotions are under control."

Liz looked at Jenna, who shrugged. "No clue. Never been married."

"Well, I'll tell you. I have several months to go before my wedding and I already need Valium." Liz glanced over at Tara and Maggie. "Don't look to me to help calm your nerves. I plan to have a bottle of Patrón in my purse that day."

Jenna laughed. "Glad it's you all and not me."

"Don't you laugh over there," Tara said. "Your day will come."

"Are you kidding? I'm not even dating anyone."

"That's not what Ty said."

Her gaze turned to Liz. "What did he say?"

"He told me you shot him down, refused to go out with him, and then you said you were seeing someone."

All eyes settled on her. Fortunately, it was her turn to try on her dress, so she hightailed it into the dressing room in a hurry so she wouldn't have to admit that she wasn't, in fact, seeing anyone. But when she came out with her dress on, Tara, Liz, and Maggie were all waiting for her.

"So who's the guy?" Tara asked.

Didn't it just figure they weren't going to let that subject drop? Jenna blew out a breath. "No one any of you know."

"So why didn't you tell us you were seeing someone?" Liz asked.

"Because it's not serious. I don't tell you all every time I go out on a date."

Tara tilted her head. "Are you bringing him to the wedding?"

"No."

"Why not?" Liz asked.

"We've only gone out a couple times. Definitely not enough to sic the family on him."

"Does he have brothers?" Maggie asked. "Because I'm here alone. A date would be nice."

Jenna laughed. "No idea."

"I could set you up with someone," Liz said to Maggie. "I know a lot of sports figures."

Maggie batted her lashes at Liz. "Really?"

"Really."

"You would turn my wedding into a PR fest for one of your clients?" Tara said with a mock gasp.

"In a heartbeat, sister."

Jenna laughed.

"Hey, do whatever you want, but find me a hunky date," Maggie said. "I'm all in."

"Done," Liz said.

"And speaking of dates," Tara said, "what about Jenna's?"

Damn. She could have sworn they'd gone off topic and this would be forgotten.

"You don't know anything about his family?" Tara asked. "Mom won't like that. Neither will Mick and Gavin."

Web of lies. This is what happened when she made up boyfriends. "I don't know if we'll be seeing each other again. So Mom and Dad have nothing to worry about."

"No chemistry?" Maggie offered.

"Yeah. No chemistry." She was glad for the excuse and the out. She could kiss Maggie right now.

"Well, honey, you're gorgeous. And sexy. I'm sure if this one doesn't work out, there are likely ten guys waiting in line to go out with you."

She met Tara's confident expression and smiled at her.

She was going to have to dig up a real person to date. And by God, she would bring him to the damn wedding. One, to get her family off her back, and two, to make herself stop thinking about Ty.

For all she knew Ty might bring a date of his own. She hoped he would. That would end any residual attraction she felt for him.

After the fittings the four of them went out for dinner, fortunately not at her family's bar.

It was nice to have a night off and actually go out. Usually on her nights off she stayed home, caught up on sleep, or watched television. And she always played music and worked on writing songs. Tonight it was good to get away.

She isolated herself too much. She knew it, realized she should get out more, but she much preferred her apartment and her music.

She didn't really like people all that much, anyway.

Yeah, she was girlfriend material, all right.

"How about that guy?" Liz asked as they settled at a table and ordered a round of drinks.

It took Jenna a few seconds to realize Liz was talking to her. "Huh? What are you talking about?"

"That guy. The one at the bar who's looking at you."

She followed Liz's head motion to a suit type leaning against the bar with a drink in hand. Outstanding in the looks department, with sandy blond hair, straight teeth, and a smile that looked like it had been bleached at the dentist's office.

"Likely dating twenty girls at once and can't keep their names straight. No thanks."

"And how do you know this?" Liz asked.

"Bourbon, straight up."

Tara frowned. "What does that mean?"

"I can tell a lot about a guy by what he drinks."

"Occupational hazard?" Liz asked.

"Or a plus, depending on how you look at it. Between the way they scan a room, how they dress, and what they drink, I've got them pegged before they ever say a word."

Liz scooted her chair closer to Jenna's. "Oh, this could be fun. Hot stuff in jeans and black T-shirt, far left side of the bar."

Jenna took a look. "Cheating on his wife."

"Nuh-uh," Maggie said. "How do you know?"

"Too easy. Wedding ring mark on his left hand. And a fresh one at that. You can still see the ridges on his finger."

"What an asshole." Tara sipped her drink, then looked at Jenna. "You're good at this. I would never have noticed that."

"Most women don't, not on initial glance, anyway. They're not all assholes. But a lot of them aren't worth a second look, especially at a bar."

"Because they go there to pick up women?" Liz asked.

"And to get laid."

Tara shook her head. "So cynical. No wonder you don't date much."

"Unless I'm in the mood for sex, I don't really see the point. None of those guys are my type. And a bar isn't a place to meet men."

"Oh, come on." Liz scanned the bar. "There are some serious hotties in here."

Training her gaze into laser-point precision, she pointed it at the male traffic. "Unemployed. Gay. Mama's boy. Bully. Wimp." She turned to them. "Should I go on?"

Tara shook her head. "I think you might be just a wee bit too picky. Are you certain your system is as flawless as you'd like to believe?"

"I'll prove it to you." She smiled at the corporate type they'd singled out for her at the beginning. He graced her with his thousand-watt smile, pushed off the bar, and headed over to them, pulling up a chair and sliding into it.

"Hello, ladies. Enjoying your evening?"

Jenna took the lead. "So far."

"Can I buy you all a drink?"

"Sure." Jenna told them what they were having. Without even turning around, he raised his hand and snapped his fingers for the cocktail waitress. Jenna gritted her teeth.

They all introduced themselves. His name was Craig. He was in hardware technology sales.

"Do you travel?" she asked.

His lips curved. "Quite a bit, as a matter of fact. I'm on the road a lot."

"You must enjoy it."

"It's an adventure. And what about you, Jenna?"

"I'm a bartender."

He held up his drink and tipped it to her. "Nice. I like drinks."

She'd just bet he did.

"And what about the rest of you gorgeous women? What do you do?"

Number one sin. When you're hitting on one woman, you don't also hit up her friends. You ignore them. Craig was hedging his bet, just in case Jenna wasn't the one he decided he wanted to go home with tonight.

"Engaged," Liz said.

"Getting married in a week," Tara said.

"Dating someone," Maggie lied.

Smart Maggie.

Craig scooted his chair closer to Jenna's. Ugh.

"So you're a bartender, huh?"

"I am."

That was the last thing he'd mentioned about her. After that she endured a half hour dissertation all about himself, his career, his aspirations, and how he'd risen to the top of his company's food chain in three short years, including the big quarterly bonus that allowed him to buy his new condo he was certain she'd want to come over tonight and see. She tried to avoid yawning.

She threw some serious "help me" signals at Tara, Liz, and Maggie, who stood.

"Well, Craig, this has been fun," Liz said, "but it's girls' night out and we need to go."

He stood, too, turning to Jenna. "Wait. You're leaving? With them?"

She wouldn't laugh at the shock on his face. Really, she wouldn't. Craig must not get turned down too often. "Afraid so. Nice meeting you. Good luck with the job."

The slap of frigid air as they stepped outside never felt better.

"Wow. You were so right," Tara said.

"No wonder I never dated much." Liz shuddered. "Are all single guys like that?"

"Not all of them. But a lot of the ones I meet are."

Which meant she was going to have a difficult time finding a date for the wedding.

FIVE

FINDING A MAN COULDN'T BE THAT HARD. JENNA worked around a sea of them. Men came through the doors of the bar often enough it was like catalog shopping. All she had to do was pick one.

Easy, right? Great-looking guys poured into the bar every night. Men with charming smiles who made good conversation. All she had to do was scope them out, talk to a few of them, and then ask one out and hope he said yes.

She was hit on all the time, but usually blew them off with a smile and a gentle no.

This time, she didn't intend to say no.

She'd gotten busy after happy hour and stayed that way. No hockey game tonight, but there was a basketball game on. Anything that would bring people in to watch a game was good for business. And that meant men would come in.

She laughed. Never before had she been interested in men

coming in. She cared about customers coming in, not what sex they were. Tonight she eagle-eyed every guy who walked through the doors, sizing them up as potential dates.

When a gorgeous man with a body to die for pulled up a seat at the bar, her radar started pinging. He wore crisp dark jeans and a button-down shirt, which he covered with a dark jacket.

Medium brown hair, cut short, and killer green eyes, with an engaging smile to perfect the look. She took a deep breath, a quick glance at the back bar mirror to make sure she looked okay, and went to take his order.

"What can I get for you?"

"I'll have a glass of Chardonnay."

Crap. "Sure."

A wine drinker. Fussy and anal retentive. How could she not have noticed that his jeans had that crease down the center? He probably dry cleaned them.

It would never work.

One down, many more to go, she busied herself serving some of her regulars and scoping out a few more potential single candidates, when another new guy walked in.

Dark blond hair, leather jacket, relaxed jeans and boots, motorcycle helmet in his hand. Must be tough to be riding in February, because it was damn cold outside. His goatee and lazy grin were sexy as hell. He caught sight of her right away and headed in her direction.

She liked that.

"What can I get for you?"

He leaned against the bar. "I'll have a Chivas on the rocks."

Dammit. "Sure."

She'd been so hoping he was a beer guy. Instead, she'd gotten a rich boy playing biker. And he'd had so much potential. He probably rode a Ducati Superbike.

She refused to give up hope and went back to serving her customers and filling orders.

"Busy night."

Shivers skittered down her spine at the dark, sexy tone of the man's voice. She closed her eyes for a second and let the sound of Ty's voice fill her senses.

She really didn't need this tonight. Not when she was man shopping.

She turned around. "Why are you here?"

"Uh, to play pool?"

She looked to the left, and sure enough, two of the other members of the Ice hockey team were already setting up at one of the pool tables.

So maybe he wasn't here to see her after all. Maybe Tyler and his friends liked the atmosphere and pool tables at Riley's.

And now she felt like an ass. An egotistical one. "What can I get for you?"

"Three beers. One light, two regular. Bottled."

She grabbed the bottles and slid them across the bar. "Want to start a tab?"

"That'd be great, Jenna. Thanks."

Mortified, she rang up the tab and decided she was going to ignore Ty the remainder of the night. She signaled Amber to work his table and to keep him and his friends in drinks so he wouldn't feel the need to wander over to the bar.

Then maybe she could get back to finding herself a date.

The rush slowed for the next couple hours, so she had time to survey the crowd.

Maybe she was being too picky. Damn her liquor as predictor theory. This was why she didn't date much. It was an accurate theory and weeded out the losers.

"Can I get a beer?"

She looked up and saw her savior in front of her. Nice looking, dark hair, a little long, just the way she liked it. He had on a tight-fitting shirt and worn jeans, a day's worth of stubble on his jaw, and spectacularly sexy brown eyes.

Yum.

"Bottle or draft?"

"Draft. Regular."

Bingo. A beer drinker.

She poured his beer into a mug and he paid her in cash. No fancy credit card. So far, so good. He walked away and she watched to see if he met up with a girlfriend. He didn't. He also wasn't watching sports. He sat at the other end of the bar with a group of friends—all guys—talking.

Okay, this dude worked for her. Which didn't mean anything. He could still have a girlfriend or even a wife, and this could be guys' night out.

She gave him his space, waited on her customers, washed glasses, and when the time was right, moseyed down the bar.

"Ready for refills?"

He graced her with a thousand-watt smile, one that showed interest.

"Sure." He looked at his friends. "You guys ready?"

"I have an early call tomorrow, so I'm headed out," one of them said.

"Me, too. You're on your own, Joe."

"See you, guys."

His friends grabbed their coats and left. He stood and followed her to the bar.

"Still want that beer?" she asked, figuring he'd take off now that his friends had.

Instead, he nodded. "Yeah. I'll take one more before I head out. It's been a long day."

"Coming right up." She filled his mug and handed it to him.

He paid her and tipped her well. She liked that part, too.

"Thanks."

"You're welcome." He took a long swallow, but held her gaze. "This is my first time in here. Nice bar."

"Thank you."

His brows lifted. "Yours?"

"My family's, but right now I'm running it."

"Big operation for someone so young."

She leaned over the bar, doing her best to remember how to flirt. "I manage."

He held out his hand. "Joe O'Brien."

She shook his hand. "Jenna Riley."

"Nice to meet you, Jenna."

"So what do you do, Joe?"

"I'm a doctor. Resident, actually, and new in town. I just moved here from Massachusetts, so I'm trying to find new places to spend what little free time I have. My friends and I decided to pop in here since it's close to the hospital."

She grinned. "Welcome to St. Louis. I think you'll love it here. Are you a native of Massachusetts?"

"No. Originally from Pittsburgh. But I've heard great things about Washington University, so I'm anxious to do my residency there."

"It's an awesome hospital."

They chatted awhile. She liked this guy, though she couldn't help but catch sight of Ty in her peripheral vision.

He was playing pool. He looked up to occasionally glance at her talking to Joe.

She wondered if he was jealous. Not that she cared. It wouldn't surprise her at all if he walked over and put himself in the middle of her conversation.

Except he didn't. Not even when she and Joe started laughing. It was obvious Joe was flirting with her.

Really, really obvious.

Just as it was obvious Ty was watching them. But he continued to play on, even ordered food and more drinks. From Amber.

He didn't once come over to the bar. Not even to chat with her.

"So, Jenna. Since I need a tour guide for your great city, and since you're a native, would you be up for a date? I could buy you dinner, and you could show me around."

She'd been concentrating on Ty and had almost forgotten about Joe. His question startled her. "Oh. What?"

He frowned. "I'm sorry. Do you have a boyfriend?"

"Me? No. Not at all. I'm sorry. Occupational hazard here. I was keeping an eye on my customers."

Liar. You were watching Ty.

Which was going to have to stop. Right now. "I'd love to go out with you, Joe."

Maybe she'd said that a little loud. Lowering her voice, she tried again. "Yes, I'd love to go out."

They worked out a date when they'd both be free, which was Friday night.

Perfect.

She had an actual date, with a good-looking doctor.

And even better, with someone who didn't play sports.

After Joe left, she busied herself with bar and manager duties. She wandered around to visit with her customers and to make sure everyone was happy, which also required her to mingle with the Ice players who'd apparently made Riley's their home. Keeping them happy was good for business. She needed to make sure they kept coming in.

"How's it going, guys?"

Eddie Wolkowski watched Ty line up to take his shot at the table, then grinned at her. "We're doing great, Jenna. How are you?"

"Perfect. You guys are smokin' up the arena lately. Making us all proud."

"Doing our best. Thanks for the burgers, by the way."

"You're welcome. By the way, Victor, you have a gaggle of female fans across the room dying for an autograph." She motioned with her head toward table seven, where about a half dozen women in their mid-twenties had zeroed in on Victor when they first came in and hadn't stopped looking at him since.

Victor Putinov was their left-winger on the Ice. His platinum blond hair and patrician good looks always sent the women swooning.

Victor lifted his chin. "I will go see them. Sign their papers."

"I'll bet you'll sign their papers," Ty said without looking up from the pool table.

Victor arched a brow. "It is my duty to keep female fans happy."

Eddie laughed. "Yeah, with your giant dick."

Jenna shook her head.

"I see you got yourself a new boyfriend."

She stopped and turned to face Ty, who'd taken his shot and leaned against the end of the pool table. "Not a boyfriend. A date."

"New guy?"

"None of your business."

"He's not your type."

Irritation skittered along her nerve endings. She put her hands on her hips. "Really. And why would you think that?"

He shrugged. "No chemistry between you."

"There's plenty of chemistry between us."

He reached up and grasped a strand of her hair, gave it a gentle tug.

Her breath stilled, and a tingle shivered down her spine. Everything she hadn't felt between her and Joe sizzled between her and Ty.

"Between you and me? Yeah. There's chemistry."

She lifted her gaze to his. He was right. An explosion bombarded her senses. Her breasts tingled, her lips parted. She went damp and she all but gave him an invisible road map to the promised land.

Whatever was between them was combustible, and very dangerous.

But he wasn't on her list of acceptable males to date. Or to do anything with, for that matter.

"There's nothing between you and me," she said.

"Isn't there?"

She liked Joe. She was going to go out with Joe.

"I have a date on Friday."

He let her hair sift through his fingers and took a step back, but still the shadow of a smile remained on his lips. "Have a good time."

"I will." She pivoted and walked away, figuring she'd feel a sense of triumph.

All she felt was empty.

A DATE? SHE WAS GOING OUT WITH THAT LOSER?

Why?

Ty stood back and watched Eddie take the shot, but his mind wasn't on the game anymore.

Not that it had been 100 percent on the game ever since he'd caught sight of Jenna talking to—what had she said his name was? Joe?

He took a quick glance at the bar. She was wiping it down with a cloth and laughing with one of her customers.

He liked her laugh. It was deep and gravelly, the kind of sound that got into every one of his nerve endings. He wanted to make her laugh like that. Actually, he wanted her naked and laughing.

Hell, he just wanted her naked.

He wanted more than that. He just didn't know why. He wasn't looking for a relationship, so why the hell did he care who Jenna went out with?

Except that Joe guy wasn't for her. He could tell right away it was the wrong kind of match, but if she wanted to go out with the guy, it wasn't like he had any claim on her. They hadn't even dated.

If she kept going after the wrong guys, Ty would never get a chance.

Not that he planned to give up. He'd just let her play her games with losers like Joe, and when the right time came, he'd swoop in.

Feeling better, he picked up his pool cue, ready to take his shot.

SIX

TWO DAYS LATER, JENNA STOOD IN FRONT OF HER MIR-
ror, inspecting her just to the knees, long-sleeved black dress and
black peep-toe pumps.

She chose dangling silver earrings and a long silver chain to com-
plement the outfit.

Simple, yet sexy.

Joe told her to choose a restaurant—an upscale one so he could
treat her to a nice meal since she was going to be his tour guide. He
said he'd heard Italian food was good in this city.

He'd heard right. She chose Tony's on Market Street, even
though the best Italian food was on the Hill, in her opinion.

Their reservations were for eight o'clock. It was almost seven. Joe
said he'd pick her up at seven and they'd have cocktails in the bar
before dinner.

She'd spent the day picking up the house, or at least the living room and kitchen, which had been a war zone. She'd vacuumed and dusted and put away the clutter so it didn't look like an insane person or a hoarder lived there.

Her stomach fluttered. She was nervous. How crazy was that? *Relax, Jenna.* She really had to start going out more.

The doorbell rang and she hurried out of the bedroom, stopping at the mirror for one last quick look to make sure she didn't have lipgloss on her teeth.

Everything in order, she spiked up her hair and went to the door, taking a quick, calming breath before opening it.

Joe stood there with flowers in his hand.

Nice touch.

"Hi. Come on in."

He smiled at her and handed her the flowers. Roses. How utterly . . . unoriginal. But still, sweet.

"These are for you. Thanks again for offering to show me around."

"You're welcome. And thank you for the flowers. Let me put these in some water."

He slipped off his coat. He wore dark slacks, a white shirt, no tie, but a jacket. Kind of relaxed, but still dressy. He looked incredible.

He was a good-looking guy. A really good-looking guy.

So why wasn't she tingling?

Likely because she was starving. She'd had a busy day, had run into the bar to see to a few things, do some bookwork, make sure everything was set up for tonight with her assistant manager before rushing home to clean the house and get ready for her date. And she might have forgotten to eat lunch.

So she was stressed. And really hungry.

She put the flowers in a vase of water, then came out. Joe was standing in her living room, looking around. Grateful she'd cleaned up the mess, she wandered over to him. He was examining the art on the wall.

"This is nice."

"Thanks. It's one of my favorite pieces."

"Original?"

"You could say that. Shall we go?"

"Sure."

He took her coat and helped her with it. The drive downtown didn't take long. They'd had a dusting of snow earlier in the day, so it was cold. Thankfully he used the available valet parking the restaurant provided, so she wouldn't have to worry about maneuvering the snow in her heels. They dashed inside where it was warm and cozy.

He led her to the bar and they ordered drinks.

For once it was nice to be on the other side of the bar, receiving rather than serving.

She sipped a martini and tried to settle in for a night of fun. It was time to relax and enjoy her gorgeous date, who turned his panty-melting brown eyes on her.

"So tell me what there is to do in your fine city."

"Everything. There's art, music, and theater, if you enjoy those things. There's also sports as you probably noticed from Riley's. We have a football and baseball team as well as a hockey team."

"Not much into sports, but I could get into the art museums."

Not into sports and good looking? She should be swooning by now.

"Do you like music?"

He shrugged. "Not much time to listen to music, so I'm not a big fan."

Her heart crumbled. Still, she decided to keep an open mind.

"So what do you do for fun?"

He laughed. "I've been in medical school for the past twelve years. I haven't had any fun. When I haven't been working or studying, I've slept."

"You're right. You haven't had any fun. What's your specialty?"

"Cardiology."

"Big undertaking."

"Yes, but I'm excited about it. It's all I've ever wanted to do. Being a doctor has been my dream since I was a kid."

"A family dynasty thing?"

He laughed. "Not at all. My father worked in construction his whole life. My mom worked as a secretary."

He was so interesting, so vast, so smart. He was dedicated, motivated, friendly, and definitely not at all bad on the eyes.

They moved into the restaurant for dinner, and he captivated her with his conversation, made her laugh with his stories about medical school and the horrors of life as an intern. He didn't just talk about himself, though, but engaged her and asked her about herself and her family and her goals and dreams for her own future.

He was almost the perfect man.

After dinner she drove him around and told him about her favorite places. He seemed fascinated with the history of the city, then told her what he was interested in doing.

"Will you settle here?"

"I'll be here for a few years. I don't know where I want to end up."

"Probably somewhere near your family, don't you think?"

He pulled up in front of her condo, shut off the engine. "I'm a big boy. I don't need to live so close to home anymore."

She laughed. "I guess to me family is so important. I can't imagine ever being far away from them."

"That's what makes people so different, Jenna. I like the freedom to live my own life. You like being close to those you love."

"I guess you're right."

Then the conversation was over, and he leaned in.

She waited for the swell of heat, the explosion of sensation.

His lips brushed hers and he enveloped her in his arms. She went willingly into the kiss, tangled her fingers in his hair.

His tongue swept across hers.

It was . . . nice.

Dammit. It was nice. Pleasant. No fireworks. Nothing in her body was going off like a rocket.

This guy was gorgeous, successful, funny, and she'd just had a great night with him.

And there wasn't a single hormone in her body that wanted to jump his bones.

How disappointing.

He broke the kiss and smiled at her. "Who's the guy?"

She blinked. "What?"

"Who's the guy you were thinking about when you were kissing me?"

"There is no other guy."

He gave her a look that told her he wasn't buying it. "I'm a doctor, Jenna. I might not know everything, but what I do know is biology and basic chemistry. You and I got along great."

"We did."

"But when I kissed you just now, you didn't feel it."

She looked down at her hands. "I'm sorry."

He tipped her chin with his fingers. "Don't apologize for something you just don't feel. It's either there or it isn't, and you can't manufacture chemistry. I had a great time tonight. Thanks for showing me around."

He opened the car door and went around to open hers, then walked her to her front door.

She turned to face him. "I really wish there'd been something, Joe."

"Me, too." He kissed her cheek. "I'll see you at the bar."

She watched him walk away and knew Joe would never step foot in Riley's again.

Even worse, she still didn't have a damn date for the wedding.

She turned around and went inside.

SEVEN

THE WEDDING CEREMONY HAD BEEN BEAUTIFUL. THE church had been decorated with white calla lilies and ruby roses with baby's breath and assorted greenery Jenna knew nothing about. It was beautiful. Seeing Tara walk down the white-carpeted aisle in her dress had made her breath catch. She'd looked stunning. Mick had tears in his eyes. Her big, tough-as-nails brother had shed a tear.

Her brother Mick was a married man now. Jenna still found that hard to believe. Her big brother, who had teased and tackled her and looked out for her when they were kids, had found the woman of his dreams and married her. And he had a teenaged son who he was going to officially adopt. Nathan was going to become a Riley.

Sometimes the world moved at such a fast pace it made her head spin.

Jenna had stood on the altar and listened to the priest perform the ceremony, truly listened to the words as Father Abrams told them about love and faith and finding that one person you were meant to be with. As she watched her brother and Tara look at each other, she knew for a fact that two people couldn't possibly love each other more.

Shockingly, she'd cried. She'd never thought it would happen. Strong and stoic were her fortes. But she'd stood on the altar with tears rolling down her cheeks as Mick and Tara recited their vows.

She'd have to work harder at her intestinal fortitude before Gavin and Liz's wedding.

After the ceremony the wedding party hung behind at the church to take pictures in multiple shots. Jenna had to admit that had been fun. Sometimes family could be overwhelming. Today, she couldn't get enough of them.

When there was a spare moment in between photographer shots, she hugged her brother.

"I'm so happy for you."

Mick grinned and put his arm around her. "Thank you. I'm a lucky guy."

"You are. Take good care of her. She's special."

He squeezed Jenna's arm. "I know."

The day turned out glorious. Cold, but bright and sunny. A perfect day, without a cloud or raindrop in the sky.

The bride and groom were happy, Jenna's parents were beaming with joy, and that's all she could ask for.

And the bridesmaid dresses didn't suck—thank you, Tara—so Jenna would survive the day.

She'd given up on finding a date for the wedding after that disastrous episode with Joe. The poor guy. She'd felt awful about it. No more dating for her. Not until she found someone who knocked her socks off.

Correction. Someone who didn't play sports who knocked her socks off.

That might be a tall order, but she knew he was out there

somewhere. And right now she just didn't care. She had enough to deal with today, and a man wasn't even on her radar.

Okay, one man was.

Tyler.

She'd noticed him sitting in one of the pews at the church when she walked down the aisle, couldn't help but catch sight of his dark hair as he stood and watched her, his gaze riveted to hers.

Butterflies. Giant butterflies in her stomach when she looked at him.

She'd quickly looked away, focusing on the altar instead. Today was about Mick and Tara, not her conflicted feelings about Tyler Anderson.

The wedding had been smooth and beautiful and had gone off without a hitch, allaying Tara's last-minute jitters.

Now if she could get some food and a drink, this day would be perfect.

They piled into the limos and made their way to the reception hall. The guests were already gathered there, so the wedding party was introduced, then the bride and groom to thunderous applause.

Mr. and Mrs. Michael Riley. Jenna still couldn't get used to that, but she already loved Tara like a sister, and Tara's son Nathan like a blood nephew. It didn't matter that Mick wasn't Nathan's real father. He was family to the Rileys and always would be, from now until forever.

Nathan looked so handsome in his tux. Nearly seventeen, he was going to be one serious lady-killer someday. He definitely fit in with all the Riley men. Both her brothers looked gorgeous as did her dad. Jenna couldn't help but grin. She was going to have to order a lot of pictures from the photographer.

As the bride and groom took to the floor to have their first dance, Jenna's ridiculous waterworks started up again.

Good Lord, was she a basket case today or what?

"I see you're full of tears today, too."

Her mother wrapped her arm around her. Jenna leaned against her and laughed.

"I can't seem to help myself. They're so happy, Mom."

"I know. And they deserve it. I've never seen two people more in love."

Jenna could only nod as Mick led Tara around the floor. Tara was breathtaking in her cream and pale pink strapless ball gown, a true vision with her blonde hair pulled up, diamond drops in her ears and across her throat—a wedding gift from Mick.

"She looks like freakin' Cinderella."

Her mother laughed. "She's stunning. And so are you."

"Thanks, Mom. But no comparison. This is Tara's day."

"You're gorgeous, Jenna. The ruby red dresses Tara chose bring out the blue in your eyes and make your hair stand out. And what they do for Maggie and Elizabeth's hair—I'm telling you, she chose the best dress for all of you."

"She did."

It was the bridal party's turn to dance, so Gavin danced with Maggie as best man and maid of honor, Liz danced with Mick's cousin Cole, and Jenna got to dance with Nathan.

"You look all grown up."

Nathan grinned. "I kinda feel that way. And sometimes I still feel like a kid."

She laughed. "Enjoy the feeling-like-a-kid moments. They'll be gone before you know it."

"I know. I'll be off to college soon. Only one more year of high school after this."

"I'm not sure we'll let you leave us yet."

"I'm not sure I'll be ready to go."

"Oh, trust me. You'll be ready. Too much of the Rileys can be suffocating. You'll have your bags packed and sneaking out the door in the dark of night so we can't tie you to us."

He squeezed her hand. "I like having you all for family, Jenna."

"We all like you, too, Nathan. A whole lot."

He turned her so they were facing Mick and Tara. "My mom and dad look happy."

"They are. And they will be. Forever."

She felt him relax.

The night flowed smoothly. She ate, finally, so she was content. Everyone danced, and she wandered around to greet the guests.

"Hello, gorgeous."

She was picked up and whirled around. When she was set down, she whirled around with a glare. She rolled her eyes when she saw her cousin's smug grin.

"Cole. Don't you know it's impolite to annoy the crap out of a lady?"

"First, you're not a lady, you're my cousin. And second, annoying the crap out of women is what I do."

Her cousin Cole was and always had been a big pain in her ass, second only to her brothers in that department. A jock just like Mick and Gavin, Cole played in the NFL and was one of the best wide receivers currently playing for Green Bay. And he had the giant ego to go with his giant talent. But she loved Cole nearly as much as she loved her brothers, despite all the years he'd spent tormenting her when she was a kid.

Her uncle and her dad must have been a hell of a duo when they were kids, because they sure passed it on to their sons.

"Shouldn't you be off doing shots with the guys?"

"On my best behavior tonight. I promised my mother and Aunt Kathleen."

"And when have you ever kept a promise?"

"Never. But since they're both here with their eagle eyes, I don't have much of a choice."

"Aren't you just a boy scout?"

"Yeah, until about midnight when I ditch this shindig and head to a club. I've got some babes waiting for me."

"And the media will be right behind you, waiting for you to get into a fistfight or some new scandal that'll make headlines. The new bad boy of football."

Cole shrugged, then grinned, the dimples in his cheeks doing nothing to diminish his rugged good looks. No wonder the media loved him.

"Hey, not my fault I'm photogenic."

"Yeah, your mug shot was charming. I'm sure Uncle Jack and Aunt Cara were thrilled with that."

"That was bullshit. And I've got great attorneys, and that was thrown out of court."

She shook her head. "It pays to make money, I suppose, but you're pushing thirty now, party boy. Isn't it time to grow up?"

He laughed. "Just call me Peter Pan. It'll never be time to grow up."

She waved him off with a shake of her head. Cole was trouble with a capital T. Great football player, but he did like his social life. Maybe a bit too much.

She grabbed a glass of champagne and was watching Gavin and Liz and Mick and Tara dance when she felt a warm presence behind her.

"You're not dancing."

Tyler. She'd successfully managed to avoid him for the past couple hours. She turned to face him.

Oh, did he ever clean up nice. Dressed in a black suit and tie that fit him as if it had been tailored for him, his dark hair spilled over the collar, making her want to sift her fingers through it to see if it was as soft as it looked.

"No, not dancing."

"Who was the guy you were hanging out with? Your date?"

She frowned, then realized he was referring to Cole. She laughed.

"No, that was Cole Riley, my cousin. You might recognize him from the Green Bay team. He plays wide receiver."

Tyler nodded. "Thought he looked familiar. You Rileys like to breed the sports players, don't you?"

"You have no idea."

"So where's your date?"

Refusing to rise to the bait, she said, "Didn't bring one tonight."

He cocked a brow. "Oh, you have more than one?"

She didn't answer.

"How about a dance?" he asked.

"Where's *your* date?"

"Didn't bring one tonight."

Her lips curved at the ditto. The music was hot and she wanted to dance. She'd had more than a little champagne tonight, and she felt good. So good, in fact, she tingled all the way down to her toes. Tonight was all about magic and romance. Not that there was any romance between her and Ty. But there was chemistry and he was the hottest guy here, so she might as well dance with the devil she knew.

"Sure. Let's do it."

Ty hadn't expected Jenna to say yes.

He thought the guy she was talking to was her date. He was relieved to find out it was her cousin Cole. When he found out she hadn't brought a date tonight, he got his game plan in order to get her on the dance floor, or get her alone. One way or another, he was determined to have her in his arms tonight, figuring he'd have to do some fancy maneuvering.

For it to be this easy? Hell yeah. He took her hand and led her onto the crowded floor, then watched her groove to the beat of some seriously hot dance music.

Jenna looked beautiful tonight in a red dress that clung to every curve of her body—a body she knew how to move. He wanted to put his hands on her, to feel her move like that without clothes on. She swayed her hips and pivoted around, and his dick twitched when she shook her ass. She got into the music, raised her hands in the air, undulating her body in time to the beat.

He inched up closer to her, fit his body against her, wrapped his arm around her waist, and rocked with her to the music, expecting her to kick him back. Instead, she put her arm around his and let her head fall against his chest. He inhaled her scent and tried to keep up with her since he wasn't much of a dancer, but hell, he was happy to let her take the lead since she obviously knew what she was doing.

When she turned around, she slung her arm around his neck and pressed her body against his, rocking her hips against him.

She had to notice he was getting hard. But she drew closer and ground against him.

To torture him, no doubt to get back at him for showing up at the bar and hitting on her all the time. But her gaze met his, her clear blue eyes not filled with anger, only interest.

And when the music slowed to something sexy, she didn't push off and walk away, so he took her hand in his, slid his arm around her back, and drew her in close.

He should probably say something to her, but he didn't want to break the spell. If he spoke, she might actually remember who she was dancing with, so he stayed quiet, content to breathe in the vanilla scent that seemed to always be part of her. He stroked his hand along the top of her back. Her skin was soft.

She tilted her head back and looked up at him. "You're quiet."

"I was afraid if I said anything you'd leave."

She arched a brow. "Why would I do that?"

"You don't like me."

Her lips curved into a smile. "I never said I didn't like you."

He arched a brow.

"Okay, I might have given you that impression. But the music's nice, and you feel good."

"You feel pretty good, too. Mind if we stay on the dance floor all night?"

She giggled and laid her head on his chest. "All right by me, but these shoes have to go. My feet are killing me."

He stopped. "Take them off."

She nodded. "Good idea." She slipped her shoes off one by one, and handed them to him. He held them by their straps, deciding any woman who'd wear heels this high had to have some kind of death wish.

"How do women walk in these things?"

"It's in our genetics. It's why women are the master species. We give birth and we can walk in heels."

He laughed. "No wonder your feet hurt." She slid into his arms again and they continued to dance. The deejay was nice enough to play another slow song. He'd have to remember to tip the guy.

"The wedding was nice."

She grinned. "It was. My brother and Tara are happy. They went through hell to get here, so they deserve it."

He didn't much believe in the whole happily-ever-after thing, but for some people, he supposed, it worked. He really hoped it worked forever for Mick and Tara, especially since there was a kid already involved. Tyler knew better than anyone what could happen to a teenager when what you thought was a happy family dissolved in front of you. "Yeah, I hope it lasts for them."

"It will. They've already been through all the rough stuff. The rest of forever will be easy."

He kept his thoughts to himself. No sense in bursting her bubble. She probably believed in knights in shining armor, rescued princesses, and fairy tale endings.

And love being enough to solve any problem.

All a bunch of bullshit. He didn't buy into any of it. Right now was what counted, and grabbing whatever you could while you had it. Because nothing lasted.

Including the song, and holding Jenna in his arms. The deejay cranked it up to something fast after that.

"Thanks for the dance," Jenna said. "I'm ready for a drink."

"Me, too."

Instead of walking away, she took his hand. "I know a shortcut to the bar."

She didn't ask for her shoes, so he held on to them and let her lead him to the bar. He found them two seats and ordered two drinks. He wanted soda, while Jenna ordered another glass of champagne.

She crossed her legs and the slit along the side of her dress parted, revealing an amazing length of slender thigh. Used to seeing her in blue jeans and T-shirts, Tyler looked his fill, then leaned against the bar to take a drink.

"No champagne for you?" she asked.

"Not my kind of drink."

She smirked.

"What?"

"Nothing. I just remembered something I said to the girls one night about guys and their choices of drinks."

"Yeah? What's that?"

She shook her head. "Can't tell you. Bartender trade secret."

He could imagine. "I'll bet you can tell all about a guy from what he drinks."

She frowned and laid her glass on the bar. "You think so?"

"Bartenders have keen insight. So what would you say about me?"

"You like whiskey, neat. Though sometimes you'll drink beer. That means you're independent, not easy to pin down. You like your freedom, but you're not pretentious. No expensive champagne for you. You don't like to show off, but you are choosy—no, wait. That's not the right word. Particular. That's better. You're particular. You aren't going to pick up just any girl. She has to be the right girl."

"You know all that just from the drinks I order?"

She took a sip of champagne. "Yes. And you also don't pick up women in my bar."

"Maybe because I'm waiting for you."

She tilted her head back and laughed, that sound he loved hearing. "You're so full of shit, Ty. I like that about you."

He liked listening to her talk. She had a sharp mind, and seeing the gears of it working got him as hard as seeing her move on the dance floor. "You think you know me, huh?"

"Actually, I don't think I know you at all. Most men are easy to peg. You I haven't figured out yet."

He took a couple swallows of soda. "I'm glad. I'd hate to be predictable."

"You're anything but predictable. You annoy me. You like me, and you obviously want me, and you make no secret of that. I like that, because I don't much care for games. On the other hand, I don't want you to like me. I want you to go away and leave me alone so I can stop thinking about you."

He grinned. She was just a little drunk, which meant she was relaxed enough to spill more of her inner thoughts than she was aware of. Which meant this was his opportunity to take things a step further with her, if he played the game right.

"I can't stop thinking about you, either, Jenna."

She leaned her elbows against the bar. "Really?"

"Yeah."

"What do you think about when you think about me?"

This was a test. She was putting him on the spot to see if he was just bullshitting her.

Actually, he wasn't.

"I think about your mouth." He traced her bottom lip with his thumb. "I like what comes out of it when you talk to me. It's sassy and smart. And I sure as hell liked kissing it. It's soft and wet and you yield under me like you want what I've got."

Her chest rose and fell.

"I like the way you talk. Confident, but you're a bit of a smart-ass. I like that about you, too. It means you're not a pushover. I don't want a woman I can walk all over. I want a woman who can stand up for herself."

She licked her bottom lip. Damn distracting and he needed to focus on what he wanted to say to her.

"You have the most beautiful eyes I've ever seen. And you see a lot with them. You call people on their bullshit, and obviously you know men."

"Yeah? In what way?"

"You know who's true and who's full of shit. You aren't going to fall for a line."

She let out a soft laugh.

"I like these." He swept his knuckles over the many earrings in her left ear, then leaned in close. "Are you pierced anywhere else, Jenna? I spend nights thinking about it."

Her eyes went dark. Interest or desire? He wasn't sure.

"And your tattoos. Those turn me on." He cupped her wrist and caressed the tattoo of the earth, moon, and stars. "It makes me want to get you naked and explore your body. So, yeah, I think about you a lot, Jenna."

"I don't want to date you, Ty. I've told you before, you're the wrong type of guy for me."

"So you've said."

She inhaled, let it out. "The problem is, there's this thing."

"A thing."

"Yeah. A chemistry thing, between you and me. And it's interfering when I go out with other guys."

Oh, this was getting good. "A chemistry thing."

"Sex."

"Sex." He shook his head. "Yeah, that's a problem." He brushed his shoulder against hers. He understood the chemistry thing. Just being near her made his dick spring to life.

She turned in the chair to face him. "It is. What should we do about that?"

"I don't think sex is a problem for me, Jenna. You already know how I feel. The question is, what do you want to do about it?"

She slid her fingertip down the lapel of his jacket, the look she gave him burning him from the inside out.

Yeah, definite chemistry. He was surprised flames weren't sparking between them. His breathing quickened and if she didn't make a decision soon he was going to have to make a quick exit, because this woman was driving him crazy.

"I think you should come home with me tonight and we can talk about it," she said.

"Ready when you are."

EIGHT

JENNA HAD CONSUMED ENOUGH CHAMPAGNE TO KNOW she was inebriated, but not so much that she was dead drunk and unaware of what she was doing.

In other words, when this was all over, she wouldn't be able to blame this on the alcohol.

There had been something in the air tonight. Maybe it was all the love she felt between Mick and Tara, and it reminded her of her way too solitary existence lately.

She was tired of coming home alone, and why should she? She was an adult, and if she wanted to bring a guy home and bang his brains out, she was entitled.

Ty didn't seem like the fall-head-over-heels-in-love-after-one-night type of guy. She didn't think he wanted to marry her or be her boyfriend, which made him perfect. He wanted to get into her panties, and she really needed a guy to get into her panties. The two of them had abundant chemistry, so she had no idea why she kept pushing him away. She was just foggy enough that all the valid reasons why she didn't want to go out with him had fizzled away like a glass of flat champagne.

Besides, they weren't going out. They were going to have sex.

Since her parents had picked her up this afternoon and taken her to the wedding, she didn't have her car. Ty drove them to her place after she had said her good-byes. The wedding was winding down and only the die-hard partiers were left.

"Keys?"

She lifted her gaze. She and Tyler stood on the front step of her condo. "What?"

"Your keys."

"Oh. Right." She dug into her bag and produced her keys. Tyler took them and unlocked her door, pushed it open, and waited for her to walk in.

She flicked on the light switch. He closed the door behind them. "This is nice."

"You lie. It's a wreck."

"You're right. I'm shocked. You keep the bar in tip-top shape."

She turned to face him, only to find him grinning at her. And okay, she was embarrassed. She dropped her purse on the coffee table. "Yeah, well, I had to get out of here in a hurry today because my dad was laying on the horn, and I was running late." She dashed through the living room to pick up her yoga pants and socks and tennis shoes.

He grasped her wrist.

"I was kidding. Drop that stuff."

She lifted her gaze to his. "I'm not a good housekeeper."

"I don't give a shit. If you came to my place right now you'd find last night's pizza box on the table, empty beer and soda cans, and about a week's worth of laundry thrown around."

"Really?"

"Really. I don't care what your place looks like. That's not why I'm here."

She exhaled.

"Would you like something to drink? We could sit and talk."

He rubbed her wrist with his thumb. Her pulse sped up.

"Is that why you invited me here? You want to have some drinks and talk?"

She swallowed, knowing that's not at all what she wanted. Not from him. "No. I don't want to talk."

"Okay, then." He looked down at her. "You're dressed way too nice for what I have in mind to do to you."

Her heart pounded, her breasts swelling against the top of her dress. She couldn't breathe. She was primed and ready—had been for months. She felt like she'd been dancing around this with him for a long time, and she didn't want to wait just because she was in a fancy dress.

"I don't care." She wound her arm around his neck and pulled his head down.

When his lips touched hers, a lightning bolt of sensation exploded inside her. This was what had been missing from her date with Joe. This blast of heat, this chemical reaction her body had to being touched and kissed. When Ty put his mouth on her, she felt it all the way to her toes—a tingle of awareness, a promise of what he was going to give her.

Ty wrapped his arm around her waist and tugged her hard against his body, and she went up in flames.

She swept her hands over his arms, feeling the steel-like strength of him. She slid her palms over his shoulders and tangled her fingers in his hair, something she'd thought about doing for a long time.

It was just as she imagined—thick and soft, a sensual delight for her fingers. And when he deepened the kiss, his tongue sliding inside to sweep alongside hers, she grabbed a handful of his hair and held on, her entire body trembling in response.

Never had she been kissed like this. Oh, she'd been kissed before. Hard, soft, and somewhere in between, but this was a full-on assault. Ty used more than his lips in the kiss. His hands roamed all over her, pressing in gently at the small of her back with one hand and cupping the nape of her neck with the other, while the front of him—the hard, oh-thank-God-he-was-a-man front of him—pushed her against the wall.

"I've been wanting to do this for as long as I've known you," he whispered, his voice harsh with strain as his fingers flexed against her hip.

He leaned over and kissed her jaw, then her neck, moving to her left ear. She shuddered when his tongue swept across her earlobe, flicking at her earrings.

"I like these earrings, Jenna. They're sexy."

"Thank you."

He swept his tongue across her throat, then turned her around and kissed the back of her neck.

Jenna shuddered, her knees weakening when she felt the tug of the zipper.

"I need you out of this dress."

She couldn't agree more.

When he unzipped her, she started to turn around, but his hands on her hips stilled her.

"Jesus."

"What?"

"This tattoo on your back."

"My dragon."

"Yeah. It's amazing. And when I'm not so damn hard I want to explode, I'm going to lick it all over. But right now there are other parts of you I want to lick."

She sucked in a breath and could already imagine his tongue on her, on the parts of her that ached and throbbed.

He pushed off her dress, laid it over the back of the sofa. When he came back to her, he knelt, this time cupping her ankles to sweep his hands up her legs.

"Your legs are so sexy." He pressed a kiss to the back of her knees. "And your thighs. I can't wait to feel them wrapped around me." He kissed her there, too, before turning her around to face him again.

Dressed only in her panties and heels, she felt bared to him, yet utterly sexy and turned on.

Tyler was so gentle, and she didn't expect that. He was such a big guy. She expected lumbering, fumbling, inept caresses—a few minutes of foreplay and then right to the action—not these achingly sweet movements that made her want to crumble to the floor. She was damp and throbbing with desire, her nipples tight points of burning need that begged for the touch of his hands and mouth.

He caressed her legs again, the silken soft hairs of his head tickling her skin. She was ready for penetration, while he was taking a slow trek south along her body.

When he reached for her panties, he tilted his head back to look at her.

The dark desire in his gaze made her pulse race. She had no idea how she was still standing. She laid her palms flat against the wall as he dragged her panties down her hips, then left them at her thighs while he admired her sex.

"You *are* pierced here." He leaned in and flicked the tiny ring attached to her clit with his tongue. Tingling shocks of pleasure vibrated through her.

He looked at her. "You are so damn sexy, Jenna."

He pressed his mouth to her pussy, and she melted. His tongue was hot, wet, and as he began to move it against her, she held on to the wall for support, because she was sure she was going to die from the sweet pleasure of it. Warm spirals of sensation coiled deep inside her, and she lost herself in the feel of his hands flexing and unflexing on her hips as he swirled his tongue so intimately across her sensitive flesh, his tongue rolling over her clit to flick and play with the piercing.

She was so sensitive there, and it had been awhile. With her panties resting at her thighs, naked except for her shoes and him still wearing his suit, kneeling before her and worshiping her with his mouth—the mere visual of it made her want to come right then. But oh, it was so good she needed it to last. She loved his mouth, loved the way he teased her with his tongue, then took her clit in his mouth and sucked, first light and easy, then harder. And the way he'd move down and slide his tongue inside her pussy, stabbing it in and out as if he were fucking her, was painfully exquisite. She tangled her fingers in his hair and arched against him, feeding her sex to him, needing him to take her there and make her fly over the edge.

She needed this orgasm so badly. Ty had been the one in her fantasies for so long now. No one else had been there for a while. And she was going to exorcise him out of there by having him make her come tonight—over and over again.

"Yes, Ty. Right there. Suck my clit."

He took her clit in his mouth and rolled his tongue over the bud, at the same time sliding a finger inside her pussy.

The tremors built as he began to pump, her pussy squeezing his fingers as the climax rolled toward her with a force that wouldn't be denied.

She banged her head against the wall as the first hard wave of her orgasm tunneled through her.

"Oh, God, I'm coming." She arched against his face, begging him to continue as she came with a torrent of wild cries. He held on to her, fucking her with his fingers and rolling his tongue over her sex until the last contraction subsided.

Out of breath and utterly unable to hold herself upright, she sank against him.

Tyler stood, wrapped his arm around her, and held her while she caught her breath. He pushed her panties to the floor and slipped two fingers inside her.

"I like to feel you coming, to feel your body respond. I could make you come over and over again, Jenna."

The dark promise in his words kept her on the sensual high. She knew they had barely gotten started, which was fine with her. She'd been in a drought for a long time, and since they were only going to do this once, she planned to get plenty of Ty tonight.

"I need you naked," she said, running her hands over his shoulders.

"I can fix that."

He stepped back and shrugged out of his suit coat, then undid his tie and pulled it off. She slipped out of her shoes.

Looking at him made her libido peak hard. His dark hair spilled over the collar of his white shirt. He worked the buttons of the shirt in a hurry, then took it off, revealing a wide span of well-developed chest with a dark smattering of hair that made her want to splay her fingers all over him, especially the line of hair that disappeared into the waistband of his pants.

He kicked off his shoes, undid his belt, and drew the zipper down, and her throat went dry as he dropped his pants to the floor, followed by his socks and his briefs.

Naked and hard, he was everything she could have imagined. Wide shoulders, well-muscled but lean in all the right places, with taut, muscled abs and a narrow waist, he was strong and absolutely beautiful. She wanted to touch him, then taste him, and definitely look at him for as long as he let her.

But he took a step forward and swept his arm around her, dragging her against him and kissing her with a passion she thought was

reserved for the movies. His mouth on hers—the way he commanded the kiss—stole her breath and made her muscles turn lax.

He cupped her neck and bent her over his arm, deepening the
kiss, sweeping his tongue against hers.

It really was like the movies, because she was certain she swooned.

When he straightened her, he looked into her eyes.

"You taste good."

Her body flamed, but not from embarrassment. She loved sex.
Nothing about it embarrassed her. She smiled at him. "If you let me
taste you, I could give you a report, too."

He laughed. "Yeah, we'll get to that for sure, but there's so much
about your body I haven't tasted yet." He swept his hand over her
breasts. "Like these."

Her breasts were small and often overlooked by guys. She liked
that he noticed. Tyler looked at her breasts like they were a feast.
"Not pierced like your clit."

"Not yet." She gave him a grin.

He arched a brow, then cupped one breast with his hand, swiping
his thumb over her nipple.

Her breasts might be small, but they were oh so sensitive, and she
gasped.

"Yeah, that's what I thought," he whispered, then bent and took
her nipple in his mouth.

She had no idea what he thought, because as soon as he put his
mouth on her, her mind focused only on what he was doing. Sensation shot from her nipple straight south. Her clit tingled and her sex
fired to life again.

He sucked her nipple into his mouth, licking around the bud and
flicking it with his tongue while he played with the other with his
hand and fingers, tugging and pulling on it until she cried out in
pleasure.

And then he took the other in his mouth, alternating between her breasts, lavishing attention on them until she had to hold on to his arm for support because she was dying from the sheer joy of it.

Her sex ached with need for him. She reached for his cock and stroked, loving the feel of his pulsing heat in her hand. He groaned and took her mouth in a blistering kiss that left her feeling weak.

When he swept her into his arms, she was grateful, because she wasn't sure she could stand anymore. He moved them into the bedroom and laid her on top of her bed, then crawled in after her, pulling her into his arms to roll her on top of him. He grabbed hold of her butt and lifted, arching her against his erection. She braced her hands on his chest and straddled him, rising up to look down on him.

"Now that's a vision," he said, grasping her breasts in his hands to play with her nipples.

She rocked against him and his gaze locked with hers. He gave a light pinch to her nipples and she gasped.

"I like that. Put your mouth on them."

She rose up to drop a nipple between his lips. He flattened it against his tongue and the roof of his mouth, giving her just the right amount of pressure, then increased the sensation by sucking it hard.

She grabbed a handful of his hair and shoved her nipple deeper into his mouth. "Ty, I really like that."

In an instant he rolled her over onto her back, swept his hand under her to arch her pelvis against his. She slid against his cock, her juices coating him. She could come from rubbing against him, but that's not what she wanted.

"If you aren't inside me in two seconds, I'm going to bite you."

He lifted his head to look down at her. "I might like that."

She pushed against him. "Seriously. There are condoms in the drawer there." She motioned with her head.

He arched a brow. "Prepared, aren't you?"

"Always. Now put one on and fuck me."

"I brought my own."

"Now who's prepared?"

"I try to be."

He climbed off the bed and went into the other room, coming back a few seconds later with a package of three condoms.

She lifted up on her elbow. "Three?"

"Yes. Three. Hope you're not planning on sleeping tonight."

He put the condom on and nudged her thighs apart, then drew her against him to kiss her again.

Oh, man, she really liked the way he kissed, the perfect way their lips fit together. There was a thoroughness to his kisses that left her lightheaded, and it had nothing to do with the champagne she'd had tonight. He had beautiful lips that made her want to linger and kiss him for hours.

And when he held the kiss and nudged her legs apart, she went willingly, opening to him so he could slide his cock against the entrance to her pussy. He entered her slowly, letting her feel every inch of him.

She pulsed as he thickened inside her, her body adjusting to him, everything about her discovering everything about him. It was achingly sweet, a powerful aphrodisiac that made her clench around his cock.

She listened to the sound of his breathing, deep and heavy like hers. He smelled so good, like fresh winter and sexy, musky male. His body was like a plane of hard-edged muscle, yet his skin was soft. And when she ran her hands over him, she'd feel the occasional bump—scars, maybe? She'd have to discover all those later, after this initial exhilarating rush of first-time sex.

Because right now all she was interested in was the way his body moved against hers, the way he pulled out, then slid inside her again. He was easy with her at first, and she appreciated it because it had been awhile. But once her body adjusted to him, she needed more, and let him know it by arching up to meet him, accelerating the pace.

And he was obviously happy to give her exactly what she wanted, because he drew partway out, then thrust, deeper this time.

"Yes. Just like that. Harder again."

He took her hand in his and tangled his fingers with hers, and gave her what she asked for, plunging inside her, then grinding his hips against hers until she saw stars. She whimpered, her body tightening around him, squeezing him, taking her so close she had to fight not to come.

"Jenna."

She met his gaze and he lifted against her, then slammed it home, rocking against her with a strong rhythm that balanced her right on the peak several times, only to pull back and take her up again. And each time, he rocked against her clit, conscious of her pleasure, her needs.

This man was magic.

She reached up and ran her fingers through his hair. He swept his hand under her butt and held her close. Lines of strain tightened his features as he quickened the pace of his thrusts. She knew she wasn't going to be able to hold on as he began to slam against her, one right after the other.

"Tyler. That's going to make me come."

"Then let's go, babe."

He bent her knee, drew her leg up, and pounded hard, tunneling faster and faster against her. And then he kissed her, his tongue licking against hers. The sensation rolled south and the waves of orgasm rushed over her. She moaned against his lips as her climax hit her hard. She dug her nails into his skin, bucking against him as the sweetest pleasure of all rocked her. And when he groaned and came with a burst of thrusts, she held on to him, loving the feeling of him tightening and shuddering around her.

He wrapped his arms around her and held her while they both settled and breathed.

Wow. That had been . . . amazing. It wasn't like she'd never had great sex before, but that had been . . . Wow.

Yeah, they had chemistry all right.

When he withdrew he left for only a second, but came back and pulled her into his arms again.

She had an idea that maybe he'd want to leave right away. Some guys did, were uncomfortable with the after part of sex. Ty didn't, just continued to stroke her body, drawing lazy circles over her skin with the tip of his finger.

She didn't know what to do now.

She couldn't remember the last time she had a guy in her house. She was picky. And busy. And maybe she preferred her own company over just bringing home random guys. She'd done plenty of that when she'd first moved out and gotten her own place at nineteen. Her rebellious, independent stage, when she'd first tasted freedom without parents and big brothers looking over her shoulder. That had been fun, but it had grown old fast. She'd been young, but more mature than most of the guys she'd brought home.

Men were often boys in disguise, and she had very little patience for the games they played.

Not much had changed in the eight years she'd been out there dating. Men were pretty much all the same, much to her disappointment. Then again, she didn't get out much to meet different types of guys. She was usually trapped at the bar, and she already knew those types of men were not her type at all.

So why was one of those types of men lying in her bed?

Because he was tall, built, gorgeous, and she'd wanted to touch his hair.

Yeah, well, she'd touched his hair all right. Among other things.

"You've gone quiet on me, Jenna. Are you tired?"

She lifted her gaze to his. He was studying her. "Not tired. Reflective."

He propped his head in his hand. "Sex reflective or wedding reflective?"

She laughed. "Neither. Or I don't know. Maybe a little of both."

She waited for the panicked, after sex, deer-in-the-headlights look a lot of men got.

Nothing. He just seemed interested.

"Tell me what's on your mind."

"I was thinking about Mick and Tara's wedding and how much my life has changed in the past several years."

"Yeah?" How so?"

She searched his face. "Do you really want to hear this?"

He drew imaginary circles over her shoulder and seemed in no hurry to bolt. "I really want to hear this."

"I moved out of my parents' house when I was nineteen. It was such a freeing experience for me, because before then there was my parents and Mick and Gavin."

His lips quirked. "A lot of supervision, huh?"

She sat up and scooted back against the pillows. "Like you wouldn't believe. I was taking college classes, so I spent the first semester at the dorms. Hated that. The girls were all bitches, into their social worlds and clubs and partying all the time. It didn't take me long to figure out college life was not for me. The partying was too heavy and too loud and too all the damn time. I was one of those rare freshmen who was interested in getting an actual education. I couldn't study, so I moved back home. Huge mistake."

"Because once you're out, you can't go back?"

She laughed. "Yes. That was it exactly. I couldn't live with rules and people breathing down my neck anymore. Not that I was out there being wild or crazy or anything. Not then, anyway. I just needed my own space. So I got an apartment and lived alone for the first time in my life."

"That must have been fun."

"It was."

"And then did you party?"

She laughed again. "Hard. Nothing like that taste of freedom with no restrictions. So much for me ragging on the hard partiers at the dorm. I was such a hypocrite when I ended up doing the same thing as soon as I got my own place."

"Yeah. Been there. But eventually you have to grow up and be responsible."

"True. And it didn't take long for my grades to slip and for me to realize that college life wasn't for me."

"Is that how you ended up at the bar?"

"More or less. I dropped out of college after my second year, took a year off to travel and clear my head."

"Where did you go?"

"Went up to Canada with some friends, then over to Paris, Germany, and then London. More wild and crazy times."

He rubbed her wrist, then trailed his finger up her arm to where her banded tribal tattoo circled her biceps. "Is that where all the tattoos came from?"

She shivered at his touch. "Here and there."

He sat up and swept his index finger over her shoulder, across her neck, and behind her ear, fingering the piercings in her ear. "And what about these?"

"It was a whim."

"I like them. They're sexy."

She liked him touching her ear. She liked him touching her anywhere.

"And the tats? Were those whims, too?"

"They all mean something to me." She held out her arm. "The

sun, moon, and stars remind me that no matter where I am, my family is always looking at the same sun, the same moon, and the same stars. It comforted me when I set out on my own and when I traveled all those years. Despite wanting my freedom and this big sense of adventure I had, eventually I got homesick. That's when I got the tattoo."

He circled her upper arm. "This one?"

"The tribal band on my arm was a bonding experience with friends in England."

"Now tell me about the dragon."

She smiled. "He's my protector. I had a really good friend who was a tattoo artist. I'd known him since high school, and I loved his art. He drew it for me and I fell in love with Edgar at that moment, knew I'd have to have him on me."

Tyler arched a brow. "Edgar?"

Her lips lifted. "That's his name."

"You named your dragon Edgar?"

"Shut up."

"Roll over onto your stomach and let me look at him."

She frowned. "You're not going to make fun of me, are you? Edgar is special to me."

He cupped her chin and kissed her. "Jenna, I'd never make fun of something that means so much to you."

Her stomach clenched again. Damn this man for getting to her.

She was still kicking him to the curb after tonight. He wasn't the right guy for her.

"Now get on your stomach so I can see it. Him."

She smiled. "Okay."

TYLER SWALLOWED. WITH JENNA'S HAIR SHORT, THIS tattoo had always teased him. Without getting close to her, he could only catch glimpses of color and parts of a shape here and there, but he never knew what it was, only that it was green and wrapped partially around her neck. It was like a tease, because she often wore jewelry that hid the tat, which only made him want to see more.

And now that he could, now that he had her naked . . .

Of course now that he had her naked, he could think of a hundred other things he wanted to do to her body, but he still wanted to see the tattoo.

The tail wrapped around the nape of her neck, the tip ending at the side of her throat. It grew slightly thicker below her neck and weaved around the bumps of her spine.

Whoever had done the art was damn good, because it looked like it was moving. He traced it with his fingers, the color and drawing so realistic he expected to feel the dragon's scales.

There were even talons and wings.

The damn thing was beautiful. Of course it should be, since it graced the back of such a beautiful woman.

He swept his hand over her back, touching the dragon, but mostly loving the feeling of her muscles flex and relax under his hand.

Making love to her had been nothing short of everything he had imagined it would be . . .and more.

Jenna loved sex, was unashamed about her body, and he wanted to do it with her over and over again. She was slender and beautiful and responsive, and his dick got hard just thinking about being inside her again, tasting her again, touching her like this.

But he already knew he was going to have to put on the brakes because for Jenna, this was a one-time deal.

He wanted more than one time with this woman.

The dragon's talons dug into her left hip. It was nearly three-dimensional.

"This tattoo is amazing."

"Thank you."

"How long did it take from start to finish?"

"Three months."

"Wow. That's dedication, on your part and the artist's."

He massaged her back, keeping his touch light and making sure he swept his hands all the way down to her lower back, letting his fingertips linger right at the top of her butt.

He pressed a kiss to her shoulder and turned her to face him.

Her breasts were small ripe peaches, her nipples round and tight. And sensitive as hell, which he really liked. He massaged them with his hands, then swiped his tongue over one nipple, watching it tighten. Her breath caught as he dragged his tongue over the bud, then squeezed her breasts together so he could roll his tongue over one, then the other, teasing and tugging her nipples with his lips and teeth.

Her waist was slender, her hips the same, and her legs were a knockout, clearly her best feature. He touched her all over, keeping his massage light and easy, heightening the sensation for her minute by minute until she was writhing under his hands.

Smoothing his hands down her ribs and over her belly made her breath catch and her hips rise up.

She wanted more, and he wanted to give it to her. He could play with her body all night.

And when he smoothed his hand over the top of her sex, teasing his fingers just above her clit, her eyes darkened.

"Touch me."

Her whispered words made his dick throb. He slid his hand down over her sex, cupping her. She was hot, wet, and when she lifted against him, he coated his fingers with her moisture and rubbed it over her clit, concentrating his movements around the piercing. Her lips parted and she gasped when he touched her there. He petted and caressed her clit, then dipped lower and tucked his fingers inside her while rubbing the center of her universe with the heel of his hand, making sure to give her pleasure in both spots.

She grasped his wrist and pumped his fingers inside her, then raised her legs, planting her feet flat on the bed so she could lift her hips and drive her pussy against his hand.

Oh, yeah. He leaned over to kiss her, and she grabbed his hair, obviously deep in passion now as he fucked her with his fingers and drove her over the edge. Her cries and moans undid him, and he pulled his fingers out, flipped her over on her stomach, and grabbed a condom.

He wrapped his arm around her middle and lifted her onto her knees, climbed between her legs, and thrust inside her.

Her pussy was tight, still spasming from her orgasm. He paused to give Jenna a minute to catch her breath.

But that's not what she wanted because she pushed back against him, filling her pussy with his cock.

Oh, yeah, that was good. He grabbed her hips and shoved forward, burying himself deep.

"Yes," she said, dropping her head down and pushing against him again.

She had a sweet ass, and watching her in this position showed him everything. The way her pussy gripped him and pulled him in, the way she rolled against him as he pushed forward, giving her everything he had, and the way she rose up and threw her head back when he pounded against her.

She gripped the pillows in her hand and held on when he thrust hard enough his balls slapped against her, a fine sheen of sweat dampening her skin.

Yeah, it was hot in here, a fire blazing inside him as his balls tightened with every stroke. He leaned forward so he could touch her, tease her clit while he fucked her.

"That's going to make me come," she said, her voice tight with strain. "Fuck me harder."

He did, pressing his hips against her and rubbing her clit. Her pussy contracted around his cock and he knew she was going to go off.

So was he, but he wanted her to come first.

"Ty."

The way she said his name, the low, gravelly tone of her voice, stripped him bare and made him want to power inside her and let go.

And when she arched her back and shuddered, her climax gripping him with a force that shook him, he let his own orgasm rip free, lifting up to grip her hips and shove hard one last time, then held, just feeling the sensations as he came with a hard groan.

She collapsed onto the bed and he disposed of the condom, then rolled her over onto her side so he could tug her against him.

She reached behind her to cup his neck, half turning so she could kiss him.

He met her lips in a kiss. He liked her mouth, wanted to feel it surrounding his dick, but her eyes were half slits and he knew she was done for. He swept his hands over her arm and hip, content to listen to the sound of her breathing until her eyes closed.

She was asleep in minutes. He followed her a minute later.

NINE

JENNA BLINKED, OPENED HER EYES, AND FELT AN UN-
familiar heaviness pinning her to the mattress. She pulled against
the warm sensation.

Then heard a groan.

Oh.

Ty. That's right.

A smile tugged at her lips.

Last night had been . . . amazing. More than amazing. She rolled
over onto her back and looked at him. He was on his side facing her,
still asleep. The hazy light of early dawn seeped into the room,
enough that she could see him.

True to his word about doing it three times, he'd woken her in
the middle of the night, his cock hard and sliding between her
thighs. He'd put on a condom and slid into her from behind, fucking
her with slow, languid thrusts while caressing her breasts. She wasn't
sure she'd ever come fully awake, just enjoyed the hazy pleasure

while he'd held on to her hips and thrust inside her with easy, leisurely strokes until she'd felt the pleasure intensify. And when she'd come, it had made her shake all over, her body tensing with the sweetest pleasure. He'd pushed his cock into her with a deep, hard thrust, then groaned and climaxed.

They'd both fallen back asleep right after that. It had been breathtaking.

She felt no regrets as she woke up next to him. How could she after the best sex of her life last night?

A day's growth of beard stubbled his jaw, his hair was sleep and sex messy, and all she wanted to do was climb on him and have more of him. Her belly tumbled with renewed desire.

Until she caught sight of the clock.

Six thirty.

Shit. She was due at her parents by eight to have breakfast with Mick and Tara before they left for their honeymoon.

She slid out of bed and jumped into the shower, scrubbing last night's makeup—and the remnants of sweet sex—off her body. When she got out, she dried off, did her hair and makeup again, then tiptoed out to the bedroom.

Ty hadn't budged. Heavy sleeper, obviously. She shook her head and went into the closet for a pair of jeans and a sweater, then grabbed underwear, socks, and boots, and dressed in the kitchen while she brewed a pot of coffee.

She got a cup of coffee down—thank you, caffeine—before she had to go back into the bedroom.

Still asleep. Lucky man. She'd like nothing more than to climb in with him and get a few more hours' sleep. And maybe a little more sex.

Too bad she was going to get neither.

She sat on the bed next to him and grasped his shoulder. "Hey."

"Hmmm."

"Ty. Tyler."

His lids partially opened. "Yeah. Hey, you're dressed."

"I need to be at my parents this morning. A family thing."

He pushed the covers halfway down and sat up. "Yeah, sure. I'll get out of here."

"No hurry. The front door locks on its own when you shut it. I've gotta go."

He dragged his fingers through his hair and looked at the clock. "Yeah, me, too. I've got a game tonight."

"Okay. I had a good time."

"Me, too."

She started to get up, but he hauled her against him and kissed her deeply.

His body was warm, his kiss reminding her of what they'd shared last night. When he broke the kiss, she really wished she didn't have somewhere to go this morning, especially seeing the thick erection he sported under the covers. She wanted to touch him, to taste him, to play with him some more.

But she wasn't going to play with Tyler Anderson again.

"Have a good day, Jenna."

Regret made her sigh. "You, too."

She got up and made a hasty exit before she did something stupid, like ask to see him again.

TY SAW THE LOOK OF REGRET AND HESITATION IN Jenna's eyes.

He knew the score. One game only.

But he also saw the heat flare in her eyes after that kiss.

She might be determined, but so was he. And he never gave up.

He threw the covers off and went into the bathroom, then grabbed his clothes. No sense in showering in Jenna's bathroom when he'd just have to throw the same clothes on again. He'd wait until he got home. He dressed and followed the scent of coffee.

Jenna had laid a cup out for him so he filled it and drank, grateful for the caffeine perk that would get him home.

It had been a long night. A good night. He smiled remembering it. He wanted another night with her.

He was on his way out when he spotted the guitar sitting in the open extra bedroom. He paused, glanced in the room, and saw the sheet music.

It was private, he knew, and he shouldn't snoop, but she'd left him alone in here.

He walked into the room and squatted down on the floor.

There was some copyrighted sheet music, but also blank pages where she was writing her own.

Huh. He had no idea she was a songwriter.

He didn't know a damn thing about music, but obviously Jenna did. There were pages and pages of handwritten music in here.

Interesting.

JENNA THREW OFF HER COAT AND HURRIED INTO THE kitchen while she rubbed her cold hands together.

Everyone was already here and the smell of food made her stomach growl. Bacon and some kind of baked goods. She was starving.

"Morning. Am I late?"

"Right on time," her mother said. "Everyone's already in the dining room. You can take this plate of muffins in."

She kissed her mother on the cheek and grabbed the muffins.

"About time you showed up," Gavin said. "We're all about to waste away waiting for you."

She rolled her eyes as she took a seat. "It's five after eight. I don't think you're going to die."

She hugged Tara, who absolutely glowed with happiness. "Good morning, Mrs. Riley."

Tara grinned. "It's going to take me some time to get used to that. Tara Riley. I can't believe it actually happened. He's mine."

Mick came up and put his arm around Tara. "It did happen. You're my wife. No backing out now."

Tara tilted her head back and cast adoring eyes at Mick. "Not a chance. I'm never letting you go."

"You two are making my stomach hurt. Or maybe that's just hunger."

Mick and her mom sat down and they all dug into the wonderful meal Mom had made. Obviously everyone was hungry, and talk turned to rehashing the wedding.

Jenna enjoyed the conversation and listening to everyone's stories about the night before. Mick had been nervous, afraid he'd forget his vows. Tara had been ecstatic, and Nathan had been glad to get through it without tripping over his fancy shoes. Gavin and Liz were starry-eyed with thoughts of their own upcoming wedding, and her parents looked on all them with such joy it made tears spring to Jenna's eyes.

This was her family, and she loved them so much.

She poured another cup of coffee from the carafe on the table, then added cream and lifted the cup to her lips, closing her eyes and breathing it in as she sipped.

"Rough night?"

She opened her eyes and looked at Liz. "Late night, same as the rest of you."

"I don't know," Tara said, giving Jenna a thorough once over. "You've got dark circles under your eyes, yet your cheeks are pink."

The guys had all moved into the living room to watch something on television, and Mom was in the kitchen, leaving Jenna alone in the dining room with Liz and Tara.

Liz tilted her head. "Dark circles and flushed cheeks? That can only mean one thing. You had sex."

Jenna's eyes widened. "I did not."

"You did, too," Tara said. "You think we've never had sex before? We know the look."

Jenna looked around to be sure no one heard. The TV was blaring and obviously if her mother heard anything she wasn't going to come running into the room for details. Thankfully.

"So who was the guy?" Tara asked.

"I don't want to talk about this."

Liz looked at Tara. "She doesn't want to talk about it. She isn't denying it, which means she definitely had sex last night."

She raised her chin. "I plead the fifth."

Tara nodded at Liz. "I was obviously busy the entire night. Who was she with?"

Liz tapped a perfectly manicured fingernail on the table. "Let's see. She didn't bring a date, and as far as I know she isn't seeing anyone."

"No one that I know of. I could ask Mick."

"I could ask Gavin."

"Stop it, both of you. There's no one. Just a random hookup."

"Random hookup my—oohh," Liz said. "It was Ty."

Shit.

"Ty Anderson? The hockey player?" Tara asked. She turned to Jenna. "Oh, he's gorgeous. And so hot, Jenna."

"And a hockey player, and you know how I feel about sports and the men who play them."

"That shouldn't matter, if you like him," Tara said. "And if you had sex with him I assume you like him."

Liz looked from Tara to Jenna. "What does sports have to do with you staying up all night screwing his brains out?"

"She won't date anyone involved in sports," Tara explained.

Liz frowned. "Why not?"

Jenna shrugged, realizing it sounded stupid. "Because I live it in my job and I'm surrounded by it with my family. I'd just like a freakin' break when I date a guy, you know?"

"But sports are in your blood, Jenna."

"No, sports are in *their* blood." She motioned toward Gavin and Mick. "Not mine."

Tara leaned back and sipped her juice. "Okay, well I get that, really. And as someone who was the queen of denial herself, I understand about your reason for not wanting to be with Ty—"

"As stupid as that is," Liz interjected.

Tara pinned Liz with a look. "But it's her reason, nonetheless."

Liz waved a hand. "Whatever."

"So anyway," Tara continued. "Was it good?"

That got Liz's attention. "Yes. Tell us. Was it?"

Jenna shook her head. "You're as bad as men."

"Men don't gossip about sex details," Tara said.

"They don't?"

Tara shook her head. "No. Mick told me all they say to their friends is, 'I gave it to her so good last night, she couldn't walk today,' or some such nonsense. But no details. We want details."

"Huh. Well, I gave it to him so good last night he couldn't walk today."

Liz snorted. Tara tilted her head back and laughed out loud.

"What are you all laughing about in there?" Mick asked.

"Girl talk," Tara hollered to him before turning back to Jenna. "And?"

"And what?"

"Come on, Jen, we need more than that," Liz said. "Just how good was it? That man is sex on a hockey stick. I've seen him play. Hell, he's my client. His stamina on the ice is epic."

Jenna leaned back in her chair. "And you want to know if that stamina translates to the bedroom."

"Hell, yes."

Her lips quirked, remembering last night, and her body heated. "Then . . . hell yes."

Liz slapped her hand on the table. "I knew it. Not that I have any complaints. Gavin—"

Jenna held up a hand. "Is my brother and I so don't want to hear about your sexcapades with him."

"You are not fun."

She stood and grabbed the carafe. "I'm going to refill the coffee. You can share sex stories with Tara. I'll be right back."

She went into the kitchen. Her mom had just ended a phone call.

"I'm sorry, sweetie. It was Diandra, who couldn't make to the wedding last night because Bill had emergency gallbladder surgery."

Jenna refilled the carafe from the full pot of coffee on the counter. She knew Diandra was one of her mother's oldest friends. She and Bill had been over to the house so many times over the years, they were like family to Jenna. "Oh, no. Is Bill okay?"

"He's fine. Still in the hospital because they're treating him with antibiotics due to an infection, but he should go home by tomorrow. She was so upset to miss the wedding."

Jenna leaned against the counter. "Understandable considering the circumstances. I'm glad Bill is okay."

"Me, too. Now what were you girls talking about in there?"

"Nothing much. Wedding stuff."

"It was a great wedding, wasn't it?"

"The best, Mom. The absolute best."

And that was all she was going to tell her mother. It was bad enough Liz and Tara knew about Ty. Since she didn't intend to see him again, there was no point mentioning him to her parents.

* * *

DESPITE THE LACK OF SLEEP, TY WAS ENERGIZED AT the game.

They were up three to two with four minutes left in the third period. He paced in the penalty box after getting a high sticking penalty. Fifteen seconds to go and he was out of there.

Seconds ticked by like hours when he was in the box and the game was on the line. He watched the time count down, then sprang out of the box and onto the ice, taking his position back.

Wolkowski passed him the puck and he threaded it through the defenseman and back to Eddie, putting himself in position in front of the net. Eddie shot it over to Victor, who sent it sailing back to him. He slammed the shot at the net but the goalie defended, then sent it circling around behind the net.

Damn.

Adrenaline pumping, he moved backward when the Montreal center breezed toward him. He wouldn't let him past and jammed his stick against the center's, then took the puck from him, digging his skates into the ice and charging toward the opposite goal again.

His opponent slammed a shoulder into him and prevented his forward movement, and they fought for the puck. The puck slid free and Ty went after it, determined not to give it up. Every fraction of a second was a battle to be won. He wasn't going to let their center take the prize from him. They reached it at the same time and Ty swung around, turning his back to the center. He raised his stick, scooping the puck away from the opponent. He passed it to Victor, who shot it to Eddie.

Tyler skated to the net.

Eddie fought his defender for the puck and slammed it to Ty. He took the puck around the back of the net and swept it to Victor, who was in perfect position to the right of the goal and tucked it into the net.

The lights behind the goal flashed on, signaling success.

They scored, and the crowd leaped to their feet.

Tyler skated to Eddie and Victor, they piled on celebratory high fives, then finished the damn game.

After, Tyler was pumped and ready to celebrate.

"You guys ready to go out and party tonight?" he asked.

Eddie was always up for an after-game celebration. "You know it. If you're buying."

Ty shook his head. "You're a cheap bastard, Eddie."

"Yeah, but someday I'll be a rich cheap bastard, especially if I keep getting guys like you to buy my dinner and beers."

"I'll buy you dinner for that pass tonight, and Victor's dinner for that goal. You can buy your own damn beer."

"You are on," Victor said. "Beautiful women will want me after that goal tonight."

Ty patted Victor on the back. "I think beautiful women want you even when you don't score a goal."

Victor pursed his lips and nodded. "This is true."

They headed over to Riley's. Not because he expected Jenna to be there. It was Eddie's suggestion, because he liked their steaks and also because of Renee, the cute waitress he was still trying to muster up the courage to ask out. Plus, Victor had spotted a blonde there the other night that he hadn't yet managed to take to bed, so he wanted to see if she'd be there.

And if Ty was buying dinner, he had to come along, right?

Jenna just happened to be working tonight. So not his fault.

She didn't look surprised to see him walk in. She didn't look happy to see him, either, though she didn't look unhappy.

She looked tired.

Renee was working tonight and brought their drinks over. She eyed Eddie, and Eddie eyed her.

Ty elbowed Eddie in the ribs. "It's obvious she likes you. Ask her out."

Eddie blushed crimson. "Maybe I will."

"I mean, like this year, dumbass."

"Congrats on a kickass game tonight, guys," Renee said. "The shots are on Jenna for the win."

"Excellent!" Victor lifted the shot of vodka. "To the Ice."

"To the Ice," Ty said, though he looked at Jenna when he downed his shot of whiskey.

He might have seen a hint of a smile on her face. Or maybe he was just imagining it, because it was gone as soon as he saw it.

But he wasn't here for Jenna tonight. He had come to celebrate a game win with his buddies.

They ordered steaks, had a few beers, and Victor found his blonde, who was just as eager to see him again. Soon they were surrounded by eager fans happy to talk about tonight's game.

It had been a great game. Ty wanted to share his exuberance with Jenna, but it was Saturday night and the place was crowded. She was busy manning the bar, but after last night he'd be an asshole if he didn't at least go up and talk to her.

He waited until she'd filled drink orders, then leaned against the corner of the bar.

"Hey."

She was washing glasses. "Hey yourself. Good game tonight."

"Thanks."

She hadn't made eye contact yet, so he waited until she finished what she was doing. When she had, she walked to the other end of the bar to fill a customer's drink order.

Okay, she had to see to her customers. He understood that. He could be patient.

But when she came up to his end of the bar and continued to ignore him, he figured something was up.

"You look tired."

She gave him a half smile. "I am tired."

"Rough night last night?"

"No. Good night last night. But you know that's it for us."

Not offended, he leaned against the bar. "Letting me down easy?"

She gave him the kind of look he'd given to countless women before. The 'It's been great, but' look. "Tyler . . ."

He laughed. "Send Renee over to refill our drinks. And get some sleep tonight, Jenna."

Their game was over, at least according to Jenna.

If he was a sensitive kind of guy, his feelings might be hurt.

Good thing he wasn't sensitive, and it took a whole hell of a lot to hurt him.

And the game was far from over.

She thought she wanted a guy who didn't play sports?

He'd find her one.

Or maybe more than one.

TEN

THERE WAS SOMETHING VERY STRANGE IN THE AIR.

Or Jenna was giving off some new kind of pheromones, because she was getting hit on left and right lately.

For the past week she'd been surrounded by a steady stream of potential dates. It was as if someone had been advertising her availability out there somewhere.

But that couldn't be, so she just chalked it up to pheromones.

It had all started the day after she'd said good-bye to Tyler. First she'd met the hot accountant from west county who'd come into the bar and zeroed in on her like she was the only woman there. She'd been flattered when he'd asked her out, but he just wasn't her type.

The next night it was the guy who owned the car dealership. What was his name? Oh, yeah. Stan. He was great looking in a sexy, nerdy kind of way, with black-rimmed glasses and a muscle-bound body that showed how much he worked out. Plus, he was smart, and she loved smart guys. But again, there just wasn't enough chemistry between them, so she nixed his request for a date.

Then she'd met the model. Oh, dear God in heaven had he ever been good looking. He'd come in with several people—men and women who'd been just as good looking as he was. Every person in the place had stopped to take a second glance at the group, who looked like they'd just stepped off a photo shoot. And when Robert—that was his name—had leaned against the bar and flashed his thousand-watt smile at her, she'd nearly dropped the bottle of beer in her hands.

They'd talked for almost an hour. He drank beer, which showed he wasn't fussy, and told her he'd been modeling since he was a teen. He'd said modeling wasn't what he wanted to do for the rest of his life, but right now he was capitalizing on a career that paid really well. He wanted to take his money and open up an art studio. He'd showed her some of his photos on his phone. He was damn photogenic, with a body that was as good looking as his face.

She still couldn't figure out what the hell he was doing hitting on her, but he seemed nice and friendly and genuine. All of his friends were nice people, too, which just proved you could never judge a book by its cover.

And when Robert asked her out, she was determined to broaden her horizons, so she'd said yes.

He took her to the art museum, and he surprised her by being more than a little knowledgeable about art. He said she should go to New York, and she'd told him she'd seen the Louvre, so they talked about art over dinner. He said he liked to paint, which was one of the reasons he wanted to have his own art studio. He wanted to showcase his own work alongside other artists.

He was such an interesting guy. So damn good looking, talented, motivated, and fun to be with.

But when he kissed her good night—and he was a great kisser—meh.

Nothing. Not even a little twinge of interest. Nothing had tingled, peaked, exploded. Not even a tiny little pop.

Robert had smiled at her and told her he'd call her the next day, but she already knew she wasn't going to see him again, because there wasn't that burst of chemistry she'd had with Ty.

She wanted chemistry, dammit. Surely there was another guy out there she could have fireworks with.

Now that she'd thought about it, it had been a week and a half since she'd seen Ty.

Not that she'd noticed or anything. She'd been busy at the bar, had caught up on her sleep, and had been busy dealing with all the new guys who'd suddenly entered her life. Since she had the night off tonight she was headed over to her parents to see Mick and Tara, who were back from their honeymoon.

Liz was meeting them there, though Gavin was headed to Florida to get ready for spring training.

Jenna was beyond ready for spring, though in late February it was anything but spring-like in St. Louis.

She wished she were in Florida right now. But cold weather and hockey season brought people into the bar, which was good for Riley's.

As soon as Mick and Tara walked through the door, Jenna was green with jealousy.

"You're so tan," she said as she hugged Tara, then kissed her big brother. "I hate you both."

Tara grinned. "We had so much fun. We laid on the beach and soaked up the sun, went parasailing and snorkeling, swam with dolphins and scuba dived, and we even took a sunset sailing cruise that Mick booked for just the two of us. It was so romantic."

Tara tilted her head toward Mick, who kissed her.

"You two are so sickeningly romantic."

"We're newlyweds. I'm pretty sure that's how it's supposed to be," Mick said, grabbing her in for a hug and a kiss to her cheek. "But you'll always be my second favorite girl."

She shoved at him. "Oh, stop. You're being mushy and that's not like you."

He laughed a big, booming chuckle. "Hey, I'm happy and I'm in love. I'm entitled to be mushy."

"You are. It's disgusting. When will it end?"

He pulled Tara in front of him. "Not anytime soon."

She rolled her eyes and went to the kitchen to help her mother fix dinner.

"Those two are nauseating."

Her mom laughed. "They're in love."

"Yeah, isn't everyone," she mumbled low as she went to fetch the tomatoes for the salad.

"Maybe it's your turn next. Gavin and Mick have found the loves of their lives."

She tried for a smile, but knew it looked more like an expression of pain. "No thanks, Mom. Not ready yet."

Her mother, busily fixing meat and cheese on the tray, arched a brow. Jenna knew all her mother's facial expressions, so she knew what that one meant.

"Doesn't seem to me like you've been trying very hard."

"Actually, I have been trying. Trust me on this."

"You just haven't found the right man yet."

She opened her mouth, about to say that she didn't have the time to find the right man because she was always working at the bar.

But that would hurt her parents, and she wouldn't do that.

"Yeah, that's it."

Her mom paused, lifted her head. "Something's bothering you."

"No."

"Yes, there is. What is it?"

"It's nothing, Mom. Really. I'm just a little tired. I had a late night last night."

Her mother wiped her hands on a towel and came over, swept her hand over Jenna's forehead. "Are you okay?"

Jenna laughed. Sometimes around her parents she still felt like she was six years old. "I'm fine. Just busy."

"Are you feeling overworked at the bar?"

"No."

Her mother gave her a disbelieving look. "You don't take much time off. You know your dad or I can help."

"I don't need help. I have an assistant manager, and I do take time off." She laid her hands over her mother's. "Everything's fine at the bar, and my love life is good."

"Really. How good?"

Liz just had to walk in then, didn't she?

"Hi, sweetie," her mother said, beaming when Elizabeth kissed her on the cheek. "We were just talking about how tired Jenna looked."

"No," Jenna said. "Mom was talking about how tired I look. I was assuring her I was okay."

"So is this about work, or is this about a guy?"

"Both," her mom said. "I think she's spending too much time on work, and she's not dating anyone."

Liz studied her. Liz, of course, was perfect, her hair pulled up as usual, makeup done, lipgloss on and she wore some designer outfit—an oversize white sweater and pale, tight pants with killer boots—that likely cost more than Jenna made in a month.

And God, Jenna loved her. They'd had a rocky start once she and Gavin had started dating, but Liz had been family before she and Gavin had fallen in love, and she was like a sister to Jenna now.

"Well, far be it for me to criticize anyone for working too hard.

I'm the queen of all work and no play." Liz drummed her fingers on the counter. "But Mom is right, Jen. You need to go out."

"I had a date this week."

"You did? With whom?" her mother asked.

Jenna shrugged. "Some model."

Liz and her mother looked at each other. "Ooh, a model," her mother said.

"Do tell." Liz had a gleam in her eye.

"It didn't work out."

"Why not?" Her mother looked disappointed, and Jenna wished they weren't having this conversation.

"No chemistry."

"That's too bad. But at least you're getting out there." Her mom picked up the knife and went back to slicing tomatoes.

Good. Maybe they could drop the subject of her dating life.

"Doesn't mean you have to give up just because of one bad date," her mother said while slicing.

And then again, maybe they wouldn't be dropping the subject.

"Clearly you need some help."

Jenna's gaze shot to Liz. "No, I don't."

"I know a lot of guys."

"Yeah, guys in sports. You know my rule."

"What rule is that?" her mother asked.

"Jenna doesn't date guys who play sports."

She leveled a glare at Liz, who gave her an innocent look.

"What? Is that a secret?"

"You don't date men who play sports?" Her mother looked confused. "Why on earth not?"

She waved a hand. "No particular reason, Mom. Just that I'm surrounded by sports all the time, so I just don't want to date it. You know?"

"I guess so. This worries me, though." She laid the knife down again.

The one thing she never wanted was her mom's full attention. That meant she was focused on her, and that usually meant trouble.

"What's there to worry about?"

"You hate sports."

Jenna rolled her eyes. "I don't hate sports. I grew up around them. I love them. I just don't want to date them or marry them."

"Hmmm."

That was even worse. The examination by her mom when she pondered what she'd said.

She needed to escape.

"I think I'll go see what Dad's up to. You have things covered in here?"

"Sure. You go ahead."

She made a quick exit and hurried out to the living room. Her dad was in there with Tara, Mick, and Nathan, watching, of all things, hockey. And even worse, it was an Ice game.

It was either that or face more conversation with her mother about her job and her love life.

The lesser of two evils, she supposed, and this was no different than being at work and having the game on at the bar.

She flopped onto the sofa next to her dad.

"What's up, punkin?" he asked, slinging his arm around her.

"Mom and Liz are trying to fix me."

His dad frowned and looked her over. "Are you broken?"

"Nope."

He nodded. "Okay, then. Let's watch the game."

Thank God for her father. Everything with him was simple black-and-white. If you said you were okay, then you were. He believed you. Either that or he just wanted to watch the game and didn't want to be bothered with girl things.

More likely it was the latter, since he was a guy, which suited her just fine. As long as she didn't have to explain her lack of a boyfriend and why she didn't want to date anyone affiliated with sports, it was fine by her.

She settled in, leaning against her dad's shoulder.

The game was still in the first period. Normally, she'd be so busy at the bar that she'd only catch cursory glances at whatever games were on. And she sure as hell didn't watch sports on her days off.

This was the first time she'd actually had to watch Ty in action—undistracted, anyway.

"Your boys are looking good, Elizabeth," her dad said as Liz and her mom strolled in.

"Yes, Tyler and Eddie are great players. I'm very lucky to represent them."

Liz arched a brow at Jenna, who shot her a warning look. The very last thing she wanted was for anyone to know about that night she'd spent with Ty. Especially after telling her mother she didn't date sports players.

"Anderson was a good addition to the team," Mick said.

"I have you to thank for that, Mick. If you hadn't fired me, I likely wouldn't have been scrambling to pick up new talent and I would have never landed him."

"See? All kinds of good things came out of that mess. Mom and Dad ended up together. Liz and Gavin fell in love, and Liz got a whole bunch of new clients. And Dad and Liz made up and are friends again and now no one is mad at each other anymore. So sometimes bad things happen for all the right reasons."

They all looked at Nathan.

"Out of the mouths of babes," her mother said with a smile as she came into the room.

"You're right, Nathan," Mick said, ruffling the teenager's hair.

Nathan ducked. "Man. It took me a long time to get it to look like that."

"And here I thought you rolled out of bed and did nothing at all to get that style," Mick teased.

"Dude. You just don't know."

"What I do know is that if you call me 'dude' again, you'll be on toilet scrubbing duty for a week."

Nathan looked at Mick with a horrified expression on his face.

Tara smothered a laugh.

"Uh, yes, sir."

Mick rolled his eyes. "I don't think we have to go that far."

Jenna did laugh, then they all turned back to the game. She tried to watch the Ice as a whole team, but she couldn't help but focus her attention on Tyler. He had a magnificent command of the ice and seemed to always gravitate toward the puck. Part of that was his position as a center, but he was fast on his skates and didn't shy away from the hard action, which often got him double teamed or slammed up against the boards. He took a lot of elbows and hard knocks, ending up on his ass a lot of the time.

He didn't seem to mind. In fact he was as aggressive as the other players, shoving an elbow or body slamming someone, even if it cost him a penalty. He'd do whatever it took to get the puck and skate away with it or pass it to a teammate.

And often enough it resulted in a goal, so obviously his methods worked.

But the bottom line was, he was exciting to watch, and he got results.

By the end of the first period they were up by one goal.

"Dinner should be ready. Should we head in to the dining room?"

Everyone got up and headed that way. Jenna lingered, watching Ty skate off the ice.

"You've got it so bad for that guy," Liz whispered to her, bringing up the rear with her.

"I do not. I was just enjoying the game."

Liz snorted. "Oh, yeah. You being such a big sports fan and all."

She lifted her chin. "Hey, it's part of my job to know what's going on with all the games so I can talk to my customers about them."

"Uh-huh. It's more like you want to get your hands around his cock again."

Just the thought of it had her face flaming. "You are so wrong about that."

Liz directed a bullshit look her way. "Am I?"

"Totally. I'm going to start dating to get you all off my back."

"Are you? Great. I'll be sure to find you some awesome men that aren't in sports."

"You do that."

"Consider it done."

"Consider what done?" her mother asked.

"I'm going to play matchmaker for Jenna," Liz said with a triumphant gleam in her eyes. "I know a lot of men."

"Oh, that's wonderful. Aren't you sweet, Elizabeth?"

"Yeah, she's a peach," Jenna said as she took her seat at the table.

Tara cast her a hint of a knowing smile, while Liz downright grinned all through dinner.

She'd have to remember to decline the next time the family had a meal together.

ELEVEN

NOT MORE THAN TWO DAYS LATER, LIZ TEXTED HER AND told her she was sending her a guy.

Jenna felt like she was getting some bought-and-paid-for escort, but Liz insisted the guy was a friend of hers, and that he wasn't in any way involved in sports.

She had to work, but Liz said she'd bring him by after she finished with a client meeting, so it might be around eight or so, which was fine with her since she was stuck at the bar anyway.

With Ty, who had a day off.

She really wished he and his friends would find another bar to hang out in. But since it would be epically bad for her business to tell him and his friends to take a hike, she'd have to suck it up. Sports figures were a huge deal at Riley's. They made her customers happy, and anything that made her customers happy was good for Riley's.

It appeared Victor had coupled up with Lisa, the platinum blonde bar bunny who was also a regular, and Eddie had finally come up with the courage to ask Renee out, so now the two of them were dating. And since Ty, Victor, and Eddie were pretty much best friends, it made sense for Ty to hang out with his buddies.

Still, she couldn't help but think he frequented her bar because of her and his interest in her.

Though he hadn't exactly acted interested the last few times he'd been in here, not since the day after the wedding when she'd effectively shut him down cold.

God, she'd been such a bitch about it, too. Rude and dismissive, as if what they'd shared the night before hadn't meant anything at all, when it had been the best night she'd had in at least a year—possibly longer.

Which was why it could never happen again.

Seeing him again reminded her of just how good it had been, which made her want it to happen again, which just made everything worse, and made her bitchy and cranky.

Maybe if Ty saw her moving on with a new guy, he'd move on, too, and they could both get past what had happened the night of the wedding.

She hoped Liz was great at choosing men. This had to work.

Liz showed up a little after ten, later than she thought she'd be. But Dylan, the guy Liz brought with her, was worth the wait.

He was a suit, but hot as hell in a suit. Light brown hair, gorgeous blue eyes, and the kind of smile that lit up a room. Very tall and well built, and every woman stopped and stared when he walked in. He had an easygoing presence about him that commanded attention. He looked rugged and full of masculinity, but he was friendly. She liked that.

He hung out at the bar with her and Liz, but he was focused on her. She took a break, putting Renee behind the bar since traffic was light.

That meant Eddie gravitated toward the bar and kept Renee company, but as long as she did her job, Jenna didn't mind.

Dylan drank whiskey and soda.

A man's drink. She liked that about him.

He was a lawyer. Self-deprecating, funny, charming.

"I travel a lot, which doesn't leave me a lot of time for dating," he said.

"I'm always working, so the same."

He leaned toward her. "I would think you'd get hit on all the time, considering your occupation."

"Not really. I have regulars. They're pretty protective. And I don't date all that often. I'm picky."

He looked her over. "So am I."

She didn't seem at all his type. He should be running with some model or someone in the corporate world, not a girl with tattoos, piercings, and purple streaks in her hair. She wondered what he saw in her.

"What do you like to do in your off time, Dylan?"

"I go boating in the summer. I like the outdoors. Hiking, camping, water skiing, riding my bike. I'm not much for sitting around doing nothing."

"You must hate the winter, then."

He laughed. "I spend a lot of time at the gym. There's a rock wall at my gym and I climb it every chance I get. Fortunately, I have some clients in Colorado, so I do some snowboarding and skiing."

Not exactly sports, but he was a definite jock. And when Ty came over to talk to Eddie, Dylan's radar went off.

"Hey, isn't that Tyler Anderson and Eddie Wolkowski from the Ice?"

"It is."

"You know them?" He gave her a hopeful look.

"I do. I'm surprised Liz didn't mention that they were both her clients."

He turned his attention to Elizabeth. "You never told me you knew them."

Liz shrugged. "The subject never came up."

"Man, I'm a huge hockey fan. Can I get an intro?"

"Sure. Come with me." Jenna took his hand while Liz fumed silently.

This would be comical if it wasn't so ironic.

"Hey, Tyler, Eddie, this is Dylan Manchester. He's a big fan of yours."

Tyler's gaze roamed over hers before turning to Dylan. He shook his hand.

"Always nice to meet a fan. Hi, Dylan."

Eddie shook his hand, and before she knew it Dylan had abandoned her for the sports stars.

Fine with her. She had to get back behind the bar anyway. Renee took off to see to her customers at the tables, and Liz pinned her with a suspicious look.

"It's like you planned this."

Jenna rolled her eyes as she filled some drink orders. "Now how could I have possibly known he was a hockey fan? You're the one who brought him to me, remember?"

Liz studied her glass of wine. "Obviously I'm going to have to do a better job of vetting potential dates for you in the future."

"Obviously. Maybe a questionnaire?"

"You are so funny."

She smirked. "I try to be."

"But seriously, Jenna. Doesn't it annoy you that he's off with Ty and Eddie?"

"No. Should it?"

"You hate sports."

"I told you. I don't hate it. I just don't want to date anyone who loves or plays it. I get plenty of it here, as you can see."

Liz sighed. "I was so hopeful with Dylan. He's amazing eye candy."

Jenna let her gaze wander down the bar, but it didn't settle on Dylan. She couldn't help but gravitate toward Ty. Even though Dylan was drop dead gorgeous, in the middle of a pack of handsome men, it was Ty who captured her attention. He tilted the bottle of beer to his lips, and all she could think of was his mouth on hers, the way he kissed her. She watched his fingertips absently stroke the moisture on the outside of the bottle as he laughed with the guys, and remembered his touch, the way his fingers played along her skin.

She shivered.

"Sorry it didn't work out with you and Dylan."

She flipped her attention back to Liz. "No big deal."

Liz looked at the end of the bar. "Or maybe it's not Dylan you were looking at."

"Of course it was. He's hot."

"So's Ty."

"I was not looking at Ty. That's over."

Liz crossed her arms and laid them on the bar. "Is it? Why do you fight the attraction when it's so obvious?"

"It's not obvious. He's moved on and so have I."

Liz laughed. "You have not. You've been watching him the entire time I've been here."

"I haven't—oh, hell. I have been." It was pointless to deny it, when the truth was so obvious. "I can't help myself. He's like a virus I can't get rid of."

"That bad, huh?"

"He's always here."

"I don't think he's always here. It's hockey season. He plays a lot of games and he's frequently on the road. Maybe you just notice him when he is here."

"I guess. I don't know. It's hard to forget about someone you slept with when they keep showing up where you work."

"So he's bothering you."

"Not in the least. He ignores me."

"He blew you off."

"No. I dumped him."

Liz threw her hands in the air. "Then what's the problem?"

"I don't know. He's just . . . there. Reminding me."

"Of?"

She narrowed her gaze at Liz. "Are you sure you're not an attorney?"

Liz laughed. "I'm certain. But I know he's gotten to you, so what it is about him?"

"We had an amazing night together."

"So go have some more. No one says you have to marry the guy, but if you had fun with him, who cares if he plays sports? I know for a fact Ty isn't the settling-down type."

"He's not?"

"No."

Then maybe she'd been approaching this all wrong. Maybe she should just screw his brains out and get him out of her system, and then they could go their separate ways.

"You could be right. I just didn't get enough of him, and he's on my mind a lot. It's not like I care for him."

"Right. You just want more of that hot stuff he's offering."

She let out a snort. "Something like that."

"So go for it."

"If he's interested. Remember, I dumped him."

"Honey, he has a penis. He's interested. And men are different than women, in case you haven't noticed. If he was hurt over being dumped, do you think he'd still be coming here?"

"Good point." Ty didn't act hurt. He still smiled and waved at her, he was still friendly. He'd just been maintaining his distance.

It was, after all, what she'd asked for. She'd told him it was over.

But now she didn't want it to be over.

Ugh. When had she become *that* woman?

"I don't know, Liz. He might think I'm crazy."

"We're all crazy. That's what makes women so interesting. Go up and talk to him."

"In front of my date for tonight?"

"Pfft. I'll take care of Dylan. I have some legal matters to talk over with him anyway. And if Dylan had the hots for you, no hockey team in the world would have been able to pull him away."

"Huh. So you're saying I wasn't exactly his type?"

"He likes big boobs."

She gaped at her less-than-generous chest, then at Liz. "Why the hell did you set him up with me?"

Liz shrugged. "To see if you'd go through with it."

"You *are* crazy."

"See? I told you." Liz slid off the bar stool and headed over to Dylan, pulled him away from his adoration of the Ice players, and led him to one of the tables. Ever a gentleman, he went where Liz directed him.

Not that Jenna expected him to do otherwise. Liz had a dominating presence and guys tended to do what they were asked to do when she was the one doing the commanding.

In fact, it took less than ten minutes for Liz to return to the bar with Dylan and grab her purse.

"There's a few papers in my office I need to go over with Dylan, so we're heading out."

Dylan shook her hand. "Really nice to meet you, Jenna. You have a great bar here."

"Nice to meet you, too, Dylan. Come back anytime."

She went around to kiss and hug Liz. "Thanks."

Liz's eyes sparkled with mischief. "You're welcome. Now make good use of your time."

It wasn't exactly in her realm of experience to make up with a guy she'd recently dumped. But in order to exorcise Ty from her life, she was going to have to get her fill of him, and that meant eating crow was in order.

Since Dylan had left and Renee was off waiting on her customers, the guys had moved back to the pool tables. Jenna didn't relish the idea of wading into a sea of Ice players to talk to Ty, and getting him alone might be problematic.

She pondered the situation, even considered giving Renee a note to give to him, then thought better of it. What if he shared it with his friends? They'd all laugh.

And this isn't high school, you idiot. Where are your balls?

Sucking up her courage, she called one of the waitresses over to cover the bar and headed over to the group.

"How's it going tonight?"

"We are great. Steaks were good," Victor said with a smile.

"Hey, Jenna."

Ty smiled at her, seemed friendly.

"Hi."

"Sorry about monopolizing your date tonight."

"He wasn't my date. He was with Liz."

"Yeah, but she brought him here for you. I guess things didn't work out?"

She bit her cheek to keep from saying something she'd regret later. "I guess not."

"Too bad." He leaned against the pool table. "Maybe next time."

"Maybe."

This wasn't going at all like she'd planned. She pivoted to head back to the bar.

"Jenna."

"Yeah."

"Was there some reason you came over here?"

Balls, Jenna, remember? You dumped him. It's up to you to get him back.

She sucked in a breath and turned around, plastering on a smile. "Oh. Yeah. I was just wondering when you had a day off next."

"Wednesday. Why?"

"Would you like to come over? Maybe have pizza or something?"

She saw his brow arch, waited for him to make some remark.

"I thought you didn't want to have anything to do with me after that night."

And there it was. She deserved it.

"I changed my mind."

He didn't say anything for the longest time.

That was it. He was going to say no and she was going to be humiliated.

Dumbass. You should have known better.

"I like pizza."

She exhaled. *Thank you, Ty.* "Great. How about seven?"

"Sure. See you then."

She swallowed, those butterflies stomping around in her stomach. Damn them.

Soon enough she'd send those butterflies off to fly around in someone else's belly. She just had to get Ty out of her system. And when she did, the butterflies would go away.

TWELVE

TY KNEW EXACTLY WHAT JENNA WAS DOING.

He'd seen the parade of guys she'd been trying to date—hell, he'd sent a few of them her way. He'd also noticed none of them had stuck around. He wasn't too unhappy about that. He'd gambled on setting her up with some of those guys. None of them had been losers. But he also knew her type—him. It had just taken her a while to figure that out.

Maybe he wasn't exactly the man of her dreams, yet here he was, driving up to her place again. At her invitation. She hadn't exactly forfeited the game, but she was obviously trying to exorcise some demons—with him in the starring role of Beelzebub.

He grinned as he grabbed a bottle of wine from the passenger seat and headed to the front door.

This should be interesting.

She opened the door and he drank in the sight of her dressed in skin-tight jeans and a loose fitting top that fell over one shoulder, revealing skin he wanted to sink his teeth into. She was barefoot, her toenails painted black and white.

Cute.

"Hey," she said, smiling as she let him in.

"Hey yourself. You look nice."

"Thanks. I'm starving, so what kind of pizza do you like?"

"Anything with meat on it."

"Good. That's the kind I like, too. I'll go order it." She looked at the bottle of Cabernet in his hand. "Wine?"

"I like wine. It goes good with pizza."

"It does, actually. Corkscrew is in the right-hand top drawer next to the sink. Go ahead and open it while I call for the pizza. Glasses are in the cabinet above the dishwasher."

He went into the kitchen, opened the wine, and found two glasses. He leaned against the counter, letting the wine breathe for a few minutes. Jenna came in.

"You know wine."

He crossed his arms. "I'm not just some dumb hockey jerk. I have a few skills. Like knowing the right wine to go with—"

"Pepperoni and sausage pizza."

He held up the bottle. "A smooth Jacob's Creek Cabernet."

"Oh. Australian. I'm impressed."

He poured the red into their glasses and handed her one. She inhaled the wine, then took a sip.

"Good choice. And you're right. Perfect for pizza. But you still don't strike me as a wine guy."

"Now what fun would I be if I was predictable?"

She walked out into the living room and he followed.

"I might have to rethink my labeling of you."

"Does that mean you have me all figured out now?"

She laughed. "Not a chance."

She took a seat on the sofa, and he sat next to her. "Good. Hopefully I'll keep you guessing."

"You'd be the first."

"How about the guy the other night? The whiskey guy? Did you have him figured out?"

"I thought I did, but then he saw you guys and became a fan boy, and that was the end of him."

"All because he likes hockey?"

"No. There was no spark between us."

He leaned over and played with a lock of her hair. "That spark's important to you, isn't it?"

"Chemistry is important. There's no point in spending time with someone if you don't have it."

"True. So that's why I'm here? The undeniable chemistry you have with me?"

She lifted her gaze to his. "Something like that."

He leaned in and brushed his lips to hers. She moved forward, balanced her wineglass in one hand, and laid her other hand against his chest.

His heartbeat sped up when she kissed him back.

Yeah, that chemistry between them was a hell of a thing. He'd never been in a drought where women were concerned, but lately he hadn't been interested enough in anyone else to even take a second look. Not since Jenna. There was something about her that was his primary focus. Maybe he had a few of his own demons to demolish.

He cupped the back of her neck and deepened the kiss, sliding his tongue in to taste her.

Wine and peppermint, a heady combination that made his cock tighten. His body heated. He wanted to pull her on top of him and take off her clothes.

He pulled away only long enough to take the wineglass out of her hand and put it on the table. She swept her tongue across her bottom lip and pulled her legs up on the sofa.

"Shouldn't we wait for the pizza guy?"

He arched a brow. "Why? Do you have some three-way porn fantasy involving the pizza guy? Is that why I'm really here tonight?"

She tilted her head back and laughed hard. "Isn't that a man's fantasy? The whole ménage thing?"

He gave her a hard stare. "I don't share."

"Good to know. I'm not much into sharing, either."

"Good. Now that we got that settled . . ."

He reached for her, but the doorbell rang.

Too bad.

Jenna slipped off the sofa, but he beat her to the door and paid the pizza delivery girl, who obviously recognized him.

"You're Tyler Anderson. I love hockey. I'm a big fan."

"Thanks a lot." He winked at her, tipped her ten bucks, which made her eyes widen, then carried the pizza into the kitchen.

"Oh, that smells good." Jenna set out plates and they piled on the pizza.

"I have a couple movies we could watch."

"Oh, yeah? What kind of movies?"

"Fantasy, action, romance, horror."

"I like any of them."

She cocked her head to the side. "You'd watch a romantic comedy."

"I like to be entertained. Whichever one you pick will be fine, as long as it doesn't suck."

She grabbed her plate and the bottle of wine and they headed into the living room. "The pressure's on now."

"What pressure?"

"To pick a movie that doesn't suck."

He grabbed a slice of pizza, then put his feet up on the table. "I'm pretty easy to please, Jenna. Just put a movie in and I'll like it."

"Okay." She got up, slid a DVD in, and pressed play.

It was a horror movie.

He loved horror movies. A lot of women didn't. A point in Jenna's favor.

They finished eating, and Jenna turned off the lights.

"Now this is how horror movies should be watched."

"I always thought so." She finished off her glass of wine, then moved next to him.

He lifted his arm and she snuggled against him.

Ty dated plenty of women, which usually meant they went out to a club, a bar, or a restaurant, and then had sex.

This was different. Staying home, having pizza, and watching a movie? He hadn't done this in a long time. At the height of his season, he was on the go all the time. What free time he had, he usually spent at the bar playing pool with his teammates. That relaxed him and let him wind down after a grueling game.

But this? It was nice. Being with a woman and doing nothing but feeling her body next to his and sinking into the plot of a grisly horror movie? Yeah, this was a whole different kind of relaxation.

Jenna tensed during the kill scenes, when the murderer leaped out of the shadows with his knife. She didn't hide her eyes, though. But by the tail end of the movie her legs were draped over his and she was practically sitting on his lap.

"Are you sure you like horror movies?" he asked when the movie was over.

She reached for her glass of wine and held it while he poured her a refill. "Oh, they scare the hell out of me. I love them. I'll probably have nightmares tonight."

He laughed and shook his head. "So you like being scared."

"With movies, yes. Anything else, no. So don't get any ideas about lurking in corners or jumping out at me. You'll give me a heart attack and I'll throw you out of my house."

"Noted." They drank wine and she put in an action comedy next. "I need to unwind after the first movie. I need something to make me laugh."

The movie was fun and action filled, with lots of explosions and car chases and great special effects. Jenna did a good job choosing movies. But he had to admit he liked the first one better, mainly because she'd stayed so close to him throughout.

Not that she'd moved all that far away during this movie. He wasn't as invested in this one, so his attention wandered to Jenna's legs, the way the jeans fit her like they were glued to her skin, outlining every one of her curves.

He played with her hair, letting his fingers sift through the softness of it.

"Have you always worn your hair short?"

She dragged her gaze away from the television. "In high school I wore it down to my waist. It was a giant pain in the ass to deal with, so when I traveled out of the country I cut it all off."

He tugged at one of the ends. "This suits you."

"Yeah? How so?"

"Your face is small, so too much hair would overwhelm you. Plus it makes your eyes stand out, and I can see your earrings. And you have really cute ears. The whole package is sexy."

She turned her head a little to the side. "Uh, wow. Thank you."

"You're welcome."

She handed him her glass and he put it on the end table. Then she climbed onto his lap and he put his hands on her hips, feeling the warmth of her body through her jeans.

"I'd be lying if I didn't tell you I've been thinking about this all night."

She palmed his chest. "Thinking about what?"

"You in this position."

"You like a woman on top?"

"I like you in my lap." He flexed his fingers, testing the give and play of her flesh. "I like being able to feel you move against me."

She slid up his lap until the crotch of her jeans aligned with the quickly tightening bulge in his pants.

"Like that?"

He lifted his gaze to hers. "Exactly like that."

"This would be a lot more fun if we were naked."

"No hurry." He knew she was ready to get started on banishing those demons, but he just wanted to feel her body on his. They'd get to the naked part later. He swept his hands up the side of her ribs and along her back, then drew her against him. Her breasts pillowed against his chest, her nose just inches from his.

He palmed the nape of her neck and pulled her in for a kiss. This time, there'd be no one to interrupt them.

The softest sigh escaped her lips as their mouths met, their lips sliding together. He kept it slow and easy to start, his fingers dancing in her hair, holding her in place as he moved his mouth over hers. He swept his hand over her back and turned her so her legs were on the sofa and he had her cradled in his arms.

Then he settled into the kiss, demanding more, sliding his tongue inside her mouth to sweep against hers. She moaned and pushed her body closer to his. He heated, hardened, and snaked his hand down her back to cup and squeeze her butt.

It would be so easy to give her exactly what she wanted—to strip her bare and fuck her—to get them both off and release the tension that drove them both.

But that would be too easy, and he didn't want anything about this to be easy.

He wanted this to be a whole lot of complicated, so she wouldn't run off and find some other guy tomorrow.

Why he cared, he didn't know. He wasn't looking for a relationship or permanence of any kind. But he still didn't want Jenna to find it with anyone else. If that made him an asshole, he'd have to live with that.

He laid her head in the crook of his arm and turned her over so he could run his hand over her breasts. She hadn't worn a bra tonight, and he'd watched her nipples harden every time she got a chill. It had been hard not to reach out and touch them, to scoop a handful of them and tease the puckered crests every time they tightened against her top.

Now he rubbed his thumb over one, then the other, watching them peak from his touch. He tucked his hand under her shirt, her stomach quivering when he palmed it. He smiled down at her, then walked his fingers along her rib cage and laid his hand over her breast.

He loved touching her, loved seeing the spark of passion in her eyes when he rolled his thumb over her nipple.

"Lift, babe."

She sat up and he lifted the shirt over her head. He had her back in his arms right away, her breasts bared. Now he could play, could lift her in his arms and flick his tongue over her nipple, could lick and suck them until he heard the sweet gasps and whimpers she made.

Oh, yeah, he liked listening to her, liked feeling her wriggle against him as she turned toward him to fit a breast into his mouth. He cupped her breast, flicked his tongue over the nipple, and sucked it between his lips, using his teeth to lightly nibble until she couldn't hold still, until she moaned and clutched his arm, digging her nails in his skin.

And when he smoothed his hand over her belly and started moving south, he heard the hitch in her breath and smiled.

Yeah, that's exactly where he was going. Right to the button of her jeans. He undid the button, drew the zipper down, and slid his hand into her pants.

"Ty."

He wasn't sure if his name was a statement, a whisper, or a plea. All he knew was her skin felt like fire under her flimsy silk panties. He dipped his fingers below her sex and touched the dangling piercing. Her body hummed, and her sweet scent filled the air around them. He slipped his fingers lower and she was damp.

"Let's get these off."

She tugged at the hips of her jeans and shimmied out of them, kicking them to the end of the couch.

Her panties had white and pink stripes and were see-through, the edges barely scraping her hip bones. She reached for them but he stopped her.

"Leave these on. They're sexy. Let me touch you."

He palmed the panties, felt her heat and wetness through them. And when he swiped his fingers over her sex, she arched against him. He spread the panties aside, sweeping his fingers over her pussy lips. She was like velvet here, smooth and silky. He wanted to lick her, to feel her sweet cream spill over his tongue until she came.

He sat her up and laid her back against the sofa, then dropped to his knees, drawing her legs to the edge. He scooped her butt in his hands and tilted her toward his mouth, then met her gaze as he licked the length of her.

"Oh," was all she said as he flicked his tongue along the piercing at her clit, then took it in his mouth and sucked her, letting the bud rest against his tongue. Her flavor made his dick pound. He wanted to hear her scream, wanted her to come in his mouth.

He lashed his tongue across her lips, then slid it inside her. She lifted against him, sliding her pussy against his face.

Her response drove him crazy. It would be so easy to take his cock out and pound it inside her right now until they both came. But this was a sweet pleasure for her, and her pleasure was more important. His would come later.

Everything about her turned him on, from the way she lifted her butt to the way her muscles tightened when she was near orgasm. He flattened his tongue against her clit and wriggled it around the piercing. She cried out with a low moan, climaxing with shudders and whispered moans that nearly shattered his control.

· He kissed her thighs and her belly, moving up to her breasts, watching them rise and fall with her heavy breathing.

She lifted her head and smiled down at him, then reached for him to plant a kiss on his mouth, licking his lips and taking a taste of herself.

"Mmm," she said, then grabbed his shirt and lifted it off him, tossing it aside. She planted her hands on his shoulders, letting her hands slide down his arms.

He liked the way she touched him, liked the way her gaze roamed over his body with a pure feminine appreciation that made him damn glad to be a man.

"Now I want *you* on the sofa," she said.

He was happy to comply.

"But first, get those pants off."

He grinned, kicked his boots and socks off, then watched as she slid to her knees on the floor.

Oh, yeah. He saw where she was going with this, and his balls tightened. The thought of her mouth on him made his dick quiver in anticipation. He wanted this, had thought about it over and over again in his fantasies about Jenna. And he had a lot of fantasies about her when he wasn't with her. Even when he was with her.

So he thought about her a lot. Didn't mean anything. Just meant she was hot and he hadn't had his fill of her yet.

It might take awhile for him to get enough of Jenna.

She rose up against him, dragging her breasts against his chest. The tease of her nipples made his cock ache for her. He widened his legs, but she drew back.

"Not yet. I have plans for you." She brushed her thumb against his bottom lip, then swiped his lip with her tongue before diving in to take a hard, hot taste of him.

He wrapped his arms around her and drew her close, skimming the soft skin of her back before snaking down to grab a handful of the sweet globes of her ass. He pulled her against his cock, needing to feel that connection. His dick throbbed. He'd tasted her, waited for her, and wanted to be inside her—now.

But Jenna had other plans, because she pulled away, planting kisses on his neck as she wound her way down to his chest, using her hands and mouth to drive him crazy. She razed his nipples with the tips of her fingers, dragging her tongue over one, then the other. He sucked in a breath as a lightning bolt of sensation shot to his cock. It jutted up between them and he rubbed it against her belly.

She laughed, lifted her head to grin at him. "I'm getting there. Be patient."

He didn't feel patient right now. He was hungry for her.

She had a body he couldn't get enough of, and the way she touched him drove him crazy. She was torturing him with her fingernails, raking them down his body, her mouth following her touch. She licked him, dragged her teeth over his skin until he lifted his hips off the sofa. He wasn't sure if he wanted more or if he couldn't stand it. All he knew was it felt so damn good and he wanted her hands and her mouth near his cock.

And when she laid her hands over his thighs and lifted her head to meet his gaze, he was ready to beg.

But he didn't have to, because she gripped his cock at the base and stroked it, winding both hands over the shaft. He laid his head back and watched as she rolled her thumb over the crest.

His balls tightened and his cock jerked as she squeezed his cock in a vise grip.

God, he could shoot his load right now just watching her hands on him.

And when she bent and put her lips over the head, he gritted his teeth, because her mouth was hot and wet and it was sweet hell from a beautiful woman.

She rolled her tongue over his cock head, then down along the underside of his shaft, teasing his balls with the tip of her tongue before flattening it and worshiping his ball sac.

"Christ, Jenna. That feels good."

She took his balls in her mouth and rolled her tongue over them, then licked back up to his cock again, flicking her tongue over every part of it before engulfing it with her mouth.

She went down on him like a goddess, like every man's dream. He leaned forward and tangled his fingers in her hair, helping her set a rhythm. He couldn't help but push her down on his cock so she'd take all of him, wondering if she'd balk.

She made sounds of approval, wrapped her hand around the base of his shaft to squeeze and stroke him. His balls quivered. He couldn't take much more of this. He gritted his teeth, his body stretched tight with the need to release.

"Oh, yeah, I'm going to come." He wanted to give her time to back up and let go of him, but she pressed her lips firmly around his cock.

He broke into a sweat as his orgasm ripped through his body, making him shudder and rock so hard his legs shook. Watching Jenna take it all, her throat working as she swallowed, heightened the intensity of his orgasm. When it was over, Jenna released him, pressing a kiss to his cock. She licked her lips and climbed up his body to kiss him. He cupped the back of her neck and slipped his tongue in her mouth, shaken by the intimacy she'd shown him.

She laid her head on his chest and caressed him, letting him recover.

"You taste good," she said.

He grinned. "So do you. And thanks. I enjoyed that."

"So did I. I've wanted to do that for a while, but you're always doing things for me."

He rubbed her back, loving the way she arched against his hand, like she wanted more. "I like kissing you and touching you. I like knowing you get off on what I do for you."

She lifted her head to look at him. "Everything you do to me gets me off. But you probably already noticed that."

"You have a responsive body."

"Not with everyone. But with you? Definitely yes."

"There are others?"

She laughed. "No. I think you know that, too. And how about you, hotshot hockey player? With Liz as your agent? She's got to be throwing women at you all the time."

"She's reformed after the mess with Mick. Said she's staying out of her clients' love lives forever."

"I believe that. Not that you'd have any trouble attracting plenty of women on your own."

Interesting that she wanted to know if he was seeing other women. And here he thought she didn't care. Maybe he was wrong.

He ran his hands down her rib cage, then pulled her up on his lap to cup her breasts. "I'm too busy to chase women."

"You've been doing a pretty decent job chasing me."

"Ah, but you're special."

"Yeah? How so?"

"I like the way you look, the way you taste, the way you come apart under my hands and my mouth." He grazed his thumbs over her nipples.

She sucked in a breath. "Oh, that feels good. Pinch them."

He grasped her nipples between his thumb and middle fingers, giving them a light squeeze.

"I like that I can touch you like this and you tell me what you want."

"God, yes, I like that. Do it harder."

He liked that she could get into a little pain, that he didn't have to treat her like a fragile flower. His cock felt like throbbing steel as he tightened his grip on her nipples. He pulled and tweaked them until she gasped.

Jenna grasped her breasts and tugged her bottom lip with her teeth. She rocked her pussy against his cock.

"Can you get yourself off that way?" he asked.

"Probably."

"Do it. I want to watch."

She surged forward, then back, sliding her wet pussy against his shaft. He caught teasing glimpses of her tiny piercing, felt it when she seesawed back and forth over his raging hard-on.

The muscles of her thighs worked as she pitched forward, then leaned back, using his cock to pleasure herself. And when she reached down to rub her clit, he couldn't stand it anymore.

He held on to her and leaned forward, grabbing the condom from his pants. He tore open the wrapper, and Jenna scooted back while he put it on in record time.

She lifted, then impaled herself on his cock, crying out when he was fully buried inside her.

His cock jerked as she surrounded him, squeezing him with tiny pulses.

"I'm so ready to come," she said, panting heavily. She leaned back, resting her hands on his thighs. "Finish me off, then fuck me hard."

He moistened his fingers with her juices and rubbed his fingers over her clit.

"Oh, right there." She met his gaze full on as he pumped into her and massaged the hard bud. "Yes, that's going to make me come, Ty."

He felt the contractions of her orgasm grip him in a tight vise. She moaned, then rode him hard as she came, throwing herself forward, lifting and slamming down on his cock.

Watching her come was magic. She went on full force, going from one peak to the next. He thrust deep with all he had until he couldn't hold back any longer. He wrapped his arms around her and took one of her nipples into his mouth, sucking it deeply as he climaxed with a hard groan. Jenna threaded her fingers into his hair and held on tight while he jettisoned his come with a shudder and a groan.

He licked her nipple, flicking it with his tongue, loving the vibration of her contented hum as they settled. He fell back against the sofa and she brushed his hair away from his forehead.

Her cheeks were flushed, her nipples swollen. The aftermath of sex with her was always fun. She wasn't shy about her body or about sex, likely why he enjoyed being with her.

"I'm hungry again," she said.

"There's leftover pizza."

She nodded. "I love cold pizza."

He slapped her on the butt. "Me, too."

She climbed off him. "Good. You'll need the protein, because I'll be ready for another round soon."

"Insatiable, are you?"

She reached for her clothes and headed toward the bathroom. "You have no idea."

THIRTEEN

JENNA DIDN'T NORMALLY CONSIDER HERSELF SEX-starved.

Oh, she loved sex, craved a good orgasm, but it was rare to find a guy who was her equal in bed.

She knew she was going to have a problem with Ty. Not only was he fun to be around, he was a sexual dynamo. He gave her everything she wanted, and then some. He wasn't needy, wimpy, metrosexual, or submissive. Surprisingly, a lot of men were. She didn't want to take charge in bed. She didn't mind on occasion, but she wanted a man who knew what he was doing with his cock. Ty definitely knew what to do with it. She got hot flashes just thinking about what he did with his cock. And his hands. And his mouth. Damn.

He also didn't fish for compliments about his sexual prowess—unsurprisingly, a lot of men did that, too. He seemed content to have sex with her and obviously enjoyed the hell out of it, just like she did. And not once did he ask her if it had been okay for her, or if he'd been good enough. He'd just assumed he'd rocked her world, which he had. She'd clearly given him evidence of that.

They made a good pair, and didn't that just suck, because her intent was to wring as much pleasure as she could out of him, then when she got tired of the game, dump him.

That sounded awful, but hell, men did it all the time. Why couldn't she?

Except he was sprawled on the floor in front of her sofa. They'd eaten pizza, had sex again, and now they were watching another movie. Ty seemed content to drink a soda and spend the night just hanging out with her. He'd made no demands other than on her body, which was sore in all the right places.

She'd had a great night, and she wasn't done with him by a long shot.

The movie ended and he tilted his head back. "Did you like that one?"

She had. And so had he. He had a great laugh and even reached up to grab her hand during the emotional, weepy part when he'd heard her sniffling. And—bonus—he hadn't made fun of her. There was a lot to be said for a man who supported a woman who cried at the sad parts of movies.

"It was a good romance."

He swiveled to face her. "It was. They both made mistakes and they did stupid shit they needed to make up for, so there was a balance on both sides. Both of them were wrong."

"That's true. They each had to grow and learn about themselves before they ended up together at the end."

He grinned. "Yeah. It was a good story. And I liked the fact that he brought her that puppy from the animal shelter."

"Awww. A sucker for animals, are you?"

"Every time. But don't give away my secret. It might ruin my macho killer image on the ice."

"Your secret is safe with me."

"Good to know. Now tell me about your secret."

She arched a brow. "What secret?"

He stood and held out his hand. Curious, she slid her hand in his and he hauled her to her feet and walked down the hall.

"I saw this the other day when you left me in your house."

He stopped in front of the music room. She frowned, and then realized what he was referring to.

"Oh, the guitar?"

"Yeah. And the music. You write."

She shrugged, determined to downplay the music thing. "Some."

He leaned against the doorway. "Looks like a lot more than some. And you obviously play."

"Again. Some." She was surprised he'd even noticed.

"Do you sing, too?"

"A little."

"Great. Play a song and sing for me."

She shook her head. "Oh, no. I only do it for myself."

"Why?"

"Because it relaxes me and it's something I enjoy doing on my off time."

"I mean, why do you only sing and play for yourself? Are you bad?"

She lifted her chin. "No, I'm not bad."

"Then play for me."

"I don't think so."

He took her hands in his. "I want to hear you, Jenna. Please play something for me."

The sincerity in his voice, in his expression, pulled something inside her. She never played for other people. Not since Europe. And that had been a long time ago.

"I don't know."

"Just one song. You have all this music here. Let me hear one song."

"Fine." She sat on the floor and grabbed the guitar.

He grinned and came into the room, dropping onto the loveseat, looking as eager as if he'd just gotten front-row seats to see Nickelback or Beyoncé or someone famous.

"I hope you're not expecting anything life changing here."

"I'm not expecting anything, Jenna. I just want to hear you."

She warmed up her fingers on the strings, then started to play. Just music at first, getting used to the idea of actually playing in front of someone again.

But as the song filled her head, she forgot Ty was there, and she did what came naturally to her—she sang, the words flowing out from her as she strummed the strings of the guitar.

It was one of the songs she'd written recently—about needing freedom, of feeling trapped and being chained. She worked into a bridge about her dreams, of all the places she'd go if she were free. It was a slow, melancholy song, but one filled with hope.

When she finished, she looked up, and Ty was leaning forward, his elbows resting on his knees.

"Wow, Jenna. You're amazing."

She felt the heat from her neck to her cheeks. "You think so?"

"Yeah. I mean, a lot more amazing than I thought you'd be."

Her lips curved. "So, you expected me to suck."

"I expected this was just something you dabbled in. I didn't expect you to be so damn good. You have an incredible voice. And that song. You wrote it?"

She nodded.

"How long have you been writing music?"

She shrugged.

"Jenna."

"A long time."

He dragged his fingers through his hair and stood, then sat on the floor across from her. "I'm no expert in music, but that was good. Really good."

"Thanks."

"How long have you been playing?"

"Again. A long time."

"Tell me about it."

"It's not really a big deal."

He looked around at the sheet music piled up and scattered throughout the room. "It's obviously a big deal to you. You write, you play. Tell me."

She sucked in a breath. "I took a couple music courses in college before I dropped out. I really enjoyed them a lot."

"And?" he asked after she paused.

"Nothing. I just liked the courses and missed the whole music thing after I was done with school. So I started writing songs."

"Sing something else."

She couldn't help the little thrill that zinged through her. "Okay."

This time she chose a song more upbeat, a popular song familiar to anyone who ever listened to the radio. It was one of her favorites, and it was in her range. She sang it all the time and it always made her feel good. When she finished, Tyler clapped and she laughed.

"Thanks," she said.

"So why aren't you doing this . . . somewhere?"

"Somewhere?"

"Yeah. Like on a stage somewhere. In public."

She let out a snort, then laid the guitar in the stand, pushed off the carpet, and stood. "Please. I'm an amateur."

He stood, too. "Amateur my ass."

When she would have walked away, he held her back by grabbing her hand.

"You're an incredible singer, Jenna. People should hear you."

She frowned. "No."

"Why not?"

"Because I don't want to." She walked out of the room and headed back to the living room, Ty's words zinging around in her head.

"You're afraid to sing in public?"

"That's not it."

"Then what is it?"

She grabbed the empty pizza box and started cleaning up. "Leave it alone, Ty."

But he followed her into the kitchen. "You have a talent you're wasting."

She ignored him and lifted the trash out of the can. He took it from her and tied it up, then took it outside, giving her a minute to inhale and blow it out in a frustrated breath.

She bit her lip to keep the tears back. She never sang in front of anyone. Not anymore. No one knew about her hobby. It had always been just for her, a way to let out her frustrations, to pour out her feelings about whatever was on her mind.

Why had she sung in front of him? That made no sense. She should have kept it to herself. Instead, she'd played for him. She'd sung not only a popular song, but one she'd written.

He liked it, had made it seem like she was really good.

He'd touched a nerve, had tapped into her dreams and fantasies, making her want things she knew she could never have.

"Where are your trash can bags?"

"What?" She hadn't heard him come back in.

"Trash bags, to line your kitchen can?"

"Oh. Right. Under the sink."

Forcing herself to focus, she turned around. "I can do that."

"Already done."

"Well, thanks."

"You're welcome."

She turned away, but he wound his arms around her and pulled her back against his chest.

"You're a great singer, Jenna. I only meant to compliment you, not piss you off."

She sighed. She was being overly sensitive. "I appreciate it. And I'm not pissed off."

He cocked his head to the side. "Somehow I think there's more to this story."

"Not really."

He turned her around to face him. "Whatever it is, you can talk to me about it."

"I played when I was in Germany. There's an awesome music scene there and I hooked up with a few bands. I was living my dream and having the time of my life, writing and singing."

He folded his arms and leaned against the counter. "Yeah? That's great."

"It was. We got an audition to do this big show. Except they only wanted the band. Not me. They hated my voice, said I was holding back the band."

"Ouch."

"The band kicked me out and that was the end of my singing."

"Jenna, rejection is part of the business, isn't it?"

She shrugged. "Maybe. I don't know. I just wasn't good enough."

He pushed off the counter and came to her, laid his hands on her shoulders. "You are good enough. You have an incredible voice. Maybe you just weren't the right voice for that particular band. It doesn't mean your voice wasn't good enough. It is good enough. I think you have an incredible voice."

She lifted her gaze to his. "It's okay. For singing in the privacy of my bedroom."

"Bullshit. It's amazing."

Her lips curved. "You're not exactly a talent scout. But I appreciate you thinking so."

"So what happened after that?"

"Nothing."

"You mean, you stopped singing?"

"No, of course not. As you can see from the mess in the office, I'm still writing songs and singing them."

"But not publicly."

"Uh, no. Not until tonight. For you. Which I guess can't be considered public singing."

His brows rose. She knew he wanted to say more, but maybe he read the pleading look in her eyes, because he smiled at her and said, "Then I'm honored. Thanks."

"You're welcome."

He bent and brushed his lips against hers. "You're a woman of many talents."

Glad the tension had dissolved, she laughed. "Yes, I am a hell of a bartender."

"Well, yeah, that, too, but those aren't the talents I have on my mind right now."

"Is that right? And what is on your mind right now?"

"Something more bedroom oriented." He scooped her up in his arms and headed down the hall toward her bedroom.

She gazed up at the obvious amorous intent on his face and smiled.

"Speaking of someone with many talents . . ."

FOURTEEN

TY ASKED JENNA OUT A FEW DAYS LATER, SURPRISED when she agreed.

After the other night, she'd been upset, though she'd been a good sport about getting over it in a hurry. She wasn't one of those women who got mad and stayed that way.

A good thing, too, because he had special plans for her tonight, and she might end up pissed off at him all over again. Hopefully, he'd maneuver this just right and she'd never know he set it all up.

He picked her up at eight. She wore jeans and a really sexy shirt, which she covered up with a leather jacket and finished off with high-heeled boots. She looked so hot he wanted to forget all about taking her out and get down to the business of peeling off her jeans and getting her naked. But that wasn't tonight's objective.

Or at least it wasn't tonight's starting objective. He hoped to end up there later. He couldn't help himself. It's where his mind wandered whenever he was with her.

She climbed into his car and made herself comfortable by stretching her long legs out and crossing her feet at her ankles. She turned toward him, her long silver earrings dangling against her neck.

"You look beautiful tonight." He leaned over and pressed a light kiss to her lips, coming away with a taste of something flavorful. He licked his lips.

"Cherries," she gave him in answer. "And thank you. You look pretty hot yourself."

He was hardly dressed up. He'd worn jeans, a button-down shirt and his own leather jacket to ward off the icy cold chill in the air. "Thanks."

He took off and got on the highway.

"So where are we going?"

"This club a few of the guys' wives and girlfriends have been talking about. Supposed to be a popular hotspot. A lot of good music, from what I hear, and some awesome games."

"It's not a sports bar, is it?"

He laughed. "Not a television screen in the entire place."

"Then I'm sure I'll love it."

The drive didn't take long since the spot was midtown in the city, which wasn't the place you'd expect to find some killer club, but the parking lot was full. They had to park halfway down the street. Ty helped Jenna out of the car, then took her hand as they walked toward the club.

"I know about this place," Jenna said as they neared the front door. "A couple of my friends mentioned coming here. Said it was hard to even get in the door. I couldn't believe it considering the location, but now I understand what they were talking about."

There was a line outside. "Fire code restrictions, I guess," he said, then looked down at Jenna.

"Maybe we should have gotten here earlier."

"We'll get in."

She laughed and scanned the line. "Yeah, by midnight."

He walked right up to the front door and grinned at the well-muscled guy guarding the door.

"Hey, Tyler."

"How's it going, Greg?"

"Good."

Greg opened the door for them. "You two have fun tonight."

"Thanks." Ty tipped him, then escorted Jenna through the door over the complaints of those waiting outside in the cold.

As soon as they stepped inside, she turned to him. "So you're that famous, or have you been here before?"

He quirked a grin. "This is my first time here. Greg does security at the Ice games. I saw him when we drove by, figured he might let us bypass the line."

"Lucky break."

"Wasn't it?" He put his hand on the small of her back and led her inside the club.

It wasn't a rocking dance club with high-tech loud music. There was a bar off to one side and a stage that centered the whole place, with lots of tables scattered around. Right now a band was on stage playing something cool and country.

"Oh, this is fun," Jenna said, turning to him as they wound their way around the crowds to locate an available table. They found one near the far side of the club and sat down. "Not at all what I expected."

"Yeah? What did you expect?"

"From the lines out there? Something louder, heavy on the lights and bass. I figured it was one of those hot new dance clubs."

He laughed. "Yeah, you're not going to find that here."

The waitress came by and they ordered drinks.

"My friends told me it was a great club, but they didn't tell me what kind. This band is good."

"They are."

They sat back and listened while they had drinks and watched everyone dance. Tyler waited for Jenna to notice the book, as well as the pencils and cards on the table. So far she was preoccupied with the band and checking out the club, as well as her no doubt natural inclination to eye the bar and the bartenders. Checking out the competition and all that.

But when the band finished their set, took their instruments, and left the stage to thunderous applause, Jenna frowned.

"That's it?"

"Huh. I guess so."

"That was short."

Until a singer came onstage, a girl dressed in jeans and a sweatshirt. She had on neon orange tennis shoes and her hair was in pigtails. She was cute.

The announcer asked them all to give it up for Marie, so everyone clapped and hollered.

Music started playing, and Marie began to sing.

She was pretty good.

Then Jenna frowned again, noticing the book on the table.

"Oh. It's karaoke or something."

"Is it? The band did karaoke?"

"I don't know." She picked up the book and flipped through it. "No, it's open mic night tonight. You can bring in your band or sing your own music or they have recorded songs you can sing to."

"Huh. That's pretty cool."

She slanted a glance his way. "You didn't know about this?"

"How the hell would I know about it? I've never been here before. Like I said, some of the women mentioned coming here and said it was awesome, so I thought we'd give it a try. You know, since it's not a sports bar and all."

She gave him a look like she didn't believe him, but turned her attention back to Marie and let the subject drop.

So far, so good.

He was going to get Jenna on that stage tonight.

And he wouldn't have to do or say anything to get her up there.

JENNA WATCHED A PARADE OF TALENT CLIMB ONSTAGE for a couple hours, admittedly transfixed and awed and appalled.

For some reason, people weren't shy about showcasing what they had—good or bad. And some people who were really awful—or really drunk—thought they sounded great, which the crowd didn't seem to care about. They were polite, sometimes teased or booed depending on who was up there, and often clapped loudly, which was to be expected considering several of the people who'd been up there were damned talented.

This still smelled like a setup, but Ty hadn't encouraged her or asked her if she wanted to go up and sing. So maybe he was being honest and hadn't known this was the kind of place where local talent could show what they were made of. All he did was sit back, drink, and make comments to her about who he thought was great and who he thought stunk.

She agreed one hundred percent with his assessments, too.

Still, she was nervous, certain at any moment he would suggest she put in a bid to sing tonight. Which she wouldn't. Couldn't. Hadn't since that awful experience in Germany when she'd been told she wasn't good enough.

She'd never go through that again.

Two hours in, he still hadn't said a damn word.

Still, she was better than half of the people who'd drunkenly sauntered up there to slur the latest Katy Perry or Miranda Lambert or Adele song.

Dammit.

I could light a fire under these people's asses and bring them to their feet.

"I'm sure you could, if that's what you wanted to do."

"What?"

"Light a fire under their asses and bring them to their feet."

Oh, God, had she actually said that out loud?

She waited for Ty to say more, to push or encourage her or some-how bully her onto the stage.

He didn't. Instead, he flagged the waitress down to order another drink.

This was her choice. If she wanted to get up there and sing, it would be her decision and no one else's. Ty obviously wasn't going to prompt or cajole her into doing it.

She chewed on her bottom lip while a band started to play and a bunch of the patrons got up on the dance floor.

"Wanna dance?" he asked.

"Sure." Anything to avoid sitting and stewing.

The band was good, played light rock music, with a female lead singer who had a grungy, hippie look about her. She liked this sing-er's voice, and when she slowed down the melody, Ty pulled Jenna close and put his arms around her. She soon forgot all about the music and tuned in to the way his body felt against hers. His thigh slid between her legs as they moved in rhythm around the crowded dance floor.

She laid her head against his chest and inhaled the crisp maleness of his scent, let her fingers travel over the hard ridges of his shoul-ders. She'd been so wrapped around her own insecurities she hadn't allowed herself the pleasure of this amazing man's company. It was only now she saw the jealous stares of other women nearby, realized how very lucky she was to be in Ty's arms. There were about ten women staring her down who'd love to trade places with her.

What an idiot she was.

It wasn't always about her.

"What do you think?" he asked.

She tilted her head back to look at him. "About what?"

"This band?"

"Oh. They're really good."

"Yeah, they are. I like the singer. I'd like to hear her without all the guitar noise, though. She's good on this song."

"Yeah, she is." He was right about the singer's voice. The band overpowered her. She had a crystal-clear voice, but too much bass and guitar muddied it. "She'd be better as a solo act."

"I think you're right. Some voices are better without a band behind them."

The band got a good response, but not as great as that singer would have gotten had she showcased her awesome voice as a solo act.

And that's when Jenna knew she just had to get up there and sing. Not that it would mean anything to anyone but herself, but she had to do it.

For herself. Just to see what kind of reaction she'd get. Just to prove to herself that maybe she wasn't a total loser.

It had been a lot of years since Germany. For all these years she'd hidden her voice in her house, when all she really wanted to do was sing, to have people hear her. To be judged, just one more time. And if she got booed off the stage, then she'd know.

When the song was over, she and Ty went back to their table and Jenna ordered a shot.

Ty arched a brow. "Ready for some hard drinking?"

She steeled her nerves and directed her gaze at him. "I'm going to sing."

"Really." He leaned back in his chair. "What song did you choose?"

"I have no idea." She grabbed the book and flipped through it, looking for songs she recognized enough she'd be comfortable standing in front of a crowd singing. She found a few she loved that were in her vocal range, then grabbed a card and penciled one in. Before she lost her nerve, she carried it up to the deejay and handed it over.

That's when panic set in. She went back to her chair and flopped into it. Her heart pounded and her palms began to sweat as nausea swelled in the pit of her stomach.

"You going to live?"

She jerked her head up. "I'm not sure yet. Why?"

"You look pale. You don't have to do this."

"I want to. It'll be fun."

"Yeah, you look like you're about to go live on national television."

She leaned her head against her hand. "Shut up."

"In case you throw up on the stage, I'll run a bucket right up there."

She glared at him. "You are so funny."

She had to wait through three more singers, and then her name was called. The dread in her stomach turned into hot and cold flashes. Her feet felt numb as she pushed the chair back.

Ty stood and grasped her hand, forcing her attention on him. "Have some fun, Jenna. You really can sing."

She nodded and walked up onstage, not realizing how many people were crammed into this club until she looked out over the sea of expectant faces. The deejay handed her the microphone, introduced her and the song she was about to sing, then stepped back, leaving her alone in the spotlight.

What if she failed tonight and people laughed, or even worse, booed her? Tyler said she was good, but she was having sex with him, so his vote didn't count.

This was the real test, and as the music started up, she knew there was no changing her mind now. She lifted the microphone and started to sing, the song as familiar to her as her own name. She'd sung it hundreds of times before. It was a twenty-year-old song, but one of her favorites. A sweet pop song about love and romance and the man of her dreams.

Her legs were shaking. Hell, everything on her quivered, but her voice didn't, thank God. She gave the song everything she had, pouring herself into the lyrics, singing to the crowd, forcing herself to look right at them. She found Ty out there, saw him smiling at her. She latched on to his face and stayed focused on his gaze, relaxing her body and sinking into the music, making it through to the last note.

When she heard the thunderous applause and cheers, she couldn't quite believe it was real. She thought maybe she had dreamed this entire night. She was sure she'd wake up any minute in her bed.

She finally forced her feet to move as she backed away.

"You have a killer voice," the deejay said as she returned the mic to him. "I hope that's not the only song you'll sing for us."

She grinned and hugged him, then left the stage, soaking in congratulations on her way back to the table, where Ty scooped her up in his arms. She kissed him, pouring her relief and gratitude into the way her lips moved against his.

"Whoa," he said when they pulled apart. "Who knew that singing turned you on so much?"

She finally relaxed enough to smile. "I'm just glad I got through it."

"You were incredible. Did you hear the crowd? They were one hundred percent behind you."

They sat and she took a long drink of water. "It was unbelievable. I would have never thought . . . You know, I loved it back in Europe. The crowds seemed to love me. But I always sung with bands. Never alone. I never knew it could be like this. And then when they cut me and told me I wasn't good enough . . ."

"Well, now you know you are good enough. You're amazing, just like I told you."

Adrenaline kicked in, and she suddenly couldn't sit still. She wriggled in her chair and she was ready to leap back onstage and wrestle the mic away from the guy who'd just gotten up to sing. "I might want to do it again."

He leaned back in the chair. "I imagine you would. Who doesn't love an audience? I know I do. It makes me skate faster."

She laughed. "Is that why I'm shaking all over and I want to kick everyone else off the stage and take over for the rest of the night?"

One side of his mouth lifted in a knowing smirk. "Exactly."

"It's a powerful feeling."

It was, and she hurriedly scribbled down the next song she wanted to do, and waited impatiently for her turn, barely hearing the singers and bands who got up before her. She couldn't contain her excitement when her name was called. It was so much easier to get up there the second time, and she soaked in the applause when she stood on the stage. This time, she did an upbeat contemporary pop song, delighted when people got up to dance while she sang. She was so comfortable onstage. A live band to work with would be better—she was used to that—but she'd take what she could get. At the end, everyone applauded and whistled for her.

She couldn't have been any giddier than if she were drunk, which she wasn't. She went back to her seat and downed an entire glass of water.

"I'd say you're a hit tonight."

She grinned. "A lot of the acts tonight are hits."

"I think you had the loudest applause."

"You're my date. You have to say that."

He took a swallow of soda, then studied her. "No, I don't."

Okay, so he didn't. He could have been polite and non-encouraging. He hadn't pushed her, but he had told her she was a good singer.

"Thanks. I appreciate your belief in me."

"Hey, I'm no music mogul, but I know a special voice when I hear it. So what are you going to do with it?"

She snorted. "Nothing."

"Nothing?"

"Yeah. I mean, what else would I do?"

"I don't know. Do something with your talent."

"Like what? Go on one of those reality show singing contests? That's not my thing."

"Not what I meant. But there's a lot you can do with a voice like yours. You could have a career as a singer."

"I already have a career."

"You have a job. It's not the same thing."

She shrugged. "I'm doing fine. I got up and sang in public for the first time in years. That was monumental. It was enough."

"You're settling, and it isn't the same thing at all. Haven't you ever thought about doing something you loved?"

She'd thought about it a lot. She'd had this dream since she was a child. A dream that had been shoved aside again and again. She refused to let herself wonder about things that were never going to happen.

Until tonight, when she'd finally released her crushed dreams from the locked box she'd held them prisoner in for so many years. Now that she had, her mind whirled with possibilities.

Time to lock up her dreams again, because it wasn't going to happen.

"You could—"

"No, I couldn't. I don't want to talk about this. It's getting late, I'm tired, and I want to go home."

She stood and headed for the door, not knowing if Ty followed her or not.

When she walked outside, he was there at her side, grasping her hand despite her initial refusal to hold his as they crossed the street.

She was being petty, pouting despite the great night she'd had.

Her mood had soured and she had no idea why. There was no reason to blame Ty. None of this was his fault.

God, it was freezing out, the icy chill biting right through her clothes. Her ears stung and she wished she'd thought to bring her hat.

They walked to his car and he held the door for her, then climbed in and started the engine. She wrapped her coat tighter around her to ward off the cold. Heat filled the vehicle after a couple minutes and she finally stopped shivering.

As Tyler drove, she focused on the road ahead, though she chanced glances at Ty.

He should be mad at her. She acted like a child in the club, running out of there because she hadn't wanted to hear what he had to say.

"I'm sorry," she finally said.

"About what?"

"I was abrupt in the club and I hightailed it out of there without even asking you what you wanted. You might have wanted to hang out there longer."

"I was fine with leaving."

Which didn't tell her anything about how he felt about her behavior. She laid her head against the headrest. "This whole singing thing gets to me."

"Obviously. But why?"

"It's been nothing more than a hobby for so long. Just a fantasy to me. No one knows about it except you. And then tonight . . ."

"It became real."

She studied the silver ring on her thumb. "Something like that."

"Did you have fun?"

She turned her head and looked at him. "I did."

"Then that's good enough for tonight, isn't it?"

"You're right. It is."

But it wasn't good enough, because now she felt unsettled, as if she'd stood on the edge of a cliff tonight and had a glimpse of heaven, and all she had to do to get there was fly. She had been poised on the edge of that cliff, ready to take a leap of faith. The problem was, there was a good chance she could also drop like a rock straight to the bottom. She wasn't confident about her wings. Hell, she didn't know if she even had wings.

And in her way was a sheer rock wall. Immovable. Impenetrable.

She didn't want to think about this, didn't want to dream about what she was never going to have.

It was a stupid dream, anyway. She was never going to be famous, and she was never going to be a singer. She ran her family's bar. That's all she was ever going to do.

Ty pulled into the parking space in front of her condo and turned off the engine. She put her hand on his.

"No reason to turn that off. Your car will get cold."

"In other words, you don't want me to come in."

"It's late. And you have a game tomorrow."

He arched a brow. "I'm a big boy. I can stay up late. If you want to get rid of me, Jenna, use plain language and tell me you don't want me to come in."

She swallowed. "I don't want you to come in."

He opened his door and came around to her side to let her out.

"I'll still take you to the front door."

She didn't know what kind of mood she was in, but it wasn't a good one. She was taking it out on Ty, which she absolutely hated since he hadn't caused any of this.

She fished her keys out of her bag and turned to him. "I'm just tired. It's been a long day."

He smiled down at her and took the keys from her hand. "You don't owe me any explanations." He opened her door and handed the keys back to her, then pulled her to him and brushed his lips against hers.

A fire burned low in her belly and started a flame as the kiss—meant to be brief—turned into something hotter. Despite the bitter cold outside, she held on to his arms and didn't want to let go.

Ask him in, idiot.

But something stopped her.

He didn't deserve her mood. Some other time.

She pulled away and licked her lips. "Thanks for tonight."

His dark gaze made the barely banked flame inside her roar to life.

"You're welcome. Night, Jenna."

She hovered at the doorway as he walked to his car, and everything in her wanted to call out to him and ask him to come back.

But she stopped herself, and when he climbed back in his car, she went inside, shut the door, and leaned against it.

Yeah, another thing she wanted and wouldn't allow herself to have.

FIFTEEN

TY ATTACKED THE PUCK WITH A VENGEANCE, SHOVING the defender with his shoulder as he advanced down the ice.

This was a tough game against Vancouver, and he was sweating inside his gear. The team was kicking their ass and they were down by two goals, but the one thing he never did was give up. Neither did his teammates. It was the beginning of the third period, which meant there was a lot of time to go. All they had to do was stay focused, tie the game, then go for the win.

One goal at a time.

He moved the puck in the center, swept it around the defender, and passed it to Victor. Ty pushed hard, skating toward the net, hustling back and forth with his opponent as Eddie fought the defender to get into position.

Come on, man. Work with Victor and Jerry.

The defender slid the puck behind the goal and it screamed around like a pinball and headed toward Vancouver's side of the ice.

Dammit. Huffing and puffing, he reversed, on the defensive now, using his stick to stop their center from the attack.

But it was two on one and they skirted around him. Jerry and Steve were there, the goalie in position.

They took a shot. Missed. The defenders pushed the puck back out on the ice and Jerry brought it to him, sliding it in his direction.

Ty took it, this time Victor joining him as they volleyed it back and forth, keeping the opponents scrambling. Victor passed it to Eddie, and Ty got in position with Victor near the goal.

He was slammed into but held the puck within his stick, refusing to give up the prize, battling to hold on to it as he skated toward the goal. He shot it to Victor, who plunged it toward the net. The goalie shoved it out, but Eddie was right there and slammed it back in.

One goal down. Yes!

Now they had to hold them.

Ty and his group took the bench while the next went in. It was hard to sit the bench when he always wanted to be out there playing.

They were getting more shots on goal than Vancouver. They should be kicking their asses, but they'd been sluggish in the first period and Vancouver had pounced on them. Stupid. Now they were paying for it. They needed two more goals in or they were going to lose a game they needed to win. He looked at the clock—eight minutes left.

"Czenzcho is sluggish tonight," he said to Eddie and Victor as they waited in the box for their turn. Tyler had read about Vancouver's star defender recovering from a bout of the flu. He'd noticed it was slowing him down. "If we lean on him, double team him, we can get a shot past him and score these two goals."

Eddie nodded.

"We will do that," Victor said as if the goals they needed were already a foregone conclusion.

"Good. Pass it on and let's get the job done."

After Vancouver incurred a penalty for cross checking, they had the power play and now it was their chance to strike. Victor went after Czenzcho with a fury, Eddie right with him. Tyler circled back, crowding the goal, muscling in with the other defender, just waiting for the opportunity to slide the puck into the net.

Victor got the puck and shot it his way but it was deflected by the defender. Eddie was on it, slamming Czenzcho and scooping up the puck and taking the shot on goal. It was deflected by the goalie but the rebound hit air and dropped.

Ty was right there and sailed it into the net for the score.

They were tied, and the adrenaline hit a fever pitch.

Two minutes later, Eddie slid one in between the goalie's legs on a two-man breakaway, and that was all she wrote.

Damn satisfying comeback. They'd worked their asses off for this win, and they'd really needed it. They'd lost three out of four on this road trip, and that just flat-out sucked. Tyler was drained and ready to get back on home ice again. Maybe it would help their mojo.

He hit the showers, shoving his head under the steaming hot water to tune out the sound of celebration from his teammates. Not that he didn't want to take part—he would. Later. Right now he needed to be in his head, thinking about what the hell was wrong with his play the last few games.

He'd done everything right. Hell, they all had. But something wasn't clicking. He just didn't know what wasn't working. Their shots on goal were above average, but they were being outscored and it pissed him off. He couldn't blame the defense or their goalie, because they won or lost as a team.

He was going to have to study the game films to figure it out. In the meantime, he'd take tonight's win as a turnaround, be damn glad they were grabbing a flight home, and that he had a couple days off to regroup before a stretch of home games.

He grabbed the soap and scrubbed down, his thoughts moving to Jenna.

He hadn't seen her since the not-so-subtle brush-off she'd given him that night after they'd gone to the club.

Something about singing had bothered her. He didn't know what kind of demons she wrestled with, but he knew about needing distance and time alone to think, so he hadn't pressed it. But he'd missed her, which kind of surprised him. He enjoyed being with her, but he'd figured it was just a fun thing to do—that she was a fun thing to do to pass the time while he was hanging out at the bar.

She wasn't like a lot of the women he usually dated. She was complex and interesting, and he wondered about her beyond the sex part of their relationship to what she thought and how she felt about things.

He turned off the shower and dragged his fingers through his hair.

Yeah, he couldn't wait to get back home.

But this time, he was going to play a different kind of game.

"TWO MARGARITAS, ONE WITH EXTRA SALT. ONE BLOODY Mary, one Dewar's neat, one dirty martini, and three Budweiser drafts."

Jenna nodded and hustled to fill the waitress's order, while at the same time sliding two bottles of beer across the bar to her regulars and cashing out a customer who was headed home.

It had been like this since happy hour started.

Work was hell. Hockey had been on every damn night, and the Ice had been traveling, which meant the televisions at the bar had been turned on to the games. She'd been forced to endure Ty's face and body on multiple screens.

Even worse, she'd felt miserable when they'd dropped the first three games. Try as she might to ignore the games while she tended to her customers, their groans and curses made her look up and see just how badly the Ice had played. And because the media loved to focus in on despair, she'd seen close-up shots of Tyler's dejected face—along with the other players.

By the end of game three, the frustration and anger had shown on his face, and her stomach had been in knots. She wished it had been a home game so he and the other guys could have come to the bar after for some solace.

All she could think about was how she had dumped him and run like hell that night. He'd been so nice to her, so encouraging about her singing, and she'd only thought of herself. And when he'd needed her she hadn't even had the courage to pick up the phone and offer verbal support.

Thank God they'd won that fourth game, in an amazing come-from-behind victory, too. The entire third period had been nail-bitingly exuberant. She hoped it was an amazing turnaround and they'd hop on a winning streak with the start of their home games.

Yeah, and what if they hadn't won? What if they'd lost the entire road trip? What would she have done then?

Nothing.

Some friend she was. Though she was more than a friend, wasn't she? And that was the problem she'd been wrestling with, and why she continued to hold herself back, why she hadn't picked up her cell phone and called or texted him. Their relationship was in some kind of limbo. She wasn't his girlfriend, but she was more than just a friend to him.

She had no idea what to do.

Yeah, right, Jenna. You're so afraid of getting involved with him that you've reined yourself in, refusing to show Ty that you might actually care about him.

She was such a coward. In more than one way.

Disgusted with herself, she tossed the wipe-down rag in the bin and refused to face her own failings. Thankfully the bar was busy and she lost herself in work, but thoughts of Ty kept creeping in despite her best efforts to shove them aside.

She was going to have to face up to it—to him—and deal. There would be no more hiding.

It was an off night, so she fully expected him and the other guys to show up here. They'd all receive moral support from the patrons in her bar, and maybe she'd have a free minute to pull him aside and talk to him.

They were friends, she'd tell him. They'd had some fun, but it was time for her to pull back and remind him that's all it was going to be between them. She'd already gotten too close and allowed herself to get emotional about him, to feel bad when he lost. For the love of God, she'd been watching hockey, had been invested in the outcome of the games.

That couldn't happen. Her life—her future—was here at the bar. She might not have any control over that, but she could control who she fell for, and it wouldn't be for someone who played sports.

The loud cheers alerted her to the front door, where Eddie, Victor, and a few other Ice players had walked in. It was so crowded she couldn't see everyone, and she was so swamped she couldn't get away to greet them until an hour later when she pulled Renee behind the bar and took a break.

She hadn't seen Ty, but then again Riley's was wall-to-wall people and the guys were playing pool at one of the tables in the far corner of the bar, out of her line of sight. Now she circled the bar, visiting with her customers, stopping at all the tables to ask everyone how their night was going. She stayed a little longer with the regulars because she knew them, and many knew her mom and dad so they asked how her dad was faring after his surgery last year.

It took her almost an hour to make her way over to the pool tables, where she had to put up with flirting from some of her regular guys. It was always harmless fun, because they all had her back and treated her like a sister. But her gaze skirted to the Ice players at the far end of the pool room.

She didn't see Ty. Maybe he was off talking to someone in another area of the bar.

She finally extricated herself from the group of guys and made her way to the Ice players, sliding in between Eddie and Victor.

"I see you finally won a game."

Eddie rolled his eyes. "Oh, man. It was a great game, too. Did you watch, Jenna?"

She patted him on the back. "Don't I always? You really pulled that one out of the trash bin. It wasn't looking good before that."

"I know. We were on a nose dive, but we're going to kick ass now that we're back on the home ice."

The sound of cheers went up all around them, and the players lifted their beers to salute the fans.

Jenna hovered around and chatted with them awhile, but Ty didn't make an appearance. Finally, she had no choice but to ask.

"So, where's your other best player tonight?"

"Ty? He didn't come. Said he had other stuff to do."

"Oh."

"Or some*one* to do," Victor said with a knowing smirk, and the guys laughed.

"Enjoy your night. Next round is on me."

She left to the sound of cheers again and shook her head, waving at the guys, but her stomach clenched.

He didn't come tonight. Other stuff to do.

What kind of stuff?

She relieved Renee and went back behind the bar, grabbing empty beer bottles and slamming them into the recycle bin with decided satisfaction.

So what if he had a date tonight? She'd made it clear they had no future together. They'd had sex only a couple times, and she'd totally blown him off that last night they had together. What had she expected, that he'd come running back to her and beg for more of the same treatment?

Yeah, right. Men love that.

Except that's exactly what she'd expected. She'd been so smug and so sure of herself, certain he'd be back no matter how she treated him.

Only he wasn't back, and now that he wasn't, she missed him. She missed how he smelled, she missed how he felt, and she missed his sexy grin. She missed talking to him.

So what are you going to do about that, Jenna?

Normally she'd do nothing. She never chased a guy.

But she wasn't finished with Ty just yet.

SIXTEEN

TY HAD HIS FEET UP ON THE SOFA, THE GAME CON-troller resting on his stomach as he stalked the enemy.

"Yeah, you bastard. You can run, but you can't hide, because I know exactly where you are."

He was as quiet as a rolling storm cloud as he snuck up behind his target, not even hesitating as he drew his knife and slit the enemy's throat. Blood spurted from his victim's neck and he fell to the ground.

He laughed as kill points rolled up against his online opponent.

"Kicked your ass, Warlord." Whoever Warlord was. Probably some twelve year old who had no business playing a game this violent, but hey, he wasn't the kid's parent. He tossed the game controller on the sofa and stood, raking his fingers through his hair.

That game was so disgusting. Yet strangely addicting. If he ever had kids he wasn't going to let them anywhere near video games. He was going to drag their butts out of the house as soon as they could walk and make them play sports.

Yeah, right. He'd probably sit side by side with them on the sofa and play those same violent war games with them.

Or, God forbid, he'd have girls and he'd end up playing some games that had to do with rainbow ponies. Or Barbie. Or something Disney related.

Yikes. Though the thought of a little girl with a long ponytail kicking around a soccer ball or becoming a skater like him—figure skater, though—didn't horrify him as much as it would have a few years ago.

What the hell was wrong with him? He wasn't going to get married, and he sure as hell wasn't going to have kids.

Not anytime soon. No, not ever. The thought of screwing up some kid's life the way his parents had done to him? No. He wouldn't be responsible for that.

His cell phone rang and he frowned. He had no idea what time it was, but he knew it was late. He grabbed the phone, surprised to see Jenna's number come up.

"Hey," he said after punching the button.

"Hey yourself. I know, it's really late. Were you asleep?"

He laughed. "Uh, no."

"Are you on a date?"

Leave it to Jenna to be direct. "No. Are you?"

"Of course not. I had to work tonight."

He looked at his phone. It was only midnight. "Shouldn't you still be at work?"

"Yes. But I want to see you. Are you at home?"

He smiled. "Sure. Come on over."

"Be right there."

Interesting. And crap, his place was a cyclone. Gear in his living room, cans everywhere, and he was pretty sure the place smelled like gym socks. He did a quick pick up and vacuum, then sprayed with that stuff that took the odor out of the house. Hopefully it removed natural guy-stink.

By the time Jenna rang his doorbell, he had jumped in the shower and managed to pull on a pair of sweats and a clean T-shirt.

She looked great and he couldn't help but feel a punch to the gut seeing her at his front door.

"Hi. Come in."

She stepped inside. She smelled good, like she'd just sprayed on something that smelled wild and musky. He wanted to get closer and bury his nose in her neck to investigate that scent a little more, but he resisted the urge since he had no idea what she was doing here.

He took her coat. "Want something to drink?"

"No, I'm good, thanks."

"Okay. Have a seat. I picked up the apocalypse of a mess, but it's not pretty around here."

She laughed. "And you've seen my place, so I never would have noticed."

"Yeah, but a guy lives here. Trust me, you'd have noticed. Especially the dirty socks smell."

"Doubtful. I have two brothers, remember?"

"Oh, yeah. You win that round." He sat on the sofa next to her.

She picked up the controller. "Playing video games?"

"Yeah."

"I would have thought you'd have been watching game films to figure out why you all played so shitty on the road."

"I watch plenty of game films with the team. And we played like shit because we were trying too hard. Hockey is a mental game as well as physical. You start getting in your own head too much, it screws with your game play."

"Do you really think that's the problem?"

"I know it's the problem. We have the best team in the league. We can win the division and go to the playoffs with the talent we have. For some reason we hit a slump because everyone started worrying about this road trip and freaking out about the caliber of teams we were going to play. At least we salvaged the last game of the road trip."

"So you did."

As much fun as it was to debrief his games, it was time to put an end to this and get to the real reason Jenna was here. "Is that why you came tonight? To analyze my game play?"

She took a deep breath. "Wow. We're getting into that already, huh?"

"You called this meeting. Might as well."

"You're right." She half turned to face him, pulling her knee up on the sofa.

She looked pretty tonight. She'd worn a knit dress that clung to her curves, and added dark tights and ankle boots. Her hair spiked up and her dangly earrings twinkled in the light cast by the lamp on his table next to the sofa. She looked soft and feminine and he wanted to gather her against him and kiss every part of her he could see . . . followed by all the parts of her skin he couldn't see.

She was quiet, obviously struggling with whatever it was she wanted to say.

But this time, the ball was going to be in her court. He wasn't going to take the lead, no matter how much he wanted to.

She leaned her elbow against the back of the sofa, then laid her head in the palm of her hand and looked around his living room, though there wasn't anything to look at. A few pictures, some crappy art he'd bought because Liz had recommended it, and a few things he'd picked up to sit on tables because he liked the way they looked. But he didn't think Jenna was admiring his art.

There was something she needed to say, but it wasn't coming out.

She studied the ring on her thumb, then circled it around with her fingers. It was painful to watch her struggle.

He stood, walked to the front door, and grabbed his jacket and her coat. "Come on."

"Where are we going?"

"Out."

WHEN TY HAD SAID THEY WERE GOING OUT, JENNA figured they'd take a drive, some fresh air so she could get past this lump in her throat and find her voice.

She had no idea they'd end up at the freaking Ice hockey arena at one in the morning.

Who knew he had that much pull that he could get them into the arena?

And now she was being laced up in skates and protective gear and thrust out onto the ice, the lights turned on, while Tyler skated toward her with two hockey sticks in his hands.

God, she had no idea how devastatingly sexy he was in his hockey gear. On television, it was at a distance, and she never went to the games. Not since she was a kid, anyway.

But seeing him come toward her, bent over in game form, sliding that puck back and forth—holy hell it was a turn on that shocked her all the way down to her laced-up skates.

"You've got something on your mind," he said, skating around her, sliding the puck between her skates and scooping it up behind her. "I do a lot of thinking when I'm on the ice. Helps me clear my head. So let's play a little one-on-one, and maybe you'll figure out what you need to say."

She could skate as well as either of her brothers, had gone to the ice rink every winter since she was a little girl, so she had no problem going toe-to-toe with him, but she was no pro hockey player. "We could have just sat on the sofa and talked it out."

He lifted up his mask and grinned at her. "My way is more fun."

He slid the puck to her and started skating backward. "Pretend I'm the defender of my goal. Now try to get the puck by me."

He was going to obliterate her. She already knew that, but she was competitive enough to give it a try. She pushed forward on her skates, feeling bulky and hindered with the gear on, and half blinded by the helmet. Still, she skated on, trying to keep the puck moving with her stick as she advanced toward Tyler, who stood at the left face-off circle, in front of where the goal would be.

And then he moved forward, skating toward her like a high-speed train. She shifted to the right, but he was on her in seconds, sweeping the puck away from her and forcing her to turn or skate backward.

She wasn't as fast backward as she was forward, so she had to turn around and that slowed her down. He was already at the other end by the time she turned.

He brought the puck around to center ice and swept it back to her.

"You're slow. Try to pick it up this time."

"If I high stick you in the balls, you'll slow down," she said, irritation piquing.

He laughed and backed away. "That would cost you a penalty."

She glared at him. "Who will you play with if I'm in the penalty box?"

"Wasn't the kind of penalty I'm talking about."

"Yeah? And what kind of penalty is that?"

He put his stick around her back and drew her against him.

"A time out."

"Bogus, Anderson." She pushed off and grabbed the puck, racing for the imaginary goal since there wasn't a net in place. She knew she was no match for Ty's speed on the ice but she intended to give it her all. She caught sight of him on her right side and dug in, giving it all she had, then reared back with the stick and slammed a shot forward, hitting the goal spot and lifting her stick in the air in triumph.

She skidded to a stop, Tyler a few feet away. She laid her hands on her knees because she was sucking wind so hard her chest hurt, but she was grinning like a crazy person. It had felt great.

He stopped beside her. She turned her head to him. "I scored a goal."

"So you did. Feel good about that?"

"I do, but I have a feeling you let me win."

He lifted up his mask and gave her a fierce glare. "Woman, you know how competitive I am. Do you really think I'd let you score on me?"

She squinted, studying him. "Hmmm, probably not. You'd likely try and kick my ass."

"You're right about that." He moved in closer, backing her toward the boards until she was cornered. He pulled off her helmet and it clattered on the ice.

"You should take better care of your equipment. It needs to protect your head."

"That's practice equipment. We treat game equipment like gold." He pulled off his gloves and pressed his hand against her neck. His fingers were cold. They felt good against her heated skin. Who knew one could sweat like this on the ice? She knew the guys worked hard when they played the game—she watched how fast they skated and wondered how they didn't exhaust themselves. Ty's muscular body told her how hard they worked at it.

When he swept his thumb over the pulse point in her neck, she grew even warmer, especially with his pad-covered body pinning her to the boards. He drew in closer, close enough to feel his warm breath ruffle her hair. Her nipples tightened.

"So," he said. "Figured out yet what you wanted to talk to me about?"

She pulled off her gloves and dropped them, then laid her palms on his chest, wishing there wasn't all this . . . stuff . . . between them so she could touch his skin. "Not really. I'm confused."

"About?"

"You and me."

"What about you and me confuses you?"

He stroked his thumb behind her ear, slid his hand into her hair.

How was she supposed to talk to him when he was touching her like that?

"Ty."

"Yeah." His gaze bored into hers, and she didn't think he was all that interested in what she had to say, which was a good thing because she didn't much feel like talking anyway.

He tilted her head back and her lips parted for him just as his mouth covered hers.

His kiss was hungry, making her muscles clench as he moved his lips over hers in a way that demanded more. This wasn't a light and easy kiss, it was hard and passionate, his tongue sliding between her teeth to lick against hers. She gasped and held on to him as he pushed her against the boards and demanded everything from that kiss, stealing her breath as he wrapped his arm around her and pressed his body intimately against hers.

Pinned against the boards, she could only hold on to him. The ice was slick and she dug the edge of one skate into the ice for balance, clutching Ty's pads while he kissed her senseless.

She was on fire, her body needing his touch, his skin against hers. She'd missed him, had missed . . . this. This connecting to him on that intimate level. She didn't want to talk, didn't want to hash out everything that was screwed up in her head, or all the reasons she didn't want to be with him, because right now none of that mattered.

She did want to be with him. Here and now, with hot and cold swirling around her, driving her into a frenzy of need and desire.

When he pulled back, his eyes were half lidded, desire darkening them to a stormy gray.

That's what she needed to see, what she focused on. The rest of it was just extraneous fluff she didn't want to make sense of right now.

Not when he gave her a look like that.

She swallowed, her throat dry. She licked her lips and he zeroed in on her mouth and kissed her again, tugging her bottom lip between his teeth until she threw her head back against the glass and moaned out of sheer pleasure. He pressed kisses to her jaw, her neck, using his teeth to graze her throat.

"Ty, please."

"I love when you say my name. Do you have any idea what that does to me?"

"No. Tell me."

"I think I'll show you instead."

The next thing she knew he had untied the pads she wore, removed his own pads and tossed them across the ice.

It was distinctly cooler without all that padding. Her dress and tights weren't warm enough.

"I'm cold. Can we go now?"

"I'll warm you up." He cupped her face with his hands and kissed her, this time a gentle brush of his lips, and then he paused. She held her breath, waiting for him to continue. He pulled back and she saw his lips curl in a smile that turned her world off balance. She reached up to rub her fingers over his lips, then arched up on her skates to reach his mouth.

He wrapped his arms around her and kissed her deeply, and she forgot all about being cold. His hands and body were like a blast furnace as he moved them over her, drawing her within his heat. His lips were hard and demanding, making her melt from the inside out. She was surprised the ice wasn't thawing beneath them, sinking them in a sea of liquid.

His hand found her breast, molded to it, and fire spread through her. She arched against his palm and he thumbed her nipple through the material. Oh, she wanted to be naked, but there was something so primal about being here on the ice, fully clothed, with him touching her like this. He shifted his thigh between her legs and held her there, his mouth doing delicious things to her lips while he touched her breasts.

She was on fire. That, coupled with standing on the cold ice, was a study in contrasts that inflamed her senses and sent her spiraling into arousal. She wanted more than this fully clothed petting. She slid her hand under his shirt to touch his bare skin, to feel the warmth of his back.

He pulled his mouth away from hers and stared down at her, touching his hand to her cheek. Her breath caught and held as he moved his hand down her neck and across her breasts. He mapped a casual trek down her body, making her gasp as his touch snaked south, teasing her by not touching her where she wanted to, where she was throbbing with need. He grabbed the hem of her dress and lifted it, then slid his hand over her sex to cup her through the thin material of her tights.

She gasped as he rubbed his palm back and forth over the ache that had settled there. She arched against him, trying to balance on her skates. He held her firmly in his grasp, more comfortable on the ice than she was.

"Here?" she asked.

"Yeah. Right here."

"How?"

"We'll make it work. I want you, Jenna."

Their gazes fused and she saw the fierce need in his eyes, in the tight set of his jaw, his muscles tensing under her hands. It catapulted her desire to feverish levels. The idea of making love with him here on the ice suddenly seemed perfect.

He slipped his hand inside the waistband of her tights, finding the heat of her center. Her breathing quickened as the icy cold of his fingers found the warm wetness of her sex.

She clutched his shoulders and held on as he fingered her pussy, flicked the ring around her clit and caressed her there.

"Your fingers are cold."

"Sorry."

"Don't be. God, it feels good. Put them inside me."

He slid two fingers inside her, pumping them in and out of her until she thought she was going to die from the sheer pleasure of it. She melted around him, convulsed as he rubbed the heel of his hand against her sex. She arched, needing more, wanting to touch him, too. His erection was outlined through his sweats and she cupped it, stroked his shaft, each time she touched him causing him to react by sliding his fingers deeper inside her.

"I need you, Ty. No more foreplay."

He gave her a wicked smile, then bent and grabbed her tights, pulling them down to her ankles. He pulled a condom out of the pocket of his hoodie and drew his sweats down, revealing his swollen cock.

She licked her lips and swallowed, impatient as he put the condom on and pressed her against the wooden boards. He raised her dress and held on to her butt, spreading her legs as wide as they could go considering the problem with her tights and skates.

When he slid up inside her it was heaven. Cold and hot, she felt like the ice was melting around them. She cried out and held on as Ty plunged into her, brushing her clit with every thrust. With her legs practically closed, she felt every part of his cock inside her, every part of him touching her, spreading her, driving her crazy.

"Oh, it's good. Yes, like that."

His fingers bit into the flesh of her ass as he held her, taking easy strokes at first, but she wanted so much more.

"Harder. Make it hard and make me come."

He bent and powered up into her again, then ground against her, sending sparks of pleasure to her core. She bit down on her lip as he pushed into her, felt him swell inside her. His cock jerked and quivered and she was close. Oh so close. She dug her fingers into his shoulders and slammed against him, causing him to groan and give her more of what she wanted.

"I'm going to come in you, Jenna."

His words spiraled her out of control, made her quiver with her oncoming orgasm. "Yes. Fuck me harder. I'm going to come."

He banged her against the boards with a punishing thrust. She fought to dig her skates into the ice, but it was Ty holding on to her with his strength, Ty keeping her upright as he tunneled into her, pistoning his cock into her pussy.

It hit her like a blast. She came with a wild cry that shattered her.

Ty kissed her, groaning into her mouth as he emptied himself, shaking and holding her.

She panted against him, sweating, her legs shaking, and if Tyler let her go she'd drop right on the ice. But he held her firmly in his grasp, and finally withdrew, pulled up his sweats, and dropped to the ice to pull up her tights.

He stood, wrapped his arm around her waist, and pressed a warm, sweet kiss to her lips that made her tremble.

She laid her head against the glass and looked at him, so shaken that for a moment she couldn't speak.

Then she grinned at him. "You take all your girls to the ice for a little sex action?"

He frowned. "I've never had sex with any woman in the arena, or on the ice before. Just you."

He pushed off and started gathering up the gear.

Well. Damn. She felt special.

And now she was right back where she'd started, not knowing what the hell to say.

SEVENTEEN

LIZ LAID HER HEAD IN HER HANDS. "I'M BORED."

Jenna grinned and refilled Elizabeth's glass of wine from the bottle sitting at their table. "You're not bored. You have an awesome job that keeps you running all the time. Your problem is that you miss Gavin."

"Of course I do, though I'd never admit that to anyone but you." She picked up the glass and took a sip. "Spring training sucks. Baseball sucks."

Jenna fought back a laugh. "You agreed to marry him. You know what he does for a living. Hell, he was your client until you two got engaged and you had to give him up because of conflict of interest."

"Yeah, that part sucked, but what could I do? I can't negotiate on behalf of someone I'm in love with. I can't be objective where he's concerned. But I got him a great agent. Not as great as me, of course."

"Naturally."

Liz had called her this morning and asked for a lunch date, and since Jenna had the day off, it was perfect. After her last encounter with Ty, she needed some perspective and girl talk, and Liz was a no-bullshit straight shooter. Jenna didn't confide in many people, but Liz was one of those people she trusted.

"You could fly down to Florida and visit him."

"I'm a distraction and he needs to focus on work."

Jenna dug into the bread on the table and pulled out a piece, waving it at Liz for emphasis. "And I'm sure he misses you as much as you miss him. He'd probably play better if you were there."

Liz shrugged. "Maybe. Maybe not."

"Are your friends Haley and Shawnelle down there?"

"Shawnelle is. Haley couldn't make it because she has classes this semester."

"Then Shawnelle could probably use a friend, too. You should go."

Liz leaned back in the chair and grabbed a piece of bread. "I should." She looked up and met Jenna's gaze. "God, I'm a mess, Jen. Who knew I'd fall so ugly in love with a guy? He's made me a sloppy romantic. All I do is think about him. When he's on the road we text, we sext—"

Jenna held up a hand. "Way too much information. Gavin's my brother, remember?"

Liz grinned. "Tough. You're my friend so you have to listen to the sex parts, too. Just pretend he's someone else. I can't get enough of him. I thought I was old enough to get past the infatuation, that it would ease off after we were together for a while, but it hasn't. If anything, it's stronger now than it ever was. Not just the hot sex, though that's still spectacular. But the romance, the way I feel when he looks at me or holds my hand. It's like a goddamned fairy tale."

Jenna's heart did a flip. "It's love, honey. That's what it's supposed to be like."

"I guess. I just never knew." Liz reached across the table and squeezed her hand. "I'm going to get all sappy here and tell you that when it hits you, it's going to be a lightning bolt to your heart and you're never, ever going to be the same. It'll change you."

Jenna laughed. "I don't think everyone falls in love the same way."

Liz took up her glass and sipped, then slathered butter on her bread. "Don't they? Look at Tara and Mick. Their wedding was like watching a freakin' Disney movie. I've never seen two people more in love with each other. Gavin and I are like that. You can't tell me lightning doesn't strike twice." Liz gave her a direct look. "Or three times."

Jenna shrugged. "I'm not in love."

"Maybe not yet, but it's going to happen for you, and when it does, you're going to feel it right down to your toes. And that's when you know that no other man in the universe will ever do it for you like that one man does."

"You make it sound so easy."

Liz laughed. "Easy? Hell no, it isn't easy, because he's the only one who will ever have the capacity to hurt you. And oh, goddamn, when it hurts, it hurts so bad. But he's also the only one you're going to love with your whole heart."

"Good God, woman, you've got it bad."

"I know, right? I told you I was ugly in love."

Jenna laughed. And as she and Liz ate their lunch and Liz chatted about her and Gavin's wedding plans, Jenna thought about that whole love thing.

That was the stuff of fairy tales, and Liz had stars in her eyes because she was over the top in love with Jenna's brother. Jenna couldn't be happier about that, but she wasn't sure she bought into the fantasy about finding that one soul mate, that one person you were meant to be with, and when you found that person you'd know it and you were done—that was it, and you'd never look at anyone else ever again.

It was nice in theory, but she didn't believe it in reality.

It just didn't happen like that for everyone. It had for Liz and Gavin and for Tara and Mick, and she was happy for them, but so far, no one had turned her world upside down and made her heart sing love songs.

But she had sung for Tyler. She hadn't even sung in front of her own family, the people she trusted the most. Yet she'd sung twice for Tyler.

Which didn't mean she was crazy in love with him or anything.

And maybe her stomach fluttered whenever she saw him, but that was just sexual attraction, and it would wane after she screwed his brains out a few more times, because she'd never had a relationship with a guy that lasted longer than a few weeks. She and Tyler were right up there on the few weeks mark. Hell, she'd known him for months, even though they hadn't been sleeping together that long. She was bound to get bored soon.

"Maybe we need to find you an awesome guy."

Jenna looked up from her plate. "What? No. We tried that already. No, thanks."

"Hey, I can't help myself. I want you to be as happy as I am. You haven't found a guy who rings your bell yet, right?"

She refused to answer that question.

Liz arched a brow. "You're seeing someone?"

"Not really. Well, sort of."

"What does that mean?"

"Tyler Anderson and I are kind of dating."

"Really?" Liz's eyes widened. "Tyler? I thought that whole sexfest the night of Mick and Tara's wedding was a one-time thing."

She pushed her plate to the side, her appetite evaporating. "So did I."

"What happened? I know you were eyeing him at the bar that night. Is he rocking your world?"

"I have no idea. He just keeps popping up, so I keep having sex with him."

"Interesting." Liz took another sip of wine. "It must be really good sex."

"It is."

"But you're bothered, so there's got to be more to it than that."

Jenna shrugged. "There isn't more to it than that. It's just physical. You know how I feel about jocks. There will never be more than just the sex."

"Hmmm." Liz gave Jenna a sidelong look, then dug into her salad.

"What does that 'hmmm' mean?"

"Just that you're protesting an awful lot. If you didn't care, you'd just laugh it off and enjoy him until the new wore off, then you'd dump him. I think he gets to you."

"What he gets is into my panties, which is exactly where I want him."

Liz wiggled. "Oh, the mental visuals swirling around in my head right now."

"Stop that. You do not get to visualize Ty and me having sex."

"Why not? Just because you're icked out at the thought of your brother and me getting down and dirty doesn't mean I can't imagine Ty naked."

"He's your client, Elizabeth."

"So?"

"You are evil."

Liz grinned and lifted her wineglass in toast. "Thanks for the compliment. And speaking of Tyler, I have to meet with him after his game tonight to go over some details for a new promotional campaign. Come with me."

"To his hockey game? Uh . . ."

"What? Afraid to actually attend a sporting event?" Liz leaned forward to whisper. "Oh, my God, you might enjoy it. Wouldn't that be awful?"

She glared at Liz. "You are such a bitch."

"There you go, complimenting me again." Liz offered up a smug smile, knowing Jenna would accept the challenge.

She was right. "Fine. I'll go with you."

"Of course you will. I'll pick you up at six thirty."

JENNA FIGURED LIZ WOULD HAVE GOTTEN THEM SEATS in the owner's box or one of the club-level boxes so she could hide out in relative obscurity without a chance in hell Ty would even know she was there. Then when Liz had to meet with him after the game, she'd linger in the box until Liz finished up her business.

But when they headed down instead of up, when Liz led her all the way down to the front row and they took their seats right behind the glass, Jenna muttered a curse, especially when she realized they were seated right next to the players' box. That meant she'd see Ty coming and going from the locker room, and even worse, he'd be able to see her.

He was probably in game mode and never paid attention to the audience other than hearing their cheers when the Ice scored. She didn't have anything to worry about.

"Why these seats?" she asked as she settled in, glad she wore tights under her jeans. It was damn cold sitting this close to the ice.

"There's nothing better than being right up close to the action. Figured you'd want to see Ty slam someone up against the glass."

"Uh-huh. You know it."

"Try to act a little more enthused."

She snuggled deeper into her coat, deciding she'd need to find some coffee before the game started. "You know how I love my sports."

"Cynic."

"Just calling it like it is. I'm only here for you."

Liz leaned over and nudged Jenna to direct her attention over her right shoulder. "And I'm calling bullshit on that last comment, because there's a spectacle about to hit the stage."

She was about to hit Liz with another biting retort, but the players burst through the double doors of the locker room and Jenna held her breath. She wasn't sure if she wanted Tyler to notice her or not, but as the players filed out onto the rubber carpet and onto the bench, she couldn't deny she was looking for only one man.

And when she saw him come up, his head was turned in the other direction, focused on saying something to Eddie. He breezed right past her without seeing her.

She was relieved as he climbed up on the bench and put on his gear, then skated out onto the ice.

He'd never know she was here. She sat back and watched the players do laps around the arena to warm up, grinned when San Jose's players came in and everyone began to boo. She was so focused on watching the players she didn't notice him until he tapped his stick on the glass right in front of her, nearly startling her right out of her seat.

She jerked her attention to the glass. Ty gave her a wink and a grin, then skated away.

Guess there was no hiding now.

She couldn't remember the last time she'd seen a live hockey game. Her dad and brothers had come to the games a lot, and she'd been dragged to a few of them when Mom wanted to come along, but she hadn't been since she was a kid. Of course the games were always on television so she'd watched plenty of them. In the Riley household, you grew up knowing your team sports. There was no escape.

But she'd never been up front, her toes chilled from being so close to the ice, her fingers able to touch the glass. And when the players set up in the faceoff spot, she found herself leaning forward, hands clasped, her body tensed as the referee held the puck in his hand, teasing the drop.

The puck dropped and the game was on. The tension never lessened as they moved to San Jose's goal in a hurry. Jenna and Liz stood, cheering on the Ice as they fought to get the puck in the goal, then screamed when San Jose's defender shot it back, their team threatening to score with a shot on goal. The Ice defended, sending it back into San Jose's territory. Tyler grabbed it and Eddie, right with him, soared again toward the goal.

It went back and forth like that for the entire first period, the teams fairly equal. The first period ended with no score.

Jenna flopped in her seat and watched the players file out. Tyler looked as frustrated as she felt and didn't make eye contact with her. She understood he needed to keep his head in the game, not flirt with her.

She turned to Liz. "That was intense."

"Girl, don't you go to the games?"

"Uh, no."

"Never?"

"Not since I was a kid."

Liz rolled her eyes. "You are so missing out. There is nothing as breathtaking as being at a hockey game." She held her hands out toward the ice as evidence. "Case in point—this first period. I don't think I breathed the entire time."

"It was interesting."

"Interesting my ass. You were riveted. I'll bet you twenty bucks you scream and jump up and down during one of the Ice's scoring drives tonight."

Jenna turned to her, certain she wouldn't do that. "You're on."

The second period started with San Jose defending on their side of the arena, which meant when the Ice threatened to score, Jenna could see Ty close up. And when he and one of San Jose's defenders fought for the puck along the boards, they'd get slammed against the glass right where she and Liz sat. Instinct made her want to reach out for him, to let him know she was right there, but she resisted the urge.

But damn this was a rough game, and when San Jose scored the first goal, her stomach dropped.

"Damn."

They fought so hard, had more shots on goal than San Jose. They just weren't getting the puck in the net.

Liz patted her hand. "Don't give up on these guys. They're fierce."

She wasn't about to give up on them. She might not come to the games, but she'd watched plenty of them at the bar. She knew this team. They worked magic when they were down.

True to form, they tied it up on a power play goal late in the second period, a sweep from their left wing Meyers to Lincoln, the other center on the Ice. It stayed that way into the third period, and Jenna was about to climb out of her skin. The action had been intense, and the play had been brutal. Ty had gotten bloody on a slam to the boards that had resulted in a fight with the opposing player. It had ended with them trading fists on the ice. Jenna laid her hands on the glass, wishing she could be there to help him out. Her heart leaped in her throat as they pounded each other and the refs just stood there. She knew that was part of the game—that the fans loved it— but this was her guy involved and the fight was taking place just across the arena.

The referees finally stepped in and broke up the fight. Jenna exhaled when Ty got up, seemingly unharmed except for blood on his uniform and another attempted charge at the defender. The referee interceded and sent both him and the San Jose player to the penalty box.

She was furious. Ty hadn't started that fight. What the hell had he been penalized for? She'd crossed her arms, tapped her feet, and counted down the longest two minutes of the night until he was sprung. When Ty vaulted out of the box and back onto the ice there were three minutes to go.

They had to win. They were going to win. The action was intense, moving from San Jose back to the Ice, possession changing every few seconds. Both teams wanted this badly.

Ty took the puck on a sweeping pass from Victor and charged toward the goal, the defense right on him. He slipped it to Eddie, who shot it back to Victor.

Jenna was on her feet as Ty put himself in position in front of the net, fought off the defender, and when Victor sent the puck sailing, Ty pushed in front of the defender and shot the puck into the goal for the score.

"Yes! Yes, yes, oh, hell yes!" She screamed, jumped up and down, and pumped her fists in the air, joining the roar of the crowd.

She watched the seconds tick down as San Jose tried to advance, but the Ice held and won the game. Jenna was hoarse from her shouts and screams.

When she turned, Liz held out her hand. "I'll take my twenty bucks."

Jenna rolled her eyes and reached into her bag for her wallet. "Bitch."

"I love you, too. Now let's go wait for your boyfriend."

She followed Liz up the stairs. "He's not my boyfriend."

"You know what Shakespeare said about the lady protesting too much."

It would be childish to stick her tongue out at Liz's back, but Jenna really wanted to.

She followed Liz downstairs to the locker room. They waited outside in the hall while the media did their thing with interviews and the players began surfacing. When Ty came out, he grinned and came over to Jenna, wrapped his arms around her, and lifted her off her feet, then planted a hot kiss on her lips that made her stomach flutter. He put her down, then smiled at Liz.

"Thanks for coming to the game."

"It was a great game," Liz said as they made their way upstairs. "Took you guys long enough to pull it out."

He put an arm around Liz's shoulder. "Hey, the fans like a little suspense."

"The fans like a blowout."

"They like to be entertained. A close game keeps them on the edge of their seat."

"Bullshit. You guys want to be up by three or four goals in the first period, too, so you can run defense the rest of the way. Don't blow smoke up my ass, Anderson."

Jenna's lips quirked as Ty and Liz argued all the way to one of the private clubrooms, where Liz pulled some papers out of her bag. Jenna helped herself to a soda while they talked PR business.

Freshly showered, Ty's hair was still wet, the ends curling against his neck. She sipped her soda and watched as he bent over the table, the Henley he wore stretched tight against the muscles of his back.

Watching him play showcased his amazing power, the incredible strength and stamina it took to play this game. She saw it in his finely honed body and in the scars he bore. The play was rough and not without its physical hazards. She was glad he was in good shape, but oh, man, it had been a tough game and he'd been slammed against the glass several times. Seeing it on television was one thing—up close was something altogether different.

She itched to go over and run her hands over his shoulders, to remind herself of his strength and to reassure herself he was okay. She wanted to feel the heat she knew would pour off him in waves. Even on the cold ice the other night his skin had been hot, his body all muscle. After a shower he smelled cool and crisp, like the ice. She wanted to put her face in his neck and breathe in his scent.

Her nipples tightened and her sex quivered.

She sighed and took a sip of her soda. Okay, so clearly she hadn't had quite enough of him yet. She was going to have to work double time to get him out of her system.

Finally, Liz stood. "Okay, that's it. Jenna, are you coming with me?"

Jenna looked at Ty.

"She's coming with me."

Liz's lips quirked in a knowing smile. "Great. I'm out of here, then. You two have a fun night."

She waggled her fingers at Jenna and headed out the door.

Alone again. With Ty.

EIGHTEEN

THE ROOM GOT QUIET AS TY CAME OVER TO WHERE SHE was sitting. He caged her between his body and the barstool. "What did you think of the game?"

She shrugged. "It was okay. Kind of boring."

He leaned in and pressed his lips to the side of her neck. "Is that right?"

"Yes. Liz had to nudge me awake a few times."

"So you didn't see the goal I scored?"

Her breathing quickened when he licked her earlobe. "No. Missed that part. Sorry."

"That's okay. Like you said, it was a pretty dull game."

She pulled back and framed his face with her hands. "It was a great game. I enjoyed it very much."

"For someone who doesn't like sports."

She allowed a small smile. "Yeah. Rough game, though. You get banged up?"

He laughed. "I always get banged up. I'm tough. I can take it."

She swept his hair away from his forehead and noticed the cut above his right eyebrow. It had a butterfly bandage on it, but it was swollen. Helmets had gone flying off when he and the other guy had gotten into a fight.

"A fistfight, huh?"

"I've had worse, and not on the ice."

"Really. I'd like to hear about those."

He grabbed her hips and pulled her to the edge of the cushioned seat, drawing her between his legs. "Maybe I'll tell you about my childhood sometime."

"Did you live on the streets, fighting for your survival?"

He snorted out a laugh. "Uh, no. But I did get into fights a lot."

She leaned back, putting her arms on the chair. "Must be in your nature."

"Maybe. My parents put me in sports to take some of the attitude out of me. I liked hockey because it was aggressive. I played it from the time I could stand upright on skates. And sometimes we used the sticks for more than just moving the puck around."

She studied him, wondering what kind of child he had been, what that play must have been like. "Swords?"

His lips curved. "Something like that. You can playact a lot of battles with a hockey stick."

"I can only imagine."

"Can you? Just how tough are you?"

She raked her nails down his arms. "Just as tough as you are. I played football and baseball and basketball and hockey with my brothers and their friends and I gave as good as I got."

He squeezed her legs and the room got hotter. "So you can get rough with the guys, huh?"

"You bet."

"You're not one of those sissy girls who can't take a little heat."

"Hell no."

"How much can you take?"

Her breasts ached and her pussy quivered with the knowledge that she wanted him and she knew exactly where this was going. "How much have you got?"

He hauled her off the chair and into his arms, his mouth coming down on hers in a hard, hot kiss that swallowed her gasp. She tangled her fingers in his hair and yanked on the strands while he grabbed her ass. She wrapped her legs around his hips, clamping tight while he walked the short distance to a table and set her on top of it.

She was panting when he let go of her. "Aren't there going to be people coming in here?"

He left only long enough to flip the security lock on the door, then grabbed the remote, clicked a button, and closed the blinds overlooking the ice, shading them in complete privacy.

He turned back to her. "Take off your pants."

She kicked off her boots and slid out of her jeans and tights, leaving her in only her panties and shirt. He hovered over her, then bent to kiss her knee. She sifted her fingers through his hair, loving its softness, so incongruent with his overall toughness.

He kissed his way up her thighs, and when he dragged her butt to the edge of the table, she leaned back on her hands, desperate for him to touch her, to taste her, to make her come. Her pussy quivered in anticipation of what she knew he was going to do. This was so forbidden, the thought of someone coming to the door exciting her beyond measure.

"I think about you when I'm not with you," he said as he pressed a kiss to her inner thigh. "I think about your smile, your laugh, and how beautiful you are."

He swept his hand across her panties and she let out a breath.

"I think about your pussy and how sweet it tastes, and how you look when you come." He slipped his hand under her butt to lift her, parted the material of her panties aside, then put his mouth on her.

"Oh, yes, that's what I want," she whispered, laying her hand on his head as he swept his tongue across her clit. Warmth exploded inside her as he caressed her sex with his lips, then dragged his tongue across her pussy lips, fucking her with his tongue until she was sure she'd die from the wave of sensations.

She arched against him, wanting more and more, but she wasn't going to last because he found her piercing and tugged at it with his teeth, flicked it with his tongue, and the vibration sent her right over the edge. He sucked her clit and she came, whimpering, trying to hold it in because they weren't somewhere she could let out the scream she bit back. He held on tight to her, his tongue against her clit as her climax rolled in sweet pulses that made her shudder.

He pulled her off the table and kissed her, letting her taste her own salty sweetness. Her legs were shaking and she held on to him for support, her thigh brushing his erection, which only heightened her renewed arousal. She reached down to rub his cock through his pants and was rewarded with his thick groan.

He pulled back and dragged her panties off and bent her over the table, then unzipped his pants and released his cock.

"Let's see how rough you really like it."

Her pussy quivered as he tore open a condom and positioned himself behind her.

He spread her legs apart, caressed her butt, spreading her ass cheeks, petting her and sweeping his fingers between her legs to rub her pussy. She couldn't take it any longer.

She looked at him over her shoulder. "Ty. Hurry."

She felt his cock at the entrance to her pussy, teasing her as he petted her with his cock head. She lifted her ass, teasing him back until he thrust and buried himself inside her.

Ty stilled, his cock twitching as he filled himself inside Jenna's sweet, hot pussy.

She drove him crazy, challenged him to give her what they both wanted. She arched her ass against him, torturing him with hot moans and whimpers that rocked his balls.

And when he reared back and thrust deeper, the low moans she made obliterated whatever bit of control he'd been holding on to. His fingers bit into her ass as he reared back and plunged in harder again, rewarded when she threw her head back and said, "Yes. Oh, God, yes."

"You have a sweet ass, Jenna." He gave her butt a light tap with his hand, and her pussy squeezed around him while she moaned in response. She laid her head on her hands, her fingers gripping the edge of the table.

He smacked the other globe and fucked his cock into her. She shoved her pussy back against him, asking for more.

She was going to make him come hard tonight. His cock swelled thick, his balls drawn up so tight he was ready to explode.

He gave her another swat, harder this time, and she moaned louder, her pussy spilling moisture over his balls. He reached around to rub her clit with one hand, and smacked her ass with the other.

"Oh, God, I'm going to come. Fuck me harder, that's going to make me come."

He found the hard nub, pistoned his cock in deep, then swatted her ass, feeling her pussy contract around his dick.

She drove her pussy against his cock and tilted her head back, crying out as she came. Feeling her muscles clench around him, watching her as she climaxed, was the hottest thing he'd ever seen. He lost it, grabbing hold of her hips and driving deep into her as he came, letting loose a battle cry of his own.

He put his arms around her and laid his head on top of her back to gather his breath, then turned her to face him. He kissed her and smoothed his hands over her butt cheeks.

"Did I hurt you?"

She lifted a brow. "Of course not. I told you I was tough."

He laughed. "Yeah, you are."

"I enjoyed that, Tyler."

He shuddered out a breath. "Me, too."

They got dressed and left. He took her home and she invited him in. They were both hungry so she made them some eggs and bacon. After, she sang for him again as they sat in the living room sipping juice. He was surprised she didn't object when he asked her to. Maybe she was getting more used to the idea.

When she finished a song, he smiled at her. "That was beautiful."

Her lashes dipped down across her cheek. She obviously still wasn't used to hearing someone praise her voice. "Thank you."

"Why don't you ever sing for your family?"

She shrugged. "I don't know."

"You know how to play guitar. That has to be something your family knows about."

She laid the guitar against the sofa. "Actually, they don't. I didn't take guitar lessons until I moved away from home. I learned how to play when I was out of the country."

"And they've never heard you sing. Not even when you were a kid?"

"Oh, sure. I was in church choir when I was a kid. But solo? No."

There was more. He knew there was more. "Didn't your parents notice your amazing voice, even when you were a kid?"

Her lips lifted in a hint of a smile. "You blend in with the choir."

He studied her. "There's something you're not telling me. What is it?"

"It's nothing. Nothing important."

"Everything about you is important. I told you before you can tell me anything."

"It's petty."

"So?"

"I wanted to take singing lessons when I was a kid. I asked my parents about it, but Mom was a dance teacher, and of course me being the only girl meant I was the one stuck taking dance lessons. Ballet, tap, jazz, the whole thing."

"Okay. But what about singing lessons."

"You have to understand. There was Mick and Gavin and all their sports. Every night of the week. And then my dance lessons. And Mom and Dad had to work. There just wasn't time. And then there was money. All these activities were expensive. Singing lessons were expensive. The dancing lessons were free because Mom was the teacher."

Now he understood. "Oh. I see. Everyone's needs and wants were a priority, and what you wanted got shuffled to the end of the line."

"It wasn't like that."

"Don't make excuses for it, Jenna. You didn't get to live your dream, while your brothers did."

"They played school sports. It was much cheaper."

"That's all bullshit. You wanted to sing. Did you tell them you wanted to sing?"

She looked down at her hands. "I asked. Once."

"And?"

"Mom explained that with dance and the boys in sports, there just wasn't the time. Or the money. They said maybe some other time, once there was more money for singing lessons, but I never asked again."

"And your dream went up in a puff of smoke."

She didn't say anything, but Ty could imagine what it must have been like for her. If he hadn't been allowed to play hockey, it would have crushed him. He brushed her hair away from her face. "I'm sorry."

"It's no big deal. We can't always have everything we want."

"It is a big deal. It's what you loved."

"I liked dancing, too."

"Yeah, well I liked playing basketball, but it wasn't what I loved. I got to do what I loved."

She lifted her gaze to his. "So did I, when I went to Europe."

And then someone crushed her dream again. He ached for her. "Now you have another chance."

"Oh, I don't think so. I have a career now."

"You have a job. You have a great talent, Jenna. Why aren't you out there showing it off?"

"Because I'm happy to just sing. I don't need anyone else to hear it."

"Are you really content with that? You write all these songs and you hide in your office singing them. And you're happy with you being the only one hearing them."

She didn't answer, but he saw her flicker of a glance over to the guitar.

"You're afraid."

She snapped her gaze back to his. "No, I'm not."

"Yeah, you are. You're afraid you won't be good enough. You're still letting that rejection hold you back."

"That's bullshit." Her gaze narrowed. "And why is this so important to you, anyway?"

"Because I've been there."

She leaned forward. "What do you mean?"

"Playing professional hockey is a lot different than doing it for fun or even in college. It's doing it for money, making a career out of it. Do you think I wasn't afraid of failing? I'm not big on failing."

"So you once thought about not doing it?"

"Yeah. I was good and I knew I was good. I had a gut feeling I could make it, but I wasn't being branded as some future superstar with a guarantee of success. If I didn't make it, I didn't know if I could handle the rejection."

She reached for his hand, clasped it between hers. "It's hard to put yourself out there. The potential for failure is difficult for a lot of people to deal with. I don't blame you for being cautious."

He laughed. "Honey, I wasn't just cautious. I nearly walked away from it all on the off chance I wouldn't become a success. It was the dumbest thing I almost did."

"So what changed your mind?"

"My mom. She said everything always came easy to me, and I had real talent. I'd always been a winner and that was great and all, but until I failed at something I'd never appreciate what success really meant."

Jenna nodded. "Your mother sounds like a very wise woman."

"I don't know about that. She isn't without her own faults and failures. But knowing she failed and picked herself up and started over made me believe I could do the same thing."

"Then it sounds like she knows what she's talking about. The voice of experience and all that."

"Yeah, I listened to her advice and I took the leap."

"Was it scary?"

"Scary as hell. And I did fail a few times. Got my ass kicked down to the farm clubs, had to work my way back up. Learned along the way that you have to work hard to succeed in this sport, the wrong attitude will get you sent down faster than you can spit, and the cream rises to the top."

"You've obviously had a successful career, so you've done some things right."

He nodded. "Some things, yeah. But lurking right around the

corner is failure. You can't overthink everything. Like those losses we've had recently. Spending time dwelling on them doesn't help. If all you focus on is the failures, you can't keep your eyes on success. I don't think any athlete—or any performer—ever forgets that. If they do forget it, they're likely to fail."

"So what you're telling me is I'm not the only one who's afraid."

He rubbed his thumb over her the top of her hand. "No, babe. You're not the only one."

"I'll give it some thought."

"Maybe you could start by singing in front of your family."

Her eyes widened. "No. I can't."

He rolled his eyes. "I don't think you're giving your family enough credit. They seem really supportive."

"Yeah. They're incredibly supportive. That's the problem."

He frowned. "I don't get it."

She rubbed her temple. "I know you don't."

"Then explain it to me. Your parents seem to love all their kids. I don't think it would matter what they did. Either way, you have to start somewhere. How else will you achieve your dreams? What do you want to do?"

"I've told you before. I'm already doing—"

He put his fingers to her lips. "No, really. What are your dreams? Be straight with me. What would you really love to do with your life?"

Jenna was about to brush Ty off with another lame excuse, but they'd really gotten into a deep and heavy conversation tonight, and he'd opened up to her about some of his own fears. It was only right to be as open and honest as he'd been.

"Honestly, one of the things I've often thought about is opening a second Riley's, only this one for singing. Like the karaoke club we went to that night. But this one would be different. Instead of an occasional open mic night like they had, it would always be open mic night. And we'd bring in live bands instead of using a karaoke machine. Just a music bar. With no television screens."

He laughed. "Obviously you've given this a lot of thought."

She shrugged. "Now and then."

"I think that's a great idea. You'd have Riley's Sports Bar and Riley's Music Bar."

"Yeah. It's a pipe dream, though."

"Why?"

"Who would run it? I run the sports bar. My mom and dad are mostly retired now. They hardly ever show up at Riley's, and they never work the bar anymore. I run it single-handedly. I'm responsible for the bar."

"Does it have to be a family member running the sports bar? You have a couple assistant managers, don't you?"

"It's kind of a family tradition that the bar is owned and operated by family, so yes. That's always the way it's been. And I do have assistant managers, but they're not family. I would never think to ask Mom and Dad to turn the operation over to them. They're not family members."

"I think you're too wrapped up in this whole family thing. The main focus is on the bar and how it's run. If you have people who run it efficiently, who cares if their last name is Riley or not? Your assistants run the bar on your nights off."

She lifted her chin. "That's different. It's not on a permanent basis and our regulars know that a Riley manages the bar. That's what they expect. That's what my parents expect. What my dad expects. After his heart attack last year, I don't want him to think he needs to come back to work just so I can open another bar."

Ah. There it was. "So again, your dreams are on hold."

"Not on hold. I have my path and I'm living it."

"You put way too much pressure on yourself to be what everyone else needs you to be, instead of what you want to be. Why can't you have what you want?"

"Because I can't, and that's just the way it is."

It sounded more to him like she was afraid to ask for what she wanted, afraid to take that step forward to grab her dream.

And there wasn't much Tyler could do to push her. Jenna was going to have to take those steps herself.

DAMN TYLER FOR PUTTING THE IDEA OF A SECOND BAR in her head. It was all she could think about now.

A crazy idea, one that would never, ever happen but now that it had been dredged up from the dark recesses of her dreams and fantasies folder, she couldn't shove it back down again.

She'd started drawing up plans for a new bar a week ago. Ty was out on a road trip again, so when she wasn't working, she had idle time on her hands. Her mind wouldn't let the idea go.

Talking to him, really opening up to him about her childhood and what had happened, and singing for him was doing strange things to her. She'd never told anyone about her childhood. She'd never told anyone about Europe.

Why had she used Tyler as her personal confessional? Because he knew all the right questions to ask, or because he'd made it so easy to tell him? She had no idea. Admittedly, it was kind of nice. But she knew better than to stake any kind of permanence on their relationship. It was nice for right now.

Funny how things had changed so quickly now that she was sort of kind of seeing Tyler in a not really dating, but no longer just sleeping together kind of way.

When he was on the road, he texted and called her every day. She got used to hearing from him and missed him when he traveled. He told her on the phone that the next time the Ice played in Chicago she was going to have to go with him so she could meet his parents.

She told him she was horrified that their relationship had progressed to "meet the parents," and no way in hell. He laughed at her and told her he'd kidnap her in the dead of night and throw her on a plane, but she was going to Chicago with him.

Truthfully, she was curious about his family and she was already anticipating his next game with Chicago to see if he was serious about that or not.

Today she was meeting Tara and Liz for lunch, something they tried to do at least once a week. They were eating at a midtown restaurant since Liz had a client meeting in a couple hours and Tara had an event that night she had to rush off to prepare for after lunch. Jenna had a few hours before she had to be at the bar, so this was going to be a relaxing lunch for her.

"Now that you're married, it's a wonder Mick lets you out of his sight," Liz said to Tara after they ordered.

"I won't see him at all when camp starts up in the summer. I'll be a widow like you are now," Tara said.

Liz nodded. "I know. This is miserable. The week down in Florida was amazing, though."

"You are nice and tan," Jenna said. "I'm jealous."

"As tan as someone with my fair skin can get after I lather up with a fifty-plus sunscreen."

"And how is my brother doing?"

Liz sighed. "Your brother is spectacular."

Tara laughed.

"Gag. TMI." Jenna made a face. "Not the information I was looking for. I meant at spring training."

"Oh, his stats are great. In and out of the bedroom."

Tara snorted.

"Is that all you think about?" Jenna asked.

"When you aren't getting it regularly, yes. It's all I can think about. If I wasn't so damn busy with my own job I'd be parked at the beach house in Florida, naked and spread-eagled, ready for him after every game."

Jenna laid her head in her hands. "I give up. I should stop coming to lunch."

"Speaking of people getting it regularly, how's it going with Ty?"

Her head shot up and she caught sight of the surprised look on Tara's face, followed by the smile.

"Oh, you're still seeing Ty? Details, please."

"Again," Liz said to her. "Not a big secret, right?"

"I guess not now that you've spilled, you blabbermouth."

Liz shrugged but didn't look at all apologetic, so Jenna turned to Tara. "Yes, I'm still seeing Ty."

"And?" Tara asked.

She sighed. "It's good. Nice. We're having fun. That's all."

Tara took a sip of water. "Hmmmm."

Liz waved her fork at Tara. "That's exactly what I said. But let me tell you, the sparks that ignited between the two of them after the last hockey game I took her to nearly set me on fire. So I think there's a lot more than 'nice' going on between the two of you."

She swallowed a bite of food and laid down her fork. "He asked me to go to Chicago with him to meet his parents."

"He did? Oh, my, that is big." Tara looked to Liz, then back at Jenna. "That sounds serious."

She shrugged. "I don't know. We're not serious. It really is just a fling."

"Yeah, that's what I thought it was between Gavin and me," Liz said.

"I thought the same thing about Mick and me," Tara said, flashing her wedding ring. "And look what happened."

Jenna laughed. "We are not getting married. We aren't in love. It's just sex."

"Honey," Liz said. "If a guy is casually fucking you, he doesn't bring you home to meet his parents. He's serious about you."

"You think so?"

"Definitely," Tara said. "The question is, are you serious about him?"

"I don't know. No, I'm not. He's not my type."

Liz snorted. "Yeah, there are so many things wrong with him."

"So true." Tara lifted her fingers and started counting on them. "He's ugly. Poor. Bad job. Zero personality."

"Horrible hair. And that body . . . ugh," Liz continued. "That smile is wretched. No sense of humor. He's so unfriendly that kids and dogs run screaming . . ."

"Oh, shut up, both of you. You know what I mean. He's not the kind of guy I would have chosen for myself."

Tara let out a soft laugh. "They rarely are. But they sneak up on you and surprise the hell out of you, and suddenly, you're head over heels in love and there's a not a damn thing you can do about it."

Was she falling in love with Ty?

God, she hoped not. This was not in her plan at all.

NINETEEN

JENNA WAS ON A DAMN AIRPLANE HEADED TO CHICAGO.
How the hell had that happened?

She blamed Liz and Tara for this. Somehow, over lunch that day, they had convinced her she might be falling in love with Ty. Or if not love, then something that at least required she stay checked in to this relationship for a while longer. So when Ty actually made good on the offer to go to Chicago and meet his parents, she hadn't run screaming in the other direction.

Ty had arranged everything, including a first-class ticket on the flight. She decided she was going to look on this as a mini-vacation away from her responsibilities at the bar, and nothing more.

The flight landed and she was met at baggage claim by a gentleman holding a placard with her name on it. He escorted her by private car to one hell of a luxury hotel. She had club seats for the game tonight, where she'd be seated with some of the Ice players' wives and girlfriends who had also traveled up for the game.

She had just enough time to shower and dress for the game when it was time to meet the women downstairs to take the car over to the event center where the Ice would be playing Chicago tonight.

Admittedly, she was excited. She'd talked up Crista and Leslie on the plane, so she sat next to them when they got to the center. Leslie was married to Jeff Lincoln, the other center on the Ice, and Crista was engaged to Ruddy Meyers, one of their wings.

Leslie was a pistol, as full of fire as Jeff was cool and reserved. She was tall, statuesque, and built with an amazing body, with raven hair that fell straight down her back. She looked like a Victoria's Secret underwear model when in fact she was a middle school math and science teacher. Jenna could well imagine the pubescent boys fantasizing about Mrs. Lincoln.

Crista was a beautiful blue-eyed blonde. Jenna found out Crista was a librarian, and so smart Jenna felt inadequate. But Crista's knowledge level was so damned amazing, Jenna couldn't help but ask her a million questions since she'd all but grown up in libraries as a kid, so they shared their love of books and had talked nonstop on the plane.

"It still shocks me the two of you are in love with sports players," Jenna said as they took their seats.

"Why?" Crista asked.

"I don't know. I guess I have this idiotic delusion that sports guys attract—"

"Bimbos?" Leslie finished for her.

"I didn't want to say that without insulting all of us."

Crista laughed. "I met Ruddy in college. We shared an art history class. He's so intelligent. I fell in love with his brain first, but God, I love sports."

"Me, too," Leslie said. "There's only so much math and science I can handle. And when school is out, sports are my outlet. I played basketball in high school and I love tennis, but there's something about hockey that's so . . . primal."

"It gets my motor running," Crista said. "Seeing my guy out there, whether he's trying to score or fighting for the puck against a defender. It's just hot. Huh. Maybe I am a bimbo."

Jenna burst out laughing. "If you are, we all are."

Listening to these two amazingly intelligent women talk about hockey and their men was a revelation to her. Then again, they didn't have her life or her past or her job.

It was different for her.

Still, when the game started she was caught up by their enthusiasm and she had more to root for than just Ty. She found herself keeping an eye on Crista and Leslie's guys, too. Observing their reactions to their men was a study in relationship dynamics. These cool professional women became crazed hockey maniacs, screaming at the opposing team and cheering for the Ice with fist pumps.

Jenna joined right in, unable to help herself. It was infectious once the action started. The Ice went up two goals after the first period, and she wanted to make sure that somehow Ty could hear her when he had that puck, that he could somehow feel her support when he fought a defender or got slammed up against the boards, or when he and Eddie had that two-on-one breakaway. She wanted him to know she had his back, and if she lost her voice screaming, then she'd do it.

Chicago came back and tied it, but the Ice ended up winning the game by one goal. It was a triumph and she, Crista, and Leslie were ecstatic.

After the game, they were taken back to the hotel.

"Who needs a drink? I certainly do," Leslie said, leading them to the hotel bar. "I'm wrung out after that game."

Jenna followed and they found a table. Leslie ordered a bottle of wine and soon they were drinking and laughing as if they'd known each other forever. A few of the other women came in and joined them, and suddenly another bottle of wine was ordered.

Jenna poured. They all drank. As a bartender, she knew how to monitor her own drinking, while making sure everyone else had a great time. And why not? They weren't driving tonight, so she wanted all the women to have a great time. The guys would be showing up soon enough.

"You aren't drinking." Leslie narrowed her gaze.

Jenna held up her glass of wine. "Yes, I am."

"Not as much as the rest of us." Crista picked up the wine bottle and refilled Jenna's glass.

"Not much of a wine drinker, actually."

"Oh? And what do you drink?"

"Whiskey."

Leslie snapped her fingers and the waitress, sensing a big tip, was right there.

"How do you want it?"

Jenna laughed and shook her head. "On the rocks is fine."

"Bring this lady what she wants. Top shelf."

Three whiskeys later, Jenna turned to Crista and Leslie. "I think you two are trying to get me drunk."

"Of course we are," Crista said. "You can't stay sober while the rest of us are getting hammered."

"I have a very high tolerance for alcohol. I run a bar, you know."

Leslie pointed a finger at her and weaved back and forth in her chair. "Which has nothing to do with your ability to withstand the effects of alcohol."

"True that. But I still have a high tolerance, while you're both getting toasted."

Crista looked at Leslie. "She's so right. We're drunk. I'm so ashamed."

Leslie burst out laughing. The place was getting loud and Jenna couldn't recall when she'd had more fun.

It got even more fun when all the players showed up.

Ty grinned when he saw her. He came over to her and pulled up a seat.

"Having fun?"

"They're trying to get me drunk by feeding me shots of whiskey."

He picked up the drink in front of her and downed it in one swallow. "Is it working?"

"Not really."

One corner of his mouth lifted. "You are tough."

"Told you."

They sat and visited with the players and women for a while, rehashing the game. A few of the players and their wives and girlfriends decided to go to dinner.

"You want to go?" Ty asked.

Jenna shook her head. "I want to be alone with you. We can order room service."

"Sounds good to me." He stood and held out his hand for her.

They headed to the elevator. Once the doors closed, Jenna pressed Ty against the wall and rose up on her toes.

"You sure you're not drunk?"

"Maybe a little." She laid her hands on his chest, then wound them down his stomach. "Mmmm, hard here."

"It's about to get hard lower."

"Is it?" She palmed his erection, sliding her hand back and forth.

"You're going to make me walk to our room with a hard-on."

She tilted her head back and smiled at him. "Yup."

"You're a mean woman, Jenna Riley."

The elevator doors opened and Ty put Jenna in front of him, just in case someone was outside waiting to get on. She felt the ridge of his erection brushing against her butt.

She giggled.

"I'll make you pay for this." He gave her a gentle nudge out of the elevator and they walked the short distance to the room.

Once inside, he shut and locked the door, then pressed her against the wall, hitting the switch next to her, bathing the room in dim light.

"Now it's my turn."

He slid her jacket off her shoulders, letting it drop to the floor, then raised her arms over her head, pinning her wrists together. He roamed down her arms and across her breasts, lingering there for only a second, knowing she loved having her nipples touched. She arched against his hand, but he swept it lower, across her stomach, teasing her by dipping his fingers inside the waistband of her pants for only a few seconds before taking his fingers away.

"Ty."

The room spun. She licked her lips, waiting for him to touch her again.

He looked down at her, his face slashed with harsh lines of determination, his eyes stormy pools of desire. She saw a hunger there that never failed to make her wet and needy.

She struggled against him, wanting to touch him, but he wouldn't let her go. Instead, he leaned in and pressed his lips against her neck, dragging his tongue across her throat until he found that sensitive spot near her ear and licked her there.

He spread her legs, rocking his hard-on against her hip. She rode his thigh, her clit so sensitive she dropped her head against his chest and rubbed against him.

He tipped her chin with his fingers.

"Look at me."

She swallowed, and he cupped her neck, then took her mouth in a hot, hard kiss, using his tongue to claim hers and leave her weak and defenseless, until all she knew were the raging desires of her own body. He let go of her hands and she wrapped them around him, her nails digging into his shoulders, the passion building inside her until she tore at him with her fingers, pulling at his shirt until he lifted his arms and she drew it off him.

She dragged her nails down his back and bit down on his bottom lip. He growled and jerked at her blouse, fumbling at the buttons until he got tired of it and ripped, the sound of each button scattering across the marble floor echoing in the spacious room.

Her bra went next, it too tearing as he lost patience with anything that wasn't going to come off easy.

He dragged his pants off while she removed her shoes and pants, sliding her panties off just as he finished getting naked. He pulled her into his arms and they got only as far as the living area carpet before he laid her down and was on top of her, opening the condom package in a split second.

And then he was inside her and she cried out as he filled her, needing this—needing him—so much that tears pricked her eyes. She blinked them back as he lifted up to look at her while he plunged inside her again, bending her knee to widen her so he could thrust deeper, so he could grind against her so intimately she thought she might explode.

She scored her nails down his chest and he gritted his teeth, then bent and took one of her nipples into his mouth, flicking and biting it until she came over and over, until she thought she'd die from the unbearable pleasure.

But he didn't finish; instead he held and waited until the pulses eased. Then he began to move inside her again, taking her slow and easy, building the pressure again until she was right there with him. And when he draped her legs over his shoulders and penetrated her deeply, she arched against him, giving him everything he asked for and more.

She reached between her legs and rubbed her clit, needing to go over that cliff again—with him this time.

"Fuck. Yes," he said, pumping into her deep and hard while she made herself come. This time when she climaxed, he went with her, dropping her legs down so he could put his lips on hers and absorb her cries, mingling them with his groan.

It had been intense. Earth shattering. And each time it cemented a bond between them she was afraid to acknowledge, but knew was becoming stronger every day.

TY DIDN'T KNOW WHY HE'D INVITED JENNA TO COME TO Chicago.

He never brought women home to meet his parents. His family was . . . fractured. Flawed. The last people on earth he'd want a woman he cared about to meet.

A woman he cared about.

Yeah, that's where he was headed with Jenna. He cared about her. Beyond that, he had no clue what the hell was going on. And now he'd invited her home to meet his family.

What a joke. He must have been insane to do this, but now she was here so there was no going back.

He had so much to explain to her, to warn her about. He should have never brought her here.

But his parents—who they were, why they were who they were—said a lot about who he was. And if they were going to go any further in this relationship, it was important to him that she know where he'd come from.

They'd toured the city and seen all the highlights. It was fun showing her Chicago. Too bad it wasn't summer, or he'd take her on walks by the lake. But there were still things to do, so they'd gone to the museum and seen a few of the historical sights. She'd enjoyed that. And of course, he'd taken her to a few of what he considered Chicago's best restaurants and bars.

You didn't get out of Chicago without having great pizza, so they'd done that. Of course she'd challenged him and they'd entered a long discussion of St. Louis's Italian pizza versus Chicago-style pizza.

One of the things he liked the most about her was she wasn't a wallflower, the kind of woman who'd agree with everything he said just to keep him around. She loved to argue with him. She liked being right. And he enjoyed arguing right back with her, but there was no viciousness in their arguments. Neither wanted to hurt the other, they just enjoyed the banter and were both willing to stand up for what they believed in.

Such a difference in his relationship with her, versus the relationship between his parents.

And speaking of his parents, now that he and Jenna had seen the sights and eaten the food and taken in the clubs, he couldn't avoid that they were going to his mom's house for dinner. He owed it to Jenna to at least prepare her in advance.

She was getting dressed so he headed into the bathroom.

He walked in and leaned against the doorway, watching her look at herself in the mirror. She'd put on a dress—so uncharacteristic of Jenna. It was black and very pretty, with fancy boots and dark tights that made her look so sexy he wanted to undress her on the spot.

She was busy fussing with the long silver chain she wore around her neck.

She saw him and turned. "Do I look okay?"

He pushed off the doorway and went into the bathroom. "You look more than okay." He kissed the side of her neck. "You're beautiful."

"Thank you."

"Come here. I need to talk to you." He took her hand and led her into the bedroom and sat her on the bed.

"Uh-oh. This doesn't sound good."

He took a seat in the chair across from the bed, delaying the inevitable by glancing out the window at the city below. It was a cloudy day today. It might snow.

He felt a touch on his knee and turned to Jenna.

"Ty. What's wrong?"

"Your parents have this amazing marriage. You're part of a really happy family."

She didn't say anything. He was grateful for that.

"I thought I was part of a happy family. Me, my mom, and dad. It was all great until I turned ten. Then the fighting started. They'd try to keep it down low, or wait until after I went to bed at night, but sound travels, and you can't hide shit from kids. Kids are smart. They know when the balance is upset in their universe. Anyway, I heard them fighting. At first I thought it was just a one-time thing, but then it was the next night, and the next. And then it spilled over into the daytime. They wouldn't fight in front of me or anything, but they stopped talking to each other. The tension in the house grew until it was choking the life out of me. I started to tiptoe around them, sure if I was on my best behavior they'd stop fighting and everything would go back to the way it was before.

"It affected every part of my life. My friends stopped coming over. My grades started to drop and I didn't want to be around them anymore. They hated each other so much."

He saw the tears well up in her eyes and hated that he'd put them there.

"I can't imagine what that must have been like for you, for a child to have to go through. You realize what happened with them wasn't your fault."

"I do now. Back then I didn't. I was sure that if I just spoke softer or acted better, I could influence their behavior. And after awhile I just didn't care anymore, because they didn't seem to care anymore. That's when my behavior took a downward slide."

"Did you have any aunts or uncles you could talk to or go to about this?"

"Yeah, but there was nothing they could do about it. They couldn't stop it any more than I could. And they took sides, too, so it wasn't any better going to them."

"When did they finally divorce?"

"When I was fourteen."

"That's a lot of years of unhappiness."

"Yeah. Anyway, we're going to have dinner with my mom today. She still lives in the house I grew up in. My dad remarried and he lives in a condo near the lake. We'll meet him and my stepmom later for drinks."

"Okay."

"The thing is, I love my parents, but my mom is still in denial over a lot of this, so you need to prepare yourself. She's bitter about it, but she's kind of Stepford about the whole thing, if you know what I mean."

Jenna wondered if Tyler's mother was the only one bitter about it. She wanted to ask what broke up his parents' marriage, but the question was too intrusive, and maybe he didn't even know. She still saw the pain on his face, the rigid tension in his jaw. This wasn't easy for him.

She couldn't imagine her parents not being together. The idea of it hurt, which made her hurt for him. But the reality of it was, a lot of parents divorced, and the impact hit the children in ways that lasted for years.

She stood and wrapped her arms around him. "I'm sorry."

"For what?"

"For what you had to go through. For the end of your parents' marriage."

He laid his head against hers. "It was a long time ago."

"I'm sure it still hurts."

He shrugged and ran his fingers through his hair. "The thing is, they just weren't right for each other. My mom is very quiet and understated, likes to stay home and be with family. My dad is bois-terous and loves to entertain, always liked going out. It was a person-ality clash from the get go. I can see it now. I'm not sure what brought them together in the first place."

She slipped her hand in his. "Sometimes opposites attract in the beginning. It's not until later they realize they can't make it work, that it's those opposite qualities they found so attractive in each other at the onset of the relationship that start to grate on each other later."

He nodded. "I think that's what happened to the two of them. There was no affair, nothing scandalous that ended their marriage. They just realized they weren't right for each other anymore."

Jenna ached for the loss of Ty's parents' marriage, and the end of the stability he once knew. Divorce was never easy on a kid. She'd seen several of her friends go through it, and the havoc it wreaked on their lives. "Unfortunately, there's no test of compatibility to see how couples will survive together, despite what they say on those online dating sites. There's always a risk you take when you agree to spend the rest of your life with someone. Sadly, sometimes the kids are the ones most affected."

She leaned into him and he used his finger to tip her chin up, pressing his lips to hers. "I'm okay, babe. It was a long time ago. But thanks for understanding. You ready for this?"

She managed a bright smile. "Sure. I'm looking forward to meet-ing your parents."

He let out a short laugh that made her wonder what she was going to be dealing with tonight.

They got into the car Ty had rented and he drove to this amazing neighborhood filled with tiny row houses tucked close together. He parked in front of a narrow-frame, two-story pale blue house with white shutters on each window. Jenna instantly fell in love with it.

She wanted to take pictures of it. She wanted to live in it. The atmosphere was warm and homey and she could already imagine children running up and down this street. No wonder Ty's mother had stayed in this house, in this neighborhood.

"What are you doing?" he asked as they stood on the sidewalk in front of the house.

She tilted her head back and looked at him. "Seeing you here as a kid."

"Yeah?"

"Yeah. It fits."

Tyler slid his hand in hers. A small bay window sat off to the right side of the porch. She wondered what room that was. If it was the living room, she could imagine the Christmas tree lit up, twinkling in greeting as people walked down the street. All the homes sat close, so it must be a tight community.

Then again this could be nothing more than fantasy she'd conjured up in her own mind.

They walked up the painted blue steps to the small front porch.

"I love this house," she whispered to him, and he squeezed her hand.

She could see him jumping off that porch onto the narrow side yard or into the bushes. Boys did that.

He opened the door and walked inside. The rooms were cozy and warm, the ceilings high. There was a vintage feel to the home even though an oversize, flat-screen television sat in the living room. And yes, the bay window belonged to the living room.

A diminutive woman came rushing in, wiping her hands on the apron she wore.

"Ty," she said in a quiet yet excited voice.

Jenna stood back and watched as Ty swept his mother up in an embrace, kissed her cheek, then set her back on the floor.

His mother was nothing short of stunning. China doll features, she had dark hair that she wore pulled back in a ponytail. She wore a beige dress that had to be expensive, and pumps. Jenna was happy she'd dressed up.

"I'm so glad you're here." His mother beamed up at him, and the pride Jenna saw on his mother's face was evident. "Now introduce me to your friend."

Jenna also noted the word "friend." Not girlfriend, but friend. His mother wanted distance between Ty and Jenna. Duly noted.

"Mom, this is Jenna Riley. Jenna, this is my mother, Louise Davis."

Not Anderson? Tyler hadn't mentioned his mother had remarried, but okay.

"Nice to meet you, Mrs.—"

"You can call me Louise. So nice to meet you, Jenna."

"Nice to meet you, too, Louise. Your home is beautiful."

"Thank you. Please come in. Take off your coat and get comfortable. Would you like a cocktail?"

"No, thanks. I'd love to see the house."

"Of course. Tyler, take her on a tour. I'll check on dinner. I hope you like beef Wellington, Jenna."

Wow. "I love it. Thank you."

Tyler took her hand. "A tour it is. Let's start upstairs."

She followed him up the staircase.

He stopped at the top. "There's really nothing up here."

She pushed at his chest. "Shut up. I want to see your house."

He rolled his eyes and led her down the hall. "This is my mom's room."

It was perfect. Cozy and feminine, with a mauve bedspread, muted, earth-toned pillows, an antique dresser, and a bath off to the side. The room was painted a light beige, with eggshell wainscoting.

"I could so live in that room. Did your mom decorate it?"

"That's her thing. Seems to me like it's a different color every time I come home."

She laughed. "You know what they say about a woman's prerogative to change her mind."

"Yeah, well, Mom likes to do that plenty."

They moved down the hall to another room. "Sewing room. This is where she does that fabric and sewing machine stuff."

The room was filled with fabric. Lush jeweled colors and muted beiges. There was a sitting area and a work area, books on design and fabric. Even though it wasn't Jenna's area of expertise, the female in her squealed with delight.

"Oh, it's lovely."

"Girl stuff."

She rolled her eyes at Ty and they walked on down the hall. "This is my room. Prepare yourself."

He opened the door and it was as if time had stood still. It was precious. A twin bed sat under the double window and the room was painted a bright blue. Trophies of all kinds filled the shelves on the walls. A small desk cornered one end of the room. Photos of Ty at different ages filled several shelves on the walls. She stepped in the room and scanned the photographs of Tyler missing a front tooth, one of him with his hair falling over his eyes like it still did today, and one of him as a baby.

She put her hand over her heart and looked up at him. "This is so sweet."

"I've tried to get her to let me pack up all this stuff and put it in the attic, but she won't let me. It's creepy."

"It is not. She obviously loves you."

"She could turn this into a guest room."

Jenna sat on his bed. "Why would she?"

"Because people need to move on. I'm not a kid anymore."

"Maybe she loves these memories of you. Look at all these trophies and certificates." She stood and scanned the framed certificates listing Ty's accomplishments on the Honor roll, dean's list, even his academic scholarship letters.

She turned to him. "Weren't you a smarty?"

He crossed his arms. "Not just a dumb jock, ya know."

She was learning more about him every day, and she liked what she saw.

"Your mother is very proud of you."

"She could be proud of me by putting my crap in a scrapbook."

She laughed. "My parents have the trophy room in our house. Stuff from Mick and Gavin and my childhood, all the way through high school and college. Remind me to show it to you sometime."

"Yeah?"

"Yes. A room dedicated just to us kids and our accomplishments. So believe me, it's not just your mom. And it's as embarrassing for us as it is for you. Some parents like to show off their kids. Your mother is not creepy."

He shrugged. "Maybe not. But I'd be happier if this room had a futon and maybe an elliptical in it. Something for my mom. It's like I died or something and she's afraid to touch anything in here. She's enshrined it."

Jenna snorted. "It's a parent thing. Get over it."

They went back downstairs and through the dining room, which held a tableclothed rectangular cherry table with matching china cabinet and hutch. The furniture had to be antique. Ty led her through the doorway into the kitchen, which obviously had been remodeled. There were dark gray granite countertops, cherry cabinetry, and stainless-steel appliances as well as lots of open window space.

"Oh, I love your kitchen, Louise."

She turned and smiled. "Thank you. When I'm not sewing I'm trying out a new recipe, so I spend a lot of time in here. I remodeled a couple years ago, got rid of the ancient appliances and tacky countertops. Out with the old, in with the new is what I say."

"Except for my room," Ty grumbled.

"Hey, I like your room," Jenna said, taking the glass of wine Louise passed to her.

"So do I. Some of my best memories are of Tyler's childhood. And I want him to feel at home when he visits, which isn't often enough."

"Because I'm too tall to sleep in that twin bed," Tyler said, rolling his eyes at Jenna when his mother's back was turned.

Jenna grinned at him.

Ty's mother led them into the living room, where they sat and drank.

"You are not too tall for that bed. It's extra long," his mother said as she sipped her wine.

"My memories are fine without you leaving my room the same way it was when I was six years old."

Louise turned to her. "It's a constant point of contention between us. He doesn't like that I won't pack up his things and shove them in the attic. But I love those memories of his boyhood." She took a sip of wine. "Life was simpler back then."

Jenna slid Ty a look. He shrugged.

"I saw your sewing room, Louise. And your bedroom is amazing. Did you make the spread and window coverings yourself?"

She beamed a smile. "I did. My mother taught me to sew. It's not something I had time to do until I retired a few years ago."

"Oh, how nice for you. What did you do before you retired?"

"I was executive assistant to the president of one of the banks. Years ago I started out in clerical work, then as a secretary. Worked my way up over the years into executive work. It was nonstop busy, and I'm glad to be out of it."

"It sounds very exciting."

"Oh, it was," she said, inhaling and letting out a sigh. "But my real joy has always come from sewing. Now that I have the time to do it, I love to make things for the house. I even have friends asking me to redo some of their rooms."

Jenna saw the excitement on Louise's face as she talked about designing for her friends.

"Do you have your own business?"

She laughed. "No. It's just something I do for fun."

"You're very good at it. You could go into the design business."

She seemed to ponder the idea. "I could, couldn't I? I hadn't thought about it. It was just a hobby." Then she waved her hand in the air. "But it's too late for me to do something like that."

"No, it's not. It's never too late to start your own business. You're still young and you obviously have the talent and the ambition."

"You think so?" Her eyes lit up. "I don't know anything about starting my own business."

"My family owns their own business. I could give you some pointers on what you'd need to do."

Jenna and his mother spent the next couple hours—including through dinner—discussing small business ownership. Ty had expected the worst. His mom had never liked any girl he'd ever brought home. She'd been rude and unpleasant and had found something about the girl to pick apart. Then again, the last girl he'd brought home had been when he was in his early twenties and still in college. She'd wanted him to focus on school, not on women. And she'd still been bitter over the divorce.

He'd just assumed his mother would always be bitter.

She was different now. More mellow. Or maybe it was Jenna who brought out a different side to her. Jenna didn't hang on him or put a possessive stamp on her relationship with him. She seemed genuinely interested in getting to know his mother, not trying to make his mother like her, or trying to make his mother see that she and Ty were a couple.

But that was who Jenna was. She was good with people, knew what it took to make them at ease. That's what made Riley's so successful. She made her customers happy, and it wasn't just serving them drinks.

After dinner they had dessert, and Jenna told his mom all about her family.

"So you have brothers who play sports, too?"

"Yes. Mick plays football and Gavin plays baseball."

"Did you ever play sports?"

"I played basketball and volleyball in high school. These days I only play when the family forces me into a basketball game at the house."

His mother laughed. "I can imagine it was difficult growing up with those boys."

"It was a challenge. But I held my own."

"I'm sure you did. I'll bet you can handle my son, too."

Jenna looked at Ty and smiled. "Nothing to handle. You raised a fine son, Louise."

His mom blinked rapidly a few times. "Thank you. I'm very proud of him."

Uh-oh. He needed to get them out of there before the waterworks started. "Well, we need to go."

"So soon?"

"Sorry, yeah."

They stood and Tyler went to get their coats.

Jenna hugged his mother. "It was such a pleasure to meet you, Louise. I hope I get the opportunity to again. But you have my number. If you're serious about getting that business started, call me."

His mother hugged Jenna tight. "I will definitely be calling you." She held on to Jenna's arms. "I don't often say this, in fact, I don't recall ever saying this about any woman my son dated, but I'm very glad to have met you, Jenna Riley. And I hope I get to see you again."

"Likewise." Jenna grinned and headed out the door.

His mom pulled him into a tight hug. He bent down so she could kiss his cheek.

"I don't know where you found this girl, son, but don't let her go."

TWENTY

ONE DOWN, ONE TO GO. THEY HEADED DOWNTOWN where his dad and stepmother had a condo.

"I have no idea why you were so afraid for me to meet your mother."

He glanced over at Jenna. "I never said I was afraid."

"You intimated that she was some maternal version of Medusa."

"I did not."

"It was close."

He shrugged. "She's changed. She used to be more uptight."

"She's a wonderful, warm, and friendly woman. I had a great time with her."

"Obviously she's gotten over her bitterness about the divorce, because believe me, I expected something completely different."

Jenna laughed and patted his hand. "You worry too much."

"Probably."

"Okay, now tell me about your dad."

"He's a big, friendly bear of a man, who uses his—I don't even know how to explain this—overly sociable nature to mask any sense of unease or diffuse an uncomfortable situation. That's how it had always been. If there was stress, Sean Anderson would crack a joke to allay it. Always laugh your way out of a problem. He'll also insult you with a smile and an easy laugh. His way of thinking is, if he's smiling while he's calling you a bitch or a useless asshole, then it's okay.

"Of course it hadn't worked so well when my mom and dad had been fighting. My mother hadn't found Dad's sweep-it-under-the-rug-and-laugh-it-off way of dealing with their problems a good solution."

"Hmmm, I imagine not," Jenna said.

"But I think he's learned a thing or two over the years, because my stepmother, Gloria, is great. They've been married for ten years now."

"Do you like her?"

"Yeah, I do. A lot. She never tried to be my mother, only my friend. She knew what the boundaries were, but she had always been there for me if I needed her. And she doesn't put up with my father's bullshit, which I admire."

"Sounds like they make a good match."

"They do. But I have to warn you, you just can't prepare yourself for my dad because you have no idea what's going to fly out of his mouth."

"Uh, okay." She had no idea what that meant.

They took the elevator up to the sixteenth floor of the condominium complex. Tyler laid his hand on the small of Jenna's back as he rang the bell.

Jenna's jaw dropped as the door was opened by an older version of Ty. While his mother was petite, this man was tall, with wavy dark hair that held a peppering of white throughout and at the sideburns.

"Hey, boy, come on in."

He pulled Tyler into a hug, and Jenna noted they were about the same size, though Tyler was maybe an inch or so taller than his dad. Sean was broader, not as lean and muscled as Ty. As she walked in, she couldn't get over how similar they looked. Sean Anderson was strikingly good looking, still in great shape, and his wife, Gloria, was a knockout of a redhead with a curvaceous figure and bubbly smile.

Gloria hurried over to give Tyler a kiss and a hug and enthusiastically shake Jenna's hand.

"We're so excited to meet you, Jenna," Gloria said. "Please come on in."

The condo was modern, with white-and-black furniture and a piano that sat above the sunken living room. The floor-to-ceiling windows offered a breathtaking view of the city and the lake.

They took a seat at a table near the windows.

"I thought since you're not a native to our city, you might enjoy the night view," Gloria said. "Especially since we're lucky enough to have a clear night tonight."

"It's beautiful," Jenna said. "You must love it here."

"We do. We take walks by the lake in the summer. There's a gym downstairs that we use in the winter. Have to stay active, don't we, boy?" his dad said.

"You bet," Ty said.

His dad patted him on the back. "Of course this one stays active on the ice. Couldn't be prouder of you, even though you beat my team the other night."

"Sean," Gloria said, shaking her head before turning to Jenna. "I don't know how he can root for the other team when his own son plays for the Ice."

"Hey, I've always rooted for the local boys. Besides, Tyler gets traded a lot. How the hell am I supposed to keep up with what team he's playing for this year? I have my loyalties. Tyler understands that, don't you?"

"Sure I do, Dad. But I wouldn't bet against me."

Jenna laughed.

"That's what I keep telling him," Gloria said. "My money's on you, honey."

Tyler leaned over and kissed her cheek. "Thanks, Gloria."

"Hey, the kid's tough. He can take a little competition. And he knows I'm always pulling for him." He turned to Jenna. "So, Jenna. Tell me about yourself."

Whoa. Lightning-fast change of subjects. She found it hard to keep up, but she managed to hold her own. She told Sean and Gloria about the family bar and her part in it. They shared a few cocktails, and Sean kept them entertained with jokes and funny stories about Ty's childhood, but Jenna could see Ty was restless and uncomfortable.

"So, Sean, what do you do for a living?"

"I own several car dealerships in town. Still in business after forty years."

She could so see him in sales. "How interesting."

"He even has commercials on TV," Gloria said, pride evident in her beaming smile.

"Oh, that's exciting."

Sean grinned. "Yeah, we buy a lot of TV time. Have to keep your name in front of the people or they forget all about you." He slapped Ty on the back. "Isn't that right, son?"

"You bet, Dad."

"That's why you have that fancy agent getting you those deodorant and shampoo spots. Keep the fans interested. Get them coming to the games. Make the men want to be like you and the women want to get you in the sack." He shifted his glance to Jenna. "Whatever it takes to keep my boy in the limelight, right, honey?"

Jenna blinked. "Sure."

Ty's father was exhausting. She wasn't certain he was all that interested in Tyler's career, only that he stayed "on top." No wonder Ty was uncomfortable.

They managed a couple hours, then Ty stood.

"We've got an early flight tomorrow, so we'd better head out."

They said their good-byes.

"Such a pleasure to meet you, Jenna," Gloria said. "I hope we have a chance to see you again."

"I hope so, too."

Sean shook her hand. "You're a sweet girl. Tyler has great taste in women. Always has. Just like his old man." He put his arm around Gloria.

Tyler led Jenna to the door. "See you later, Dad."

They rode down the elevator in silence, and it was much the same on the short ride back to their hotel. When they got back to their room, Jenna came up to Tyler and put her arms around him.

"What's this for?"

"No reason." Maybe she needed it more than he did, but she figured he needed it, too.

"My dad can be an asshole."

She leaned back. "No, he's not."

"Yeah, he is."

"Your parents are night and day different. Your mom's kind of quiet and reserved. Your dad is very boisterous. I can see why they didn't mesh well."

His lips lifted. "That's being kind."

"I like Gloria."

"So do I. And my dad likes to impress people. He just doesn't know how to do it, so he comes across as a prick. His social skills need work. My mother worked for most of her life. And when she wasn't working, she was catering to me and my dad. She didn't know what to do with herself after the divorce so she stayed in the house and kept her memories of me alive like some goddamned shrine. She sews and bakes and has a small circle of friends that she's had forever, but she never remarried. She took back her maiden name because she hates my father that much. She just never figured out how to move on and carve out a new life for herself. She's frozen in that house. I think you might have helped her with that tonight. Thanks."

"You're welcome, but I think your mother has done just fine moving on. She might not have done it right away, but everyone does things at their own pace."

"I guess you're right."

Jenna swept his hair away from his brow. "You don't have to apologize for your parents. They are who they are and they have nothing to do with who you are."

He looked down at her. "They have everything to do with who I am."

"You think so? I don't believe that. I think we forge our own identities. We aren't tied to our parents, their pasts, or their mistakes. We don't have to be like them—the good or the bad."

He dragged the pad of his thumb over her bottom lip. "Maybe."

"No maybe about it. You become who you want to be, not who your parents are or were. It's all up to you."

He looked down at her and she got lost in the beauty of his face, the intensity of his eyes as he studied her.

"You're good for me," he said.

"Am I? All this time I think you've been the one who's been good for me."

Jenna pushed Ty onto the sofa in the living room of the suite. She went to the door and dimmed the lights. She came back to stand in front of him and removed her boots and tights, along with her panties, then reached inside her dress and pulled off her bra, leaving her wearing only that smoking-hot black dress. She kneeled on the rug in front of the sofa and crept in between his knees, snaking her fingers along his thighs.

Ty held his breath as Jenna shouldered herself in between his legs.

He should be pleasuring her, not the other way around, but damn if he could find a good enough reason to object to this. His dick was hard and pressing against the zipper of his pants, and her hands were inching their way to the promised land. No way was he going to stop her.

Her hair looked like midnight silver in the dim light of the room, her eyes smoky and dark as she lifted her lashes only long enough to give him a teasing glimpse before dipping her head and biting his knee.

He laughed. "You want something to bite? I'll tell you where to bite."

"I think I'm familiar enough with your anatomy to map it myself. Be patient."

She scraped her fingernails down his thighs, then reached for his belt buckle, taking her damn sweet time undoing the clasp before grasping the zipper. Each movement of the zipper caused him to grit his teeth. She was being deliberately slow when all he wanted to do was jerk the damn thing down and release his swollen cock.

Once his zipper was undone, she bent and took off his shoes and socks, teasing him by sliding her hands up into his pants.

"For a guy, you have great calves."

He couldn't even speak. His throat had gone dry. He wanted her hands and her mouth on his dick, not waxing poetic about other body parts. But this was her seduction and he was going to have to sit still and deal with it.

She pulled his pants and briefs down over his hips, dragged them off, and threw them on the chair.

His cock jutted up, ready for the taking, but she ignored it, instead rising up to undo the bottom button of his shirt . . . slowly.

Goddamn it.

"Let me do that." He reached for the buttons, but she grabbed his hands and laid them on the sofa.

"No. This is my job."

Shit.

She undid the second button, and the third, then the fourth, and he broke into a sweat. Who knew the act of undoing shirt buttons could make him even harder?

When she'd undone the last button she drew his shirt apart and laid her palms on his chest.

"I love your body, Tyler, the smoothness of your chest." She mapped her way down his ribs and over his stomach. "The way your muscles move under my hands."

His abs jerked when she got the action going lower, anticipation building when she swept her hands below his navel. She bent and kissed him there, her breasts brushing his cock.

And didn't that get his imagination going? He'd love to rub his cock head over her sensitive nipples. How would she react to that? He filed that thought away for later.

Right now he focused on her hands, the way she planted them on his thighs. Her touch was light, her nails torture as she lightly scraped them across his inner thighs. His balls tightened and he gritted his teeth, refusing to beg her to touch him, even though he really wanted her to.

She rose up and laid between his legs, lightly resting her body against him, and pressed her lips to his. He started to wrap his arms around her but she grabbed his hands again and laid them on the couch.

"No. Don't touch me. Let me touch you."

"This is going to be hard, Jenna."

She smiled against his lips. "That's the idea."

She kissed him, her tongue rimming his bottom lip before pressing her mouth against his. He tasted wine and something sweet—cinnamon, maybe. She deepened the kiss, cradling his head between her hands and moving her body against his in a seductive tease.

He wanted to touch her, to lift her dress and feel her naked ass. But this was her game and he'd play by her rules . . . for now. So he kept his hands to himself while she undulated against him and drove him crazy until all the blood—and every thought—rushed to his dick.

She moved her lips across his jaw, lightly nipping him there. He growled at her, and she gave him a low, throaty laugh that made his balls quiver in response.

"Jenna," he warned.

She ignored him, dragging her tongue along his throat and toward his shoulder. She bit him again, this time harder. He hissed, digging his fingers in the material of the sofa. If he had his way, he'd grab her, hoist her onto his dick, and fuck her until they both came. He was more than ready, and her scent filled the room. This game she played turned her on, too. He could give them what they both wanted.

But he wasn't going to have this his way.

She kissed his chest, lightly sliding her tongue across his nipples. His nipple hardened and she wrapped her teeth around one and tugged, flicking it with her tongue at the same time.

He hissed in a breath, digging his heels into the rug.

She bit down harder, then released his nipple and graced him with a devilish smile.

"Come up here," he said.

She shook her head and sunk lower, flicked her tongue out, and slid down his stomach. The silky fabric of her dress floated over his cock, her body dragging over him.

"You're trying to kill me."

"I'm trying to please you."

"It would please me if you'd climb on my dick and fuck me."

She laughed. "Later."

She sank to the carpet and kissed each thigh, each time making her way closer to his cock and balls. He held his breath whenever she got close, then expelled a disappointed sigh when she moved away.

The woman was good at torture.

But when she lapped at his balls, he let out a low groan, certain he'd died and gone to heaven. And when her tongue blazed a trail from the underside of his cock all the way to his cock head, he was sure he'd have to do some serious math to keep from blowing his load right then, because he was primed and ready to go off.

She flicked her tongue over the tip of his cock, then swallowed him whole and took him all the way to the back of her throat. He groaned, watching his cock disappear in her mouth while at the same time feeling the suction, the wet heat as her mouth surrounded him.

She cradled his balls in her hands and gave them a gentle squeeze as she trapped his cock between her tongue and the roof of her mouth, then let go, rolling her tongue over him and popping his cock out of her mouth to lick the head like a lollipop.

Watching his cock head wet from her mouth made his balls tighten up hard as knots. And when she took him deep again and squeezed him with a swallow, he knew he wasn't going to last.

"Jenna, I'm going to come in your mouth."

She grabbed the base of his cock and began to pump while bobbing up and down on his cock and flicking her tongue over him. He felt his orgasm approach like a runaway freight train and dug in his heels, shoving his cock deep into her mouth.

And when it hit, it felt like the top of his head came off.

"Oh, yeah." He exploded, filling her mouth with the spill of hot come, his entire body shaking with the effort as he poured out everything he had. She sucked him hard and squeezed his balls until he was empty.

He was wasted. So wasted, he could barely draw in a breath. He couldn't do a damn thing for a few minutes but lay there, his head resting against the back of the sofa, feeling Jenna's pounding heart against his thigh. When he could finally raise his head, he smoothed his hand over her hair. She seemed content to lie there, waiting for him, but he knew there was more she needed—more he needed.

He finally pulled her up onto his lap and buried his fingers in the softness of her hair. He put his lips on hers, taking the kiss he'd wanted to take when she'd denied him. She kissed him back with a soft moan and he slid his tongue in her mouth, licking along her velvety softness. He lifted her dress and filled his hands with her sweet ass, running his fingers over the silkiness of her skin, rocking her against his fast-hardening cock.

"Touch me," she said, arching her back.

He filled his hands with her breasts, wanting her naked so he could lick and suck her nipples, but loving the sexiness of her wearing this dress. He wanted to be inside her while she wore this dress. The silk draped over his legs, teasing him with what he couldn't see. He teased her nipples through the silk, then covered one breast with his mouth, sucking the nipple through the material.

She gasped and grabbed his head, holding him there while he used his teeth to pleasure her.

"I love when you touch me like that," she whispered, and he grasped the other nipple between his fingers and squeezed.

She clamped down on him with her thighs, telling him how good it was.

He bent her backward in order to reach his pants and found the condom in his pocket.

"Let me," she said, undoing the wrapper.

She applied the condom, her hands warm and gentle as she slid it down inch by torturous inch until he was fully sheathed.

But first he wanted to make her come, wanted her shattered and shaking before he slid his cock inside her.

He lifted her dress and put his hand to her sex. She was wet, her sweet aroma intoxicating him more than any alcohol ever could. He swept his hand over her, teasing the nub with his fingertip until she tilted her head back and arched her pussy against his hand.

He dipped a finger inside her, felt her quivering and tightening around him. He rubbed his thumb over her clit and she whimpered.

He loved seeing her body respond to his touch, watching her face tighten as she fought for her orgasm. He moved his finger inside her and rolled his thumb over the piercing.

"I'm going to come, Tyler."

He quickened his finger movement and used the heel of his hand on her clit.

She came apart, dropping her head onto his shoulder as she rode the waves of her orgasm. He held his finger inside her while until the quakes lessened, then pulled her onto his lap and onto his cock.

He could still feel the contractions of her body as he filled her.

"Mmm," she said as she settled over him. "That's so good."

Her dress draped around them and he couldn't see, could only feel their bodies joined. He closed his eyes and let Jenna adjust to him inside her, let her recover from her orgasm.

When she began to rock back and forth, he opened his eyes, fisted her dress in one hand, and held on to her hips with the other, lifting her on and off his cock.

He felt thick and swollen inside her, felt the tight squeeze of her body as he pumped into her.

Her face was flushed, her lips parted as she looked down at him. She held on to his shoulders, her nails digging into him when she lifted. She'd started easy, but now the intensity built and her movements quickened.

Their slick bodies slid together in unison. He knew her body like he knew his own, felt when she began to tighten and convulse around him. He grabbed her ass, dragged her back and forth, and she splintered, her eyes widening as her pussy squeezed him like a vise, milking the come from him.

Her gaze met his and held as they both climaxed. He watched the storm ride out in her eyes and gave her back the same, her name spilling from his lips in a wild groan as he thrust deeply inside her and shuddered through an intense orgasm that left him shaking.

She fell against him, the two of them stuck together while he rubbed her back and her hair.

"I need a shower," she finally said.

Jenna leaned against the shower wall, certain she was too tired to do anything but rinse off and fall into bed. But Tyler put his mouth on her nipples and her sex fired to life again, throbbing in demanding need as if she hadn't already had two amazing orgasms.

He slipped his hand between her legs, petting her while he sucked her nipples. She grabbed a fistful of his hair and held on as sharp pleasure traveled from her breasts to between her legs. She was nothing but mindless sensation, hot water raining down on her while overwhelming pulses sizzled at her core.

And when Ty dropped to his knees and lapped at her pussy, she drowned in the sheer erotic haze of being worshipped by his tongue and lips. She looked down to watch him licking her pussy, shuddering when his tongue disappeared inside her. Her legs shook as the pressure built inside her. And when he put his mouth over her and sucked, she burst.

"Ty," she cried, bucking against his face as the force of her orgasm slammed her back against the wall. He held on to her hips while she rode it out, water pouring over her hair and sluicing down her body.

He rose and took her mouth, then entered her. She gasped, met his gaze.

"Shit. Let me get a condom."

She held him firm. "Stay."

"I'm safe. I have blood tests all the time. Team physicals. I never—"

She put her fingers on his lips. "I'm on the pill. We're fine."

"Jenna."

"Make love to me, Tyler."

He thrust into her and kissed her, swallowing her cries of pleasure with his mouth and his tongue. He swelled so thick inside her, his body grinding against hers and taking her so close to orgasm again she was shocked. But she wanted to feel him like this, so naked, so intimate, for just a few moments longer.

He lifted her leg and wrapped it around his hip, held her there while he pushed inside her with painfully sweet, slow thrusts that made her melt from the inside out. He swept her hair away from her face, his gaze so intense, so full of unspoken expression it took her breath away.

His jaw tightened and he powered up inside her harder this time.

When he kissed her, she came apart and felt the heat and power of him as his climax hit. She held on to him as he plunged inside her one last time, then shuddered against her, his mouth buried against her neck.

It had been so perfect, to feel him so raw and unsheathed inside her. Somehow she felt closer to him.

But now she was done for, exhausted, and utterly satiated.

Ty shifted her under the water to tenderly wash her off, then pulled her out of the shower. She gave him a lazy smile as he scrubbed the towel over her hair.

"I'll comb it tomorrow," she said, and he scooped her up in his arms and carried her to the enormous bed, where he laid her down and climbed in after her.

She was asleep before he turned off the light.

TWENTY-ONE

JENNA WAS IN DEEP, DEEP TROUBLE.

She sat in her parents' living room on Sunday, realizing she'd likely made the biggest mistake of her life. She'd invited Ty over for dinner.

It had happened in a weak moment. Utterly satisfied from so much mind-blowing sex, she'd invited him over while they were on the plane flying back from Chicago, figuring he'd likely say no because he had a game or would be out of town. After all, she didn't keep track of his game schedule.

He didn't have a game that day since he'd be leaving town the next morning for a road trip.

So he'd said yes.

To her family, her bringing a guy over for dinner was nothing short of a declaration of love.

Which it certainly wasn't.

Was it?

How did she feel about Ty?

That was a question she wasn't prepared to answer, or delve into at the moment, because Ty was due here in about ten minutes and she was as nervous as a bride on her wedding day.

Oh, bad, bad analogy.

"What are you fretting about over there?"

Jenna looked up to see her mother staring at her.

"Me? I'm not fretting."

"You're chewing on your bottom lip. You always do that when you're worried about something."

She removed her teeth from her lip and smiled at her mother. "I'm not worried about a thing, Mom."

"She lies. She's bringing a guy to dinner and she's panicked, thinks we're all going to give him the third degree."

Mick pressed a kiss to the top of her head, walked past her, and snatched a carrot from the plate at the center island.

Mom waved the carving knife at him. "Do that again and I'll make you do dishes."

Mick shrugged. "You'll make me do dishes anyway. You don't scare me."

He grabbed a piece of celery, winked at Jenna, and headed back into the living room.

"It's a sad day when I can't scare my kids with thoughts of dish duty."

Jenna laughed, grabbed one of the stools at the island, and started mixing dip. "He's a married man now. I'm pretty sure Tara's got him washing dishes regularly."

"So true," Tara said as she walked in and grabbed the stool next to Jenna, taking up a knife to slice celery and carrots. "Big strong hands do a great job on greasy pots."

"Jenna's nervous because her boyfriend's coming over for dinner today."

Jenna glared at her mother.

"Ty's coming for dinner?" Tara turned to her and smiled. "How wonderful. So things must be getting serious between you two."

She knew she should have cancelled on him, told him she had a cold or flu. Or leprosy.

"We're not serious. We're just seeing each other. And it's just dinner."

"But it's dinner with the family," Tara said. "That's a big deal."

"You've never invited someone over before," her mother reminded her.

No, she hadn't, and precisely for this reason. The inquisition.

"Look, it's not a big deal. We're just friends. And Ty's been over here already, so it's not like he's meeting everyone for the first time."

Liz snorted as she walked in. "You and Ty are more than friends. Mom, you should see the sparks coming off the two of them when they're in the same room. You're going to need potholders when Jenna's around Ty, because she'll be on fiyah."

"You are so not funny." Where was her sister support system when she really needed them?

Liz hugged her, then Tara. "What can I do to help?"

"Make some tea?" Mom asked.

"Sure."

The topic switched to Gavin and how he was doing in Florida. Jenna was glad not to be the focus of attention.

Until the doorbell rang.

"I'll get it," she hollered, swinging off the barstool and wiping her hands on the towel.

But by the time she hurried down the hall, Nathan had already let Tyler in and had led him into the living room. Her dad was already engaging him in hockey conversation.

"Hey," she said, tucking her hands into the back pockets of her jeans.

He looked delectable this afternoon in his faded jeans and sweater. He had a bouquet of wildflowers in his hands.

"Hey yourself."

"Are those for me?"

"No, they're for your mother."

Her dad cast a big grin in her direction.

Her heart tumbled over and over. "Oh. Well, come on back to the kitchen."

"Don't keep him in there with you women too long," her dad said.

"I won't."

They walked down the hall and Ty stopped her midway, pulled her into his arms, and kissed her until she was breathless. When he pulled away, he said, "I figured that might be my only chance today."

Her body opened to him, warmed by the kiss and being near him. "Thank you. You've made my day."

He took her hand and they walked into the kitchen, but she released his hand as soon as three sets of very curious eyes landed on them.

"Tyler. How nice to see you again," her mom said.

"Mrs. Riley. I brought these for you."

"Suck-up," Liz whispered.

Tyler turned to her and winked.

"Oh, they're beautiful. Thank you. And call me Kathleen." She went up to Ty and placed her hands on his face, then kissed his cheek. "Why don't you reach up above the cabinets and grab that vase for me."

"Yes, ma'am."

He got the vase and her mother filled it with water.

"I'll arrange them for you, Mom," Tara said, taking over for her.

"Tyler, why don't you go on into the living room with the guys. We'll be eating in a little while."

He looked at Jenna, who nodded. Then he shocked the hell out of her by leaning over and brushing his lips across hers.

"See you in a bit," he whispered against her lips before disappearing.

"Well." Her mother crossed her arms, wooden spoon in hand. "Just seeing each other, huh? No big deal, huh?"

"I don't know about the rest of you, but it just got a little warmer in here," Tara said.

"Told you so." Liz planted a smug smile on her face.

Jenna looked at all of them and shrugged. "Okay, maybe it's a little more than that."

"Oh, it's a lot more than that," her mother said.

"I'll say. You nearly swooned right off the stool when he kissed you," Tara said, fanning herself with a napkin. "And the rest of us were swooning right along with you."

Liz narrowed her gaze at Jenna. "You're in love with him."

"No, I'm not."

"Why the denial, Jenna? What are you running from?" Her mother came around the island and turned Jenna around to face her. "Is there some problem with the relationship? With Ty?"

She so didn't want to have this conversation. Not now, and especially not with her mother. "There's nothing wrong with the relationship, or with Ty. We're just not in love."

"De-ni-al," Liz said, enunciating each syllable slowly. "Ty sure acts like he's in love."

"He does? How can you tell?"

"A man does not kiss a woman in front of that woman's mother unless he has genuine, serious feelings for that woman," Tara said.

Liz nodded. "Totally."

Jenna's gaze shifted to her mother, who was nodding right along with them. "I'd have to agree with the girls. That boy has it bad for you."

She couldn't help the little thrill that snaked its way through her nerve endings.

Ty, in love with her?

No. That was just something Mom, Tara, and Liz inferred from the kiss. It wasn't true. He'd never said a word about love.

Then again, neither had she, because she wasn't going to be in love with a hockey player.

When they'd fixed the snacks, Jenna took them into the living room. The guys were watching the race. Tyler was sitting on the sofa, his forearms on his knees, just as intent on the action on the screen as her dad, Mick, and Nathan.

"Number thirty-six looks good this year," her dad said.

"No way," Ty said. "Rumor has it he and his crew chief don't get along well and the owner's looking to make a change there. He'll be lucky to make it the season in his car."

Her dad glared at Ty. "Just because you're one of those number forty-seven butt kissers doesn't mean you know all, son."

Tyler laughed at him. "Mark my words. He won't make it half the season."

"You're both wrong," Mick said. "The number fifteen is the car to beat this year."

Jenna rolled her eyes. "Now, boys. Don't fight. I brought snacks." She laid them on the coffee table. Ty grabbed her hand and pulled her down next to him on the sofa.

Not one of the guys, including her father, made mention of the fact she and Ty were snuggled up together. No one even looked at them since they were all too absorbed in the race. Two hundred miles an hour was obviously way more exciting than Ty's arm around her. Plus, they were guys. They didn't care.

She was making entirely too big a deal out of this. She needed to relax.

It was spaghetti and meatballs night, one of her favorites. Mom had made homemade bread and as it baked the smell permeated the house. By the time dinner was ready, Jenna's stomach was in full-on growl mode.

They gathered around the table and dug into the food, all conversation at a halt while everyone filled their plates and their mouths.

"So, Ty, the last time you were here it was when Gavin brought you," her dad said. "And Liz is your agent. Now you're here today as Jenna's boyfriend."

Oh, crap. Jenna paused, the fork midway to her mouth, and turned her gaze on Ty.

Way to put him on the spot, Dad. Where was he going with this?

Nowhere, obviously, since he didn't continue his train of thought, leaving Ty to somehow formulate a response to her father's non-question.

"Yeah. I'm really glad to be back. I missed Kathleen's excellent cooking."

Her dad beamed a wide grin. "Can my wife cook, or what? She's amazing. Some of the great food you eat at Riley's are Kathleen's recipes."

"Oh, Jimmy. You'll make me blush."

"Hey, it's the truth."

"I love the smothered steaks at Riley's, Kathleen," Ty said. "I eat that every time I'm there."

She exhaled a sigh of relief. Ty didn't seem the least bit bothered by the boyfriend comment.

Maybe it hadn't. Maybe being called her boyfriend didn't even register with him, or he blew it off as not meaning anything.

"You're so sweet, Ty," her mom said. "Thank you."

"No, thank you. I don't get home-cooked meals very often, so this is great."

"Doesn't Jenna cook for you?"

"She's at work and I'm usually playing games late. But she's cooked for me before."

"I don't cook," Jenna said. "I come over here."

"Well, if you two end up getting married or something, you'll have to learn how."

She cringed at her dad's comment. "We're not getting married, Dad. We're just dating."

Ty grabbed her hand, squeezed it. "Hey, I'm pretty good with a gas grill, so I don't think we'll starve."

Her dad nodded. "Good to know. That girl stays way too busy. You'd think she'd have learned how to cook by now."

Jenna gritted her teeth. So many things she wanted to blurt out, but she held her tongue. Her dad was a traditional guy in so many ways, though he didn't mind her running the family bar nearly seven freakin' days a week. If he ever bothered to come back and take it over, maybe she'd find some goddamned time to learn how to cook, or do any of the hundred other things she never had time to do.

Like get a life of her own.

She bent her head, guilt washing over her. Last year her father had nearly died of a heart attack. She had no business pointing imaginary fingers at him for his lack of duty to the bar. He could do whatever he wanted with his life. She was just damn glad he was still alive.

Ty patted her thigh under the table.

"You okay?"

She gave him a quick nod. "Fine."

"How's the bar, Jenna?" her mother asked.

She lifted her head, the smile plastered back on. "Doing great. Really busy almost every night of the week."

"Weeknights, too?" her dad asked.

"Weeknights, too. With basketball and hockey, they keep the place hopping. It also doesn't hurt that several of the Ice players have made Riley's their home away from home."

Her mom cast a warm smile Ty's way. "We appreciate you coming to the bar. Our patrons love it when sports figures show up there."

"Jenna does a great job with Riley's. It's a fun atmosphere, the food is amazing, and the people are friendly. The guys and me consider it home."

"Good," her dad said. "We hope you always feel that way. It's always been home to Kathleen and me."

"You should come up there sometime, Dad," Jenna said. "Your regulars miss you."

He shrugged. "Not as much fun as it used to be."

"Because you can't drink beer anymore," her mother teased. "Which doesn't mean you can't still have fun with your old friends."

"And you can drink the non-alcoholic beer," Jenna reminded him. "Tastes like the real thing. I'd love to have you there. So would everyone else."

"Maybe I'll pop in one of these nights, make sure my girlie here is doing as good a job as I did."

If this kept up she'd need dental work before the end of the night. Her jaw ached from clenching it.

After dinner and dishes everyone moved into the living room. Her mom picked up her knitting, and Tara and Liz huddled together working on something for Liz's wedding, while the guys watched the rest of the race.

She and Ty were putting the rest of the pots and pans away in the kitchen.

"This would be a good time for you to mention expansion," Ty said.

She handed a pot over to him. He was crouched on the floor, sliding them into the cabinet.

"What expansion?"

"Opening a new bar."

"No. Not a good time for that at all." It would never be a good time.

He took the last pot, stacked it with the others, then stood and leaned against the counter. "Why not?"

"You heard my dad. I'm not sure he even has confidence I'm running Riley's the way he likes."

Tyler chuckled. "That sounded more like good-natured teasing to me."

She pulled up one of the stools and half sat on it. "You don't know my dad. He may sound good-natured, but he's fiercely protective of the bar. And he's traditional. He'd never go for an expansion idea."

"And you'll never know that if you don't discuss it with him. How's the capital situation?"

"Plentiful."

"Then put a business plan together and present it to him. It's a good idea, Jenna, and one where you could capitalize on your natural talent."

"You're really pushing me on this. Why?"

"One, because I think your talent is being wasted on being a bartender. Two, because I think if you opened up a second bar, you could sing there, which would make you happier because you'd actually be doing something you love to do. Three, because it's a sound business investment. You already know how to run a successful bar. I think you could make this work."

Everything he said made sense. It was logical.

But she wasn't going to do it. She shook her head and slid off the stool. "Too risky. Dad would never go for it."

More important, she would never go for it.

She started out of the room, but he took her hands. "Then make him go for it. You're the most argumentative woman I've ever known. You're telling me you can't stand up to your father? Go to him armed with a sound business plan and make him listen. Sing for your parents. Take them to the club we went to and show them how this could work."

She jerked her hands away. "No. I'm not going to do this. Just because you think it's a great idea doesn't mean it's something I want to do."

"You're afraid to take this step, just like you're afraid to sing in front of your family."

She glanced down the hall to make sure no one had heard. "I'm tired of having the same conversations with you. I don't want to talk about this anymore."

But Ty obviously wasn't going to let this go. "At first I thought it was a fear of failure. Now I think you're afraid to succeed."

"That's ridiculous. I just don't think a second bar is a good idea."

"Which has nothing to do with singing in front of your family. You're afraid you're going to be so good they're going to want to hear you again. Or maybe they'll get the idea you should do something with that spectacular voice of yours. And then you'll be forced to step outside your comfort zone—this cocoon you've so carefully wrapped yourself in—and do something about being so unhappy."

"What? Where is this coming from? I'm not unhappy."

He stepped in closer. "Yeah, you are."

She moved back. "No, I'm not, and you have a hell of a lot of nerve presuming to know how I feel. I'm perfectly content with the way things are. I was content before you came into it and I'll be content after you're gone."

He arched a brow. "You trying to get rid of me, Jenna?"

"No. I don't know. Stop pushing me. I don't like it."

"I'm trying to help you."

"You're not helping me. This isn't what I want. And if you think it is, then you haven't been listening all the times I've told you."

He took a step back and raised his hands. "If that's what you think, then I'll back off."

She nodded, but felt miserable, like an invisible wall had just been raised between them.

"I'm going into the living room so they don't wonder what we're talking about in here."

"Fine."

She walked out, leaving Ty alone in the kitchen.

Well, that went well.

TYLER GRABBED A SODA FROM THE REFRIGERATOR, needing a few minutes to cool down and collect his thoughts. He took a step outside in the backyard.

It was cold out. He should have grabbed his coat. Ah, fuck it. He'd survive. He lived on the ice, anyway. The cold might clear out his brain cells, give him some clarity where Jenna was concerned.

"You training for some iron man endurance contest?"

He looked up to find Mick standing on the steps. Mick closed the door behind him.

"Uh, no. Are you?"

Mick laughed. "Hell no. It's bad enough I have to play football in the cold. Not a big fan of it."

"And here I thought you were the tough, macho quarterback."

"Hey, I like dome stadiums. Comfortable seventy-two degrees. Don't ruin my rep by leaking that one to the media, though."

"Now I have ammunition to use against you. Bad move on your part."

"Come on." Mick moved off the steps and led Tyler to the garage. They went in through the side door. It wasn't heated, but it was a damn sight warmer than standing outside with the bitter wind biting through their clothes.

Mick leaned against one of the two cars that sat covered in the garage. "So what's going on with you and my sister?"

Tyler arched a brow. "In what way?"

"In the I-heard-you-arguing-in-the-kitchen way."

"None of your business."

Mick's lips lifted and he scratched the side of his nose. "Probably what I would have said to someone who tried to interfere in my relationship with Tara."

"There's nothing going on. I care about Jenna. We just don't always see eye to eye on things."

"My parents like you, and so does Jenna. I can tell."

"Then that should be good enough for you."

"It should be."

"But?"

"You know, as the oldest, and especially having a little sister, it's always going to be my job to look out for her."

"Of course."

"But I also know she's stubborn as hell. She doesn't make it easy for guys."

Ty decided to listen and see where Mick was going to go with this.

"She can be . . . difficult."

"Understatement," Ty said.

Mick laughed. "She's independent, tough as any man, and she'll dig in her heels if you try to change her."

"I wouldn't want to change her. I like who she is."

"But she's also fiercely loyal to the people she loves. And she's never brought a guy around before, so she thinks you're something special."

Ty looked down at the ground, then gave Mick a sidelong look. "Well, thanks for that. I think she's pretty special, too. I just don't know how to give her what I think she really wants."

"What do you think she really wants?"

"That's not for me to say."

Mick crossed his arms. "Okay, now I'm confused."

"Sorry, man. There's only so much I can say without betraying a confidence."

Mick pushed off the car and slapped Ty on the shoulder. "That's okay. She trusts you with her secrets, and you keep them. That's good. And I don't know how to talk about something I don't have all the facts about, but if you think there's something she wants and she isn't going after it, push her."

"You think so?"

"Yeah."

"She'll hate that."

Mick laughed and nodded. "Yeah, she will. But do you think she'll ever be really be happy if she doesn't get what she wants?"

TWENTY-TWO

JENNA WAITED FOR A WHILE, CHEWING ON A HANGNAIL while Ty cooled his heels in the kitchen. Mick had gone in there, so she figured he was shooting the breeze with her brother.

He finally surfaced and hung out with the family for a while, but it was obvious the dynamic had changed between them. Ty took a seat next to her dad and focused his attention on the race. Jenna sat with Liz and Tara, listening to wedding planning, but she didn't give the conversation her full focus. She kept skirting glances across the room at Ty, who hadn't looked at her at all.

He was mad. Or hurt. Or something

She couldn't help that. She knew what she wanted, and what she didn't want.

Another bar would be nice—one where there'd be music and singing instead of sports, but that was a fantasy that would never come true. Ty pushing her about it wasn't going to make it happen.

She should have never sung for him, should have never allowed herself to even think it was a possibility. Then he'd never know, and they wouldn't be having this ridiculous fight.

"Jenna, would you help me in the kitchen for a minute?"

She pulled herself out of her thoughts and stood. "Sure, Mom."

Her mother had made two pies—a cherry and a coconut cream. She loved homemade pie and her mother made the best in town as far as Jenna was concerned.

"Get out the plates and the whipped cream from the refrigerator. I'll get the forks."

"Okay."

Jenna busied herself with taking plates and utensils out to the dining room. When she came back into the kitchen, her mother was slicing the pie into serving pieces.

"Did you and Ty have a fight?"

Leave it to her mother to have superpower hearing. "No. We're fine."

The look she gave Jenna told her she wasn't buying it. "Want to try that again?"

"Really, Mom. It's not a big thing. We just don't see eye to eye on a few matters."

"Let me ask you a question."

"All right."

"Is he good to you?"

"Is he what?"

"Does he treat you well?"

"Of course he does. I wouldn't be with him if he didn't."

"Is he respectful of you?"

"Yes."

"How do you feel when you're with him?"

"Mom, really."

"Just answer the question."

She sank onto the stool and swiped her finger through the

whipped cream. "All twisted up inside. Gooey, like the inside of your cherry pie."

Her mother nodded, her lips lifting in a knowing smile. "I see. And how do you feel when you're not with him?"

Jenna sighed. "Again, all twisted up inside. I miss him."

"Have you told him you're in love with him?"

God, her mother was like a master interrogator. "I'm not in love with him."

"Are you so certain of that?"

"I don't know, Mom. I don't know how I feel. I've never been in love before."

"You always were the best at hiding your emotions, at never allowing yourself to get close to someone. Love is a scary thing, my darling daughter. But you're a strong woman and I expect you to face your fears head on, like you've faced every adventure you've taken in your life. A Riley never backs down from something they're afraid of."

Well, hell. She wasn't prepared for this, hadn't expected this conversation to get so deep so fast. But now that it had, the floodgates had opened and it was all right there, spilling out.

"I don't like to fail."

"I know you don't. But if you want something that's really worthwhile, you have to be willing to take the risk."

And there it was, the opening she needed.

"Mom, there's something I need to talk to you about."

"Are you two going to serve the pie, or am I going to have to come in here and steal it?"

Dammit.

Her mom's focus turned to her dad, who was followed by Nathan, then Mick.

"Yeah, where's that pie?" Nathan asked, looking eager as he peered over his dad's shoulder.

The moment was over.

"We'll talk about this later," her mother said to her with a pointed look.

But later never happened, because after they ate pie Tyler said he had to leave, and Jenna knew she had to talk to him before he left on his road trip, so she decided she wanted to go with him.

They said their good-byes. Tyler, always the perfect gentleman as he thanked her mother for dinner and shook her dad's hand, promised to be back soon to watch some games and play hoops in the backyard once the weather warmed up.

She wondered if they'd still be a couple come spring.

Did she want that? He was already past her expiration date, and God, he pushed her way outside her comfort zone. Her life would be so much simpler without him in it.

Yet here she was, driving home with Tyler following her. If she was smart she'd kick him to the curb before he hurt her. Or she hurt him.

She pulled into her garage and got out, shut the garage door, and went inside to let Tyler in. The bite of impending snowfall blew a harsh, howling wind from the north.

He hurried to shut the door, rubbing his hands together as he stepped inside. "I saw a few flakes out there as we were driving. Snow might come in early tonight."

"I saw them, too. I was listening to the weather on the way home. They're expecting this to be a big storm. Hope it doesn't derail your flight in the morning."

He looked out the window, watched the limbs on the tree in front yard bend from the wind, then turned and looked at her fireplace.

"Do you have wood?"

"Out back."

"How about a fire?"

"That sounds like a great idea. I'll make us something to drink. What would you like?"

"Whiskey." He started toward the kitchen.

"You're going to stay tonight?"

He stopped, turned, and looked at her, and she read the question on his face. "You want me to?"

"Yes."

"Okay, then. Whiskey."

She made drinks while he went outside and gathered an armful of firewood, brought it in, and set it down near the fireplace. He got the fire started and she sat down with him near the hearth, listening to the aged wood crackle and pop as the fire got going.

"Too bad I don't have any marshmallows," she said as she took a sip of her drink.

Tyler downed his in one shot, then laid the glass on the table in front of him. "Marshmallows don't go with whiskey."

She wrinkled her nose at the combination. "You're right."

They hadn't talked about their argument earlier, but he didn't seem angry anymore. She was glad he wasn't the type of guy to hold on to his anger, or hold a grudge. She hated guys who pouted. It was much better to say what was on your mind, get it out in the open, and get past it.

Though they hadn't gotten past it, had they? It still hung in the air between them, unresolved, and that was as much her fault as anyone's.

"I'm sorry about earlier at my parents'."

"It's no big deal. I pushed. You have a right to push back."

He always made it so easy on her.

"I have been making some notes about a new bar," she admitted.

"Have you?" He got up and grabbed the bottle of whiskey, poured himself a refill. "Tell me about it."

"They're just some preliminary estimates on cost and potential feasibility. I listed what I'd want as far as inventory and desirable space, staffing needs, and things like that."

"I'd like to hear about it, if you want to share."

Surprisingly, she did want to share it with him. "I'll go get my notebook."

She sprung up and went to her office to grab her notes. When she came back, she paused for a few seconds in the doorway, struck by how utterly sexy Ty looked leaning against her sofa near the fire. The flames outlined the darkness of his hair, the masculinity of his facial features, the long lean lines of his body as he sat there with his arm balanced on one bent knee and swirled the whiskey around in his glass.

She inhaled, let it out, came into the room, and sat down.

Ty smiled at her. "Let me see."

She flipped open the notebook to where she'd started making her notes. "Some of it is scribble, so it probably won't make much sense."

He lifted his gaze to hers. "I can read scribble pretty well since that's how I write. Let me see."

Out of excuses, she gave him her book, then downed the contents of her whiskey, hoping she'd find courage in the amber brew.

He flipped through the pages, murmuring to her as he did. "Your numbers look reasonable. I like your thought processes on space requirements. Have you given thought to electrical needs for music?"

"Yeah, that's here." She flipped forward a few pages to show him the notes she'd made. "These are preliminary. I figure I'd ask an electrician and someone in the business if it came down to needing cold, hard numbers for outlets and amperage."

He looked it over. "Good idea, but your estimates look sound. What about staffing, for both, plus insurance and liquor? Would you serve food at the other, or just drinks?"

She poured another whiskey. "You think of everything, don't you?"

"You have, apparently. You've got a good list going here."

"I told you I was just jotting down notes. It doesn't mean anything."

"Why do you do that?"

"Do what?"

"Make anything you do seem . . . unimportant. Don't devalue yourself that way. This could be a big deal for you and for your family, Jenna. Riley's is a huge success. If you expanded you could double your family's income."

Putting it that way made good business sense. "But wouldn't it make sense to just open another sports bar in another part of town?"

"Maybe. It's an option. But is that what you really want to do?"

No.

As soon as the word formed in her head, she realized another sports bar wasn't at all what she wanted. What she really wanted was what she secretly thought she could never have.

Until she'd met Ty. Now she wanted things she'd never wanted before.

And she was tired of thinking about them, at least for tonight. Those possibilities gave her a massive headache.

She laid her whiskey glass down and reached for his, putting it on the table behind her, then climbed into his lap.

"Conversation over?" he asked.

"Yes. You're leaving town for a few days and I don't want to spend our last night together talking about floor plans and electrical."

"What? That's not foreplay to you?"

She laughed and brushed his hair away from his face. "Not in the least. I prefer my foreplay a little dirtier."

He squeezed her hips, his hands traveling down to cup her ass. "Floor plans and electrical can get very dirty."

"You can get very dirty. That's why I like you."

Before she knew it she was on her back on the carpet, Tyler looming over her. "Yeah? How dirty do you want me to get?"

"Very."

He lifted her sweater and pressed a kiss to her belly, rolling the sweater upward as he moved his lips across her stomach and ribs. When he got to her bra, he kissed the swell of her breasts and undid the front clasp of her bra, exposing her to his gaze.

"Firelight does amazing things to your skin. It makes you golden," he said, lifting her sweater over her head and slipping her bra straps down her arms. He bent, pressing light kisses to each of her nipples before taking one in his mouth to suck and nip with his teeth. She arched to feed her breast to him, needing him to take more of it. He slipped his arm around her back and pulled her nipple into his mouth to suck her more deeply.

"Yes. That's what I need," she said as he worked both nipples—and her—into a frenzy. Her back bowed with need as he fed on her breasts until they popped—wet and glistening—from his mouth.

Then he went to work on her pants, unfastening them and drawing them off, followed by her panties, leaving her bare. The fire bathed her in warmth as she lay there naked before him. He laid his palm over her stomach and traced a path south, taking his time to tease and torment her before he found her sex and petted her lightly, making her hips rise off the carpet to meet his searching fingers.

But he dropped down between her legs, cupping her butt in his hands. She leaned up on her elbows to watch as he put his mouth on her.

All that wet heat surrounding her made her quiver. She tuned into only him, on the way he licked around her clit before taking it into his mouth to roll the piercing around his tongue until she wanted to die from the sweet pleasure of it. Watching him only notched up the frenzy of her desire. Seeing his tongue swipe over her sex was so incredibly intimate, and the way he'd dart glances at her made her breath catch. She felt the tingles of her approaching orgasm, almost embarrassed that he could make her come so easily, but he'd become so knowledgeable about her body and her reactions that he knew just where to touch her, where to taste her, to get her there.

She lifted against his mouth, urging him to lick faster. He knew, sliding his fingers inside her because that would intensify her orgasm. And when it hit, she unabashedly cried out, letting it roll throughout her as she released in wild abandon until she completely fell back, spent and sawing out breath.

Tyler stood and began to undress. Jenna rolled to her side, content to watch.

"You could do that as a strip tease and it would be way more entertaining."

"Ha-ha. Not a chance. I don't have any rhythm."

"Liar. I've danced with you before and you do have rhythm."

"Not on a stripper pole I don't."

"Really. So you've tried and failed on a pole. Who knew you had a background as a stripper?"

"Now you know my deep, dark secret."

When he dropped his briefs, she figured he could just stand there naked and women would happily toss money his way. Even with the scars he bore from battle wounds on the ice, he was pure male beauty.

She reached for his ankle and slinked her hand up toward his calf, loving the muscle that spoke of his strength.

He dropped down to the carpet and drew her against him, kissing her until she forgot all about worshipping his body and concentrated on worshipping his mouth. She'd miss him when he was gone this week. She'd gotten used to having him with her, touching her and kissing her. She especially loved the kissing, the way he lazily brushed his lips over hers before rolling her onto her back and deepening the kiss until heat flared throughout her body. Her heart pounded against him, her pulse rate speeding up until she felt dizzy and hot. The world melted away until all she knew was his lips, his tongue, his hand sweeping down over her breasts to pluck and tease until she arched against him.

She reached for his cock, encircling it in her hand to stroke his length. She circled her thumb over the crest, using the fluid that gathered there to coat his cock head.

The groans he made when she touched him only increased her need to feel him buried inside her, and when he rolled her over onto her belly, she was ready for him.

"On your knees," he said, grabbing a condom while she got into position.

He put his hands on her butt and spread her legs with his knees. She quivered in anticipation as his cock head inched inside her, and when he smoothed one hand over her back, she arched to meet his touch.

There was nothing sexier than a woman on her knees. Tyler slid his cock home, entering Jenna with one swift thrust. She hissed and pushed back against him, her pussy clenching around him, refusing to let go as he eased out, then powered back in again.

"I love fucking you in this position," he said, smoothing his hand over her back, tracing the lines of her dragon. "I love this tattoo."

She was a wild, untamed woman, and perfect for him. She bucked back against him and he gave her what she wanted, sliding his cock deep into her, but not too hard. Not yet. He needed to wait until the end or this was going to be over too soon. She was hot and wet and milking him with her muscles, her body glowing in the firelight as she moved against him.

He leaned back to watch his cock disappear into her, to see how her pussy grabbed on to him and draw him in. He spread her ass cheeks, the tiny puckered hole enticing him. He wet his finger and teased her there, rubbing his finger back and forth over her anus as he thrust in and out of her. Her moans of pleasure told him she liked what he was doing.

When he inserted the tip of his finger, she let out a cry of pleasure, her pussy clenching around him in response.

"Where's your lube, Jenna?"

"Right-hand bedroom drawer."

"Stay just like that. I'll be right back."

He withdrew, went into her bedroom, and grabbed the lube, then came back, coating his finger with it. He entered her pussy again, and played with the little hole, making sure it was well lubricated. This time, he slid his finger in deeper.

"Oh, God," she said, lowering her head to the carpet and lifting her ass against him. "I like that."

He drew his finger in and out in rhythm to fucking her pussy. Her ass clenched around his finger, a tight sheath, her pussy convulsing around his cock as he speared her with both. His balls quivered at the thought of fucking her tight hole, of taking her there right now.

"You want this?" he asked, pushing his finger farther into her anus.

"Yes," she said, her voice breathless. "Let's go to the bedroom. I have a dildo in there that'll get me off while you're fucking my ass."

He shook his head. "You never fail to amaze me, Jenna."

She gave him a quirked smile in response. "I hope not."

He withdrew and they went into the bedroom. He washed up, then joined her.

Jenna was on the bed, a thick silicone penis in her hands. She handed him the lube.

He smiled down at her. "I'm going to fuck you in the ass and make you come. I'm going to make us both come. Hard."

She got on her hands and knees, lubricated the dildo, and slid it into her pussy. "I'm going to enjoy this."

Hell, he could just watch her fuck herself with that dildo and jack off. The sight of her on her knees getting herself off was such a turn-on he could come right now.

"Damn, Jenna," he said.

"You like to watch me."

"Yeah."

"Remind me to get myself off for you sometime."

He took his cock in his hand, stroked it. "Anytime you want, babe, I'll be a happy voyeur."

"Put your cock in my ass. I'm ready to come."

He put on the condom and coated it with lube, then poured more on her anus. He spread her ass cheeks, his balls tightening with anticipation of having her here, of feeling her getting herself off with that dildo while he fucked her ass.

He pushed his cock head past the barrier of tight muscle. She hissed.

"Tell me if you hurt."

"Just get your cock inside me," she said, pulling the dildo out of her pussy when he pushed his cock deeper into her ass.

He did it slow and easy, inch by inch, gritting his teeth as her body clenched around him, squeezing his dick in a stranglehold that made his balls tighten up and threaten to erupt.

Not yet. Not even close. He held back, then slid in all the way home.

"Oh, yes," Jenna said, then slid the dildo back in. He felt it sliding past the thin barrier between her pussy and her ass.

When she pulled it out and plunged it back inside her pussy, he started to move inside her ass.

"Oh, fuck," she said. "Yes. Yes."

That was exactly how he felt. It was tight, hot, and perfect. He pulled partway out, then thrust into her again, getting into rhythm with the dildo she used, taking her cues on when to pull out, and when to shove back inside her again.

She squeezed him perfectly, and he had to hold on until she got off. Truth was, he could come any moment. His balls quivered and he was ready to shoot. With every plunge of the dildo, she tortured him, made him ready to go off. And when she went faster, so did he, giving her exactly what she asked for.

Sweat poured down his body, into his eyes, as he held on, thrusting into her, watching her pleasure herself. The intimacy and trust she gave him undid him. He wanted this to be good for her.

"Oh, God, oh, God, Tyler, I'm going to come. Fuck me harder."

She had his cock in the iron grip of her ass, and he was going to explode. He reared back and powered into her, again and again, and when she screamed, her body convulsing around him, he let go, shouting out as his climax was wrenched from him. He wrapped an arm around her waist and held on as he shuddered and emptied until he had nothing left.

He withdrew, pulling Jenna with him into the shower.

She lay against the wall like a limp rag doll. He washed her, taking tender care with her, then turned off the shower and handed her a towel.

"I'm done for," she said, giving him a sleepy, half-lidded look as she towel-dried her hair.

"Me, too."

He looked out the window. Snow had fallen steadily, had covered the grass and sidewalks and was still coming down. He wondered if his flight would take off as scheduled tomorrow.

He set the alarm on his phone. They climbed into bed and he pulled Jenna against him, realizing how much he was going to miss her when he left town for his road trip tomorrow.

He didn't like being separated from her.

Is that what love was like? Feeling empty when you weren't with that person, as if something essential was missing from your life?

Was he falling in love with Jenna? He hadn't intended to. He never intended to love anyone. Ever. Fun times, yeah, but love? He'd seen what love could to do people who'd once claimed to care about each other.

He was sure he never wanted to do that to Jenna. Tearing apart someone you cared about? Yeah, that wasn't what love was supposed to be about.

TWENTY-THREE

JENNA DIDN'T KNOW WHAT HAD POSSESSED HER TO call Elizabeth and Tara and invite them to the music club.

Maybe she was tired of being afraid. Or maybe she needed a second opinion.

Ty, after all, was sleeping with her. Having sex with someone could skew your opinions, make you like something that other people thought was terrible. The only way she was going to be able to figure that out would be to get the opinion of two people she trusted most.

Tara and Liz would tell her if she had no talent. Okay, Tara would be polite and sweet. Liz would be blunt and tell her she sucked. Then she'd have sweet Tara to hold her hand when she cried.

She'd brought along her guitar, though she'd left it in the trunk of the car, since there was still a ninety-eight percent chance she'd chicken out and never muscle up the nerve to get up there and sing.

"Oh, I've heard about this place," Liz said as they got through the line and found a table. "It's a new hot spot. Great live music."

"I read about it in the paper's entertainment section," Tara said, looking around for a waitress. She slid out of her coat and hung it over her chair. "It's getting great reviews."

"Ty brought me here a few weeks ago."

"Did he? Was it good?" Tara asked.

"It was amazing." One of the best nights of her life. Now if only she could drum up the courage to sing again.

The music started with a scruffy-looking bearded guy who came up and sang some bluesy number that rocked her right down to her black-and-white painted toes.

"Wow," Liz said. "You definitely couldn't judge that book by its cover. That dude looks homeless. But oh, his voice."

"I know, right?" Jenna said. "He was fantastic."

A band set up after that and laid down some serious rock tunes. They played two sets. A little loud, but she loved their beat. They didn't play any covers, all original music, and they had people up on the dance floor hopping to the music.

There was a lot of talent coming forth tonight. No duds like there had been the first night Tyler had brought her. Jenna felt inadequate. Maybe tonight wasn't the best night for her to get up and try this again.

"I wish I could sing," Tara said as another band went up and started to set up. "It's a talent I'm in awe of."

"I can't sing a damn note." Liz lifted the glass of wine to her lips and took a sip. "Not that it ever stops me from belting out Beyoncé tunes in the shower."

Tara laughed. "Oh, me either. I mean, I don't suck at it, but I don't think any talent agents are going to be knocking down my door anytime soon."

"What about you, Jenna?" Tara asked. "Do you like to sing?"

Liz looked at her, too, and Jenna realized it was now or never. "Well, here's the thing, you guys. I do sing."

"Honey, we all sing," Liz said. "Are you any good at it?"

Her heart slammed against her ribs, her skin cold and clammy while her face flamed with heat. "My guitar's in the trunk of the car."

Tara's eyes widened. "What? You have a guitar? I didn't know this."

"Shut the front door." Liz pushed away from the table. "You're going to sing tonight, aren't you?"

"I've thought about it."

"Well, stop thinking about it and go get your guitar."

"I don't know."

Tara shoved her. "Don't give us that. Go get your guitar. I want to hear you."

"Okay." Trepidation was replaced by nervous excitement. She got her hand stamped so she could get back in, then rushed out to the parking lot and grabbed her guitar. She saw Tara and Liz talking nonstop to each other as she made her way back to the table.

Liz looked down at the guitar in its case, then back up at her. "I've known you for how many years, and I didn't know you sang."

Jenna shrugged. "I've never told anyone before."

"Why?"

"Because I might not be any good."

Liz sat back in the chair and crossed her arms. "We'll be the judges of that. Get your pretty ass up there and sing for us."

Jenna laughed. "I have to wait my turn. Which reminds me, I have to put my card in with the deejay."

She wrote down what she wanted to sing and ran it up to the stage, then came back, her throat suddenly so dry she had to flag down the waitress and ask for a bottled water.

"That's why you brought us here tonight, isn't it?" Liz asked.

"Maybe. I wanted you two to hear me. If I could get up enough nerve to do this. I figured you would be honest and tell me if I sucked."

"You're not going to suck," Tara said.

"Did you sing when you and Ty came here?" Liz asked.

She looked down at her hands. "Yeah. Once or twice."

"Oh. My. God. Our girl has been keeping secrets from us, Tara." Tara shook her head. "I'm shocked and appalled."

"Stop it, you two. Mom and Dad don't even know I sing."

"Shut the front door again," Liz said. "Are you serious?"

"I am. I've never sung in front of anyone. Well, that's not true. I sang in Europe. But I hadn't sung again. Until Ty."

Liz slanted a glance at Tara before turning it back on Jenna. "Reallllly."

"Yes, and don't read anything into that. He found the guitar and songs I wrote—"

"Oh, my God, you write songs, too?" Tara asked.

"What else don't we know about you, Miss Riley?" Liz asked. "Do you put on a superhero costume and fight crime at night in the metropolis?"

"Yes, but only between three and five a.m."

"Oooh, aren't you the smart-ass." Liz cocked her head to the side and studied her. "There are new sides to you I'm just beginning to discover."

"I think you're going to be really disappointed when you realize I'm just an average singer who doesn't wear a cape and tights."

"Too bad. That would have been a great angle to promote you." Liz spread her hand in front of her, mimicking an arcing rainbow. "The Superhero Singer. Has a nice ring to it, doesn't it?"

Jenna rolled her eyes. "And you're in the business to promote your players? The poor guys."

Tara snickered. "Mick will be jealous he didn't get a superhero name."

Jenna laid her hand on Tara's. "I don't want Mick or Gavin to know anything about this. I just want the two of you to give me a listen and tell me what you think."

Tara frowned. "But—"

"Please."

"Okay."

A couple singers came up after the band, then the deejay called her name.

Jenna looked at Tara and Liz. "This is it."

"Kick some ass up there, sweetie," Liz said.

Nausea swelled in her stomach, but she grabbed her guitar and stepped up on the stage.

"Hey, Jenna," the deejay said. "Nice to see you again."

Surprised that he remembered her from so long ago, she nodded and smiled back at him. "Thanks."

"Gonna sing your own song tonight, I see."

"Yeah. Going to give it a try."

"Break a leg, sister."

She swallowed and headed out to the mic, grabbed the metal stool, and perched on the edge. She did her best to not look like she might throw up or pass out at any minute. She scanned the crowd and found Liz and Tara, who both grinned and clapped loudly for her.

Taking a deep breath, she settled in and began to strum the guitar, falling into the music she'd written. It was a mournful love song about a breakup, about hurt and pain and what happens when you thought you were in love, but it didn't work out, and how you found the strength to go on from there. She hoped a few people in the audience could connect with it.

She could always get lost in music, so she let it flow through her fingertips and through her voice, letting the words and the meaning pour through her soul to everyone who'd ever had love and lost it.

When she finished, she looked up, and no one moved, spoke, or said a word.

Oh, shit. She sucked.

But then everyone leaped to their feet, thunderous applause and claps and foot stomps springing tears to her eyes. She slid off the barstool and bowed, grinned, and left the stage.

The deejay stopped her. "Oh, no, honey. They want more."

"Really?"

"Hell yeah. Give them another."

She turned around and went back, stunned to hear the whistles and hollers and clapping as she took her seat on the stool once again. This time she gave them a song more happy and upbeat, about finding your first love in the middle of summer, when everything is sweet and innocent, the kind of love that could never be forgotten. It was a fun song, something they could stand and clap their hands to.

At the end, they cheered for her just as loud and she couldn't wipe the grin from her face.

"They love you," the deejay said. "Don't leave. I'm sure you're going to want to play more tonight."

"Okay, sure," she said with a laugh.

She got stopped along the way back to her table for congratulations and pats on the back.

When she got back to the table, Tara threw her arms around her and squealed.

"Holy shit you were good," Tara said. "I had no idea you could sing like that."

"Thanks."

Liz, however, sat back with her arms folded and glared at her.

Uh-oh. The true test. "You didn't like it."

"Are you fucking kidding me? What I want to know is why you're wasting your time as a bartender when you should have a recording contract?"

Jenna took a long drink from her bottle of water, then set the bottle down. "Oh, come on."

"Don't you 'oh, come on' me. Surely you have to have some inkling of how talented you are."

Jenna shrugged. "I like to sing and write music."

"And I'm an agent and know talent when I see it."

"Yeah, sports talent."

"Talent, sweetie. You are talented. Amazingly, fuck-my-brains-out talented."

Jenna shook her head. "No."

"Yes. You need to get an agent and a recording contract, pronto."

"I don't think so."

"Did Ty hear you sing?" Tara asked. "What did he say?"

Jenna didn't answer right away.

"Jenna," Liz said. "What did he say?"

"Pretty much what you said."

Liz threw her hands in the air. "And you, what? Ignored him?"

"I figured he was just saying nice things because we were having sex."

Liz shook her head. "You are such an idiot."

Jenna looked at Tara, who said, "I'm going to have to agree with Liz here. You are an idiot."

"You two are good for my ego. I appreciate it."

"And you're frustrating me with every second that goes by. Why don't you believe in yourself?" Liz asked.

"I don't know."

"Did you hear the crowd out there tonight?" Tara asked. "They loved you. I mean they applauded for the other acts, but they *loved* you. They stood on their feet and asked for an encore."

It was all too much to take in. "It was nice."

"Tara, talk to her," Liz said. "She's killing me."

"No, I get it, I really do," Jenna said. "I'm just not ready for . . . all that."

"You mean the chance to be famous?"

"I'm not that good."

Tara laid her hand over Jenna's. "Honey, I think you are. Liz thinks you are. Obviously the crowd here thinks you are."

Liz studied her. "Who told you that you weren't good enough?"

Leave it to Liz to be able to read her. She sighed and related the story of what happened in Germany.

"So some asshole kicked you out of a band a million years ago when you were a kid and you let that change the whole course of your life?" Liz rolled her eyes. "Come on. I thought you had bigger balls than that."

She shrugged. "I was sensitive."

"Oh, bullshit. You're awesome. And what's the name of the band?"

She told them.

Liz looked at Tara. "Never heard of them."

Tara shook her head. "Me either. So obviously they would have been better off to keep you. Honey, you have the voice of an angel. You need to be heard."

Their encouragement meant everything to her, but there were still roadblocks. Plenty of them.

"I don't want fame. I just want to open up my own club, play some music of my own."

"Ohhhh," Liz said.

Crap. Now she'd said it. She'd given voice to her dreams to someone besides Ty.

"So why don't you do that?" Tara asked.

"Because I run Riley's."

"And you can't open up a second bar because . . ."

Liz made it sound so simple, when it wasn't. "It's complicated."

"Because you're making it complicated. If that's what you want to do with your life, then don't let anything stop you."

"I'll think about it. In the meantime, please don't say anything to the rest of the family about this singing thing."

"Why on earth not?" Tara asked. "You have an amazing talent, Jenna."

"Thank you, but I'm just not ready to share it yet."

And if she kept getting this kind of reaction, she might never be.

TY WAS SURPRISED TO HEAR FROM LIZ, BUT SINCE SHE was in Los Angeles for business and he was there as part of his road trip, she suggested they meet for lunch. He didn't have to report to the arena until four, so there was plenty of time to eat and get a workout in.

Since he was in Anaheim, she picked him up at his hotel. As usual, she was in a crisp black business suit, wearing killer heels, her hair pulled up in some kind of twisty thing that defied logic. The driver of her private car took them to some trendy restaurant that took a while to get to. He guessed Liz wasn't into family friendly restaurants since they were in the heart of Disneyland.

"So what's up?" he asked after they ordered lunch.

"Jenna took Tara and me to the club to hear her sing the other night."

"She did? Good." Maybe she was finally climbing out of her shell.

"She's an amazing singer."

He took a drink of water. "Yeah, she is."

"No, I mean, her voice is killer. Like she should get an agent and cut a record."

"Is that what she wants?"

"She said she wants to open a club and sing there, plus bring in other musicians, kind of similar to the club we went to."

"Okay. So what's the problem?"

Liz waited while the waiter laid their salads in front of them, then she leaned forward. "You have heard her sing, right? She has way too much talent to waste."

He picked up his fork and dug into his salad. "And you've been down the interference road before, haven't you?"

She frowned at him and pouted her lips. "Ooh, touché, Ty. I get your point. But she's my friend, practically my sister. I just want what's best for her."

"Probably better if she decides for herself what's best for her."

"You're right. I was just blown away by her singing, and my first thought was that someone needed to make her famous."

"I don't think that's what she wants. What she really wants is a place of her own—a bar where music is played. She's not looking to become famous. She just wants to sing."

"You do realize that may not be what she gets. Say she does open a second bar—a music club. And she's in there singing. She's that good, and word of mouth travels. Some music exec happens to be in there some night and hears her, and her desire for obscurity is over."

He chewed, swallowed, and nodded. "That may be. If and when that time comes, she'll decide if that kind of life is what she wants. In the meantime, it's been hard enough to get her to go for the dream she has."

"Why?"

"I don't know, Liz. I've tried to figure it out, to talk to her about it. She won't budge. My best guess is she's either afraid to fail, or afraid to succeed."

"Pretty broad concepts."

"Yeah. Either way, I've tried to encourage her, but I'm stepping back."

"Don't do that. She needs you. She trusts you and your opinion. You're the first one she sang for. That means something. If you let it go now she might never do anything with this gift she has."

He took a long swallow of water and set the glass down. "I don't know about that. She's making progress. Look, she took you and Tara to the club and sang for you. That's a big step in the right direction."

"Exactly. And if you back down now, she may forget the whole thing. She needs encouragement—a big push."

"I'm not much for pushing people who don't want to be pushed. She's made it clear she wants me to back off."

Liz sighed. "Fine. I'll let you make your own decisions there. I love that girl and want what's best for her, but I know better than to mess in someone's business again."

Tyler grinned and patted her hand. "It all worked out in the end for you."

"Yeah, it did, but it caused a lot of pain for a lot of people along the way. And here I go again, meddling. I can't seem to help myself."

"You aren't meddling. You're trying to help Jenna."

"I want her to have what she really wants."

"So do I." He just didn't know how to make that happen for her.

Maybe Liz was right. Maybe Jenna did need a little shove in the right direction.

He'd had an idea that he thought might help, but after their last blowup he'd discarded it, decided to back away from the whole thing and leave her alone about singing.

Now that Liz had told him Jenna had taken her and Tara to the club to hear her sing, things were different. She was opening up about her singing to other people.

So maybe it was time to take that next step, open the door for Jenna and see if she was willing to walk through it.

TWENTY-FOUR

IT TOOK A COUPLE WEEKS FOR TY TO PUT HIS PLAN IN place. First, he'd had his hellish road trip, but at least they'd played well and picked up four road wins. The team was in position to make the playoffs and he needed to start concentrating on the game, not on a woman who made him crazy.

But the woman who made him crazy was never far from his mind, so no matter how hard he tried to shove her into a "forget about her for now" place in his head, she was always there, lurking.

He'd made a few phone calls to some people he knew who might be able to help him out. Liz had been instrumental there, since she had way more contacts than he did. By the time he returned home, he'd been able to get the ball rolling. It had taken a few days and trips around town to look around, but he'd liked what he saw. Now all he had to do was present the plan to Jenna, which he intended to do tomorrow.

First he had to put all his focus on the game tonight.

They were facing Nashville, a formidable opponent and one of the other teams in their division fighting for the title. Tyler needed to be on top of his game, because this was a must win. There were only three games left in the regular season schedule and they were neck and neck with Nashville. It was going to come down to these last few games. The Ice needed to win two more games, and Nashville needed to lose two of them for the Ice to win the division, and that's only if they beat Nashville tonight.

They'd had grueling practice all day today, the coach putting them through their paces. He wasn't going to accept any mistakes tonight. None of them would accept stupid mistakes. They were too far into the season and the end goal was in sight. They had to win.

By game time, he cleared his head and took the ice, his teammates as pumped as he was. He looked to the left where the seats were when he came out onto the rubber pads leading to the box, wishing Jenna were here tonight. But it was a work night for her and her assistant manager was sick, so despite him asking her to come to the game, she couldn't get away.

Probably better this way. He could concentrate on the game and not Jenna sitting in the front row watching him.

This was too important a game to let anything distract him.

He skated out onto the ice, his heart pounding. He'd never played on a winning team before, had never made the playoffs. It was so close he could taste victory.

"TY HAS NO IDEA ABOUT THIS BIRTHDAY PARTY, DOES he?" Tara asked as she put the finishing touches on the tables.

"No clue. He's so nervous about the game tonight I'm not sure he even remembers it's his birthday today."

Mick laughed as he helped Tara spread out a tablecloth. "Nothing matters when the game's on the line. He's lucky if he can remember his own name right now."

Jenna surveyed the private room that Tara had so generously offered to decorate. They couldn't close the bar tonight—with the Ice so close to making the playoffs, her regulars would be disappointed not to be able to watch the game with all their friends, and it would be bad for business. But she did shut off the private room so they could set up for the party she intended to have for Ty's birthday.

He promised her he'd come to the bar right after the game. And just in case they lost and Ty felt shitty about it, intending to drown his sorrows alone, she'd given a heads up to Eddie and Victor that today was Ty's birthday and she was throwing him a surprise party. The guys told her they'd make sure Ty came to the party, even agreed to delay his arrival to allow his teammates to get there before he did.

Everything was ready. Tara had done an incredible job setting up the room with balloons in the Ice's blue and white team colors with matching table decorations to reflect the hockey theme she'd chosen. There were miniature pucks and hockey stick drink stirrers, plenty to drink, and a lot of food because she knew the players would be hungry. Tara had worked with a cake decorator and had a hockey stick cake made. It was awesome.

Her parents and brothers would be coming in, along with all Ty's friends. She even had an ice sculpture of a hockey player staying cool in the freezer. She hoped to God the team won tonight or it would be one hell of a somber birthday celebration.

She hurried out to tend to her customers while Tara tended to the decorations. Since baseball season had started, Gavin was home again and in town, but he didn't have a game today so he showed up with Liz and Jenna's parents. Jenna barely had time to wave at them when they came in because the bar was packed with fans who were glued to the screens, watching the game and ordering beer like they hadn't had anything to drink in a week.

Fortunately her dad seemed eager to get behind the bar and help serve drinks, something she was glad to have him do. She needed as many extra hands as she could get. Her mom disappeared into the kitchen and helped out with the food orders, much to Malcolm's relief, so they had a smooth operation going. Dad served the bar patrons while Jenna filled the waitress's orders. They were going to do a hell of a lot of business tonight judging from the number of times her waitresses came running back to her with requests for more drinks. And if the Ice won, she might be calling quite a few taxis for some of her patrons.

The good thing about being busy was she barely had time to glance up at the television screens to watch the game. Even though she wanted to watch, her stomach was a knotted mass of nerves. She knew how much each of these last few games meant to the team—to Ty. Winning the division and making the playoffs was critical. She had to rely on either the cheers or the groans of her customers to let her know what was going on with the game, because it was too loud in the bar to hear the announcers.

When she heard a cheer, she'd stop and look up, knowing something good had happened for the team. The Ice had scored twice in the first period, once on a pass from Ty to Eddie, and once on a sneak shot from behind the goal by Meyers. Nashville scored on a power play, so the Ice were up two to one going into the second period.

Her stomach knotted up even tighter. It was still too close and way too much game left to play. She busied herself with her customers, not even looking up when she heard a chorus of groans and curses.

Nashville had tied it in the second period.

Dammit.

It stayed that way all through the second period. The tension in the bar was so thick she could barely wade through it, and the noise level was deafening, because the shots on goal by both teams had been insane, yet no further goals had been scored by the time they headed into the third period.

The play had been rough, with two more power plays by both teams.

"Your boy looks good tonight, honey," her dad said as he shouldered up to her to wash some glasses.

"Does he? I've barely had time to watch."

"Take a few minutes to watch. I've got this."

She laid her hand on her dad's shoulder. "I don't know if I can. I'm about ready to crawl out of my skin."

Her dad laughed. "Yeah, it's pretty tense and these are critical games. But Ty will want to know you saw him play."

He was right. And she did want to watch. She took a break and stepped out from behind the bar to walk around and visit with her customers, but no one wanted to chat. Their faces were glued to the screens, so she leaned against a wood beam and watched as Victor got hold of a puck and skated like lightning, passing it to Eddie, who got slammed against the glass as he fought the defender. Eddie dug in and passed the puck across the ice to Ty, who took it and skated toward the net, then took a shot, missed.

She let out the breath she'd been holding, realizing her heart was pounding and her palms were sweaty. She swiped them down her jeans.

Come on, guys. Time to score.

The defender slammed the puck to his wing, who passed it to the Nashville center, who took a shot but the Ice's goalie caught it in his glove.

Jenna was going to pass out if she kept holding her breath. She let it out, and decided she might be better off not watching the game. But then Ty and Eddie got a breakaway and passed the puck back and forth. Eddie defended, Tyler took the shot and it slid into the net on the left corner. The lamp lit up and the entire bar erupted, everyone coming to their feet, pounding the tables with their hands and clapping.

Jenna screamed and shot her fist in the air. She ran back behind the bar and hugged her dad, who beamed a grin.

"He did good."

She realized she had tears in her eyes. "He did, didn't he?"

"Now they have to hold them, and maybe score another."

"Oh, I hope so, Dad."

Her mom came out and watched the last six minutes of the game with them. It was more terrifying now that they were ahead, hoping Nashville wouldn't score and tie it up again. Nashville had several more shots on goal, but the defense held. And when Meyers put another one in the goal and put them two up with a minute and a half left to play, the pounding feet and cheers in the bar sounded like an earthquake. Her dad picked her mom up and kissed her, and Jenna squealed with joy as the last seconds ticked down to zero.

She'd never been happier for Ty. What a great birthday this was going to be for him. And maybe now the knot in the pit of her stomach would go away.

Two hours later she'd cleared out the bar, though most people had left after the game was over anyway, and she'd told the stragglers they were closing early because of a private party. She and her dad had handled the few grumblers and drunks easily enough. You didn't want to piss off a Riley, because if you became belligerent, you weren't invited back.

Some of the players started arriving, and she led them to the party room, where drinks and food were set up. Eddie had texted her that he and Victor would be arriving with Ty in about forty-five minutes. Media interviews were about over, and Victor was going to dawdle with protracted primping.

Jenna laughed at that because it was so believable.

She munched on a carrot stick and some dip and surveyed the set up. It was too bad Ty's parents couldn't be here, but there wasn't anything she could do about that. At least her family was here, and Ty's friends and teammates.

Eddie finally texted they were five minutes away.

"He's almost here, everyone," she said, so she went to the front door to unlock it and waited there.

When they walked in, Eddie and Victor headed into the room while she swooped Tyler up in a big, warm kiss.

"Congratulations on the game," she said.

"Thanks." He looked around. "Where is everyone?"

She shrugged. "It's a work night. We were full earlier, but I guess everybody had to get home. It was kind of dead after the game. I've got some food in the pool room, though."

"Oh. Okay."

She took his hand and led him into the room, then stepped back.

His eyes widened when he walked in and everyone yelled surprise and happy birthday.

He turned to her and she grinned.

"You knew it was my birthday."

"Of course."

Then he was swallowed up by well wishes, hugs, and pats on the back, and she didn't see him again for a while. But it was his celebration, so she let him enjoy it. She took care of his friends and her family, making sure everyone was well fed and had drinks while Tyler was surrounded the entire night by people who cared about him.

She had the sports entertainment station on so the team members could see replays of the game, and of course everyone rehashed the night's events. Her dad, Gavin, and Mick sat with the team and talked hockey, while Jenna, Liz, Tara, and Jenna's mom hung out with the wives and girlfriends of the players.

Ty finally broke away and put his arm around her.

"I didn't even know you realized it was my birthday."

"Did *you* even know it was your birthday?" she asked.

He laughed. "It wasn't high on my list of things to deal with today, but yeah, I knew. I just wasn't going to make a big deal about it."

"Well, I was."

He brushed his lips across hers. "Thank you for this."

She smiled up at him. "You're welcome."

It was after two before everyone started to leave. Tara and Mick and Liz and Gavin stayed to help with cleanup, but she pushed them all out the door after that, telling them she'd lock up. Her parents had gone home earlier, and the players would have stayed all night to party, but they all looked wiped out and had another game the day after tomorrow, so they needed to get at least a little rest.

She locked the doors, pulled the shades, and turned to Ty. "Good birthday?"

"Almost a perfect birthday."

She cocked a brow. "Almost?"

"Yeah." He took her hand in his and pulled her into the game room. "I haven't gotten my gift yet."

Her lips curled. "Oh, yeah? And what did you have in mind?"

He took one of the tablecloths and spread it out over the pool table. "I have this fantasy . . ."

Her belly tumbled. "Oh, really."

He ran his fingers over the edge of the table. "Ever done it here?"

"Nope."

"Good."

"And I haven't given you your gift yet." She kicked off her shoes, then unbuttoned her jeans, easing the zipper down.

Ty moved toward her, hunger in his eyes.

"Shouldn't you be home in bed, resting up for the next game?"

"I'd rather have inspiration for the next game." He picked her up and set her on the table, then pulled off her jeans, leaving her in her top and panties. His eyes widened at the tiny black scrap of silk she wore.

"These are nice."

"I bought them just for your birthday."

He smoothed his hands down her legs and back up, then spread her legs and stepped between them, sliding his hands under her butt and drawing her close enough she could feel the ridge of his erection.

"I like them. Thank you. They're very inspiring."

She reached between them to rub his shaft. His lips parted and she listened to his breath catch as she continued to caress him.

"I like you touching me. It makes me hard, makes my cock swell."

"I like the way you talk to me. It makes my pussy wet."

He pulled off her shirt, arching his brow at the bra that matched her panties. Black, it pushed her breasts together and made them swell over the cups of the bra.

"Very inspiring. I'll dream about this tonight." He swept his hand across her breasts, down her belly, then leaned over to press a kiss to each mound.

He undid the clasp of her bra, drawing it down her arms and casting it on a nearby chair. He rubbed his thumbs over her nipples, watching them harden.

"I don't need a whole lot of foreplay tonight, Tyler. I just need you inside me. Now."

He drew his shirt off, then undid his pants, dropping them to the floor along with his boxer briefs. His cock popped up and she licked her lips, already imagining him fucking her on the pool table.

"Hurry," she said.

He grabbed a condom and tossed it onto the pool table, then climbed on and laid on top of her, rubbing his body against hers. She loved the sensation of his skin against hers, his warm body covering hers. She wrapped her legs around him, trapping his cock against her pussy so she could slide against it.

He rolled her over so she was on top of him, and she sat up, rocked her pussy against his length.

"God, you're wet, babe," he said, making her quiver.

He pulled her forward and took one of her nipples into his mouth, flicking it with his tongue before capturing it with his teeth. She hissed at the pleasurable pain that always rocketed pleasure right to her core. She dug her nails into his shoulders and pushed her breast deeper into his mouth, craving more.

He grasped her hips and moved her back and forth across his cock, sending shards of sensation across her sensitized nerve endings. Oh, she wanted to come. She planted her feet against the edge of the pool table and rode his shaft with her clit, so close to the edge she bit her lip, lifting up so she could see his face as she catapulted over the edge.

He cupped the back of her neck and kissed her when she came, absorbing her cries with his lips and tongue while waves of pleasure rocked her senseless. She heard him tear the condom package and she moved away only long enough for him to sheath himself, then she climbed onto his cock and buried it inside her, still convulsing from the aftereffects of her orgasm.

She held still, feeling him thicken while he played with her nipples. It was always like this when he entered her—like the very first time—an amazing discovery of just how good they were together. He held on to her while she rose up, then down again, rolling her body over his in a slow, careful tease that made his jaw clench.

In this position, she had all the control, and that he let her have it said so much about what kind of man he was. She swept her hand across his jaw, his bottom lip. He grabbed her finger and took it into his mouth, sucking it, and she dropped down on his cock, grinding against his balls until he groaned.

"You're killing me, Jenna."

"I know."

He lifted her, then thrust up into her, easing down before powering into her again.

And when he rolled her over onto her back, looming over her to take possession, she welcomed him, needing him to do exactly what it would take to make her fly. He spread her legs and levered his hips against hers, their bodies as one. He buried his cock so deep she cried out, coming in a single burst that she felt all the way to her toes. She went rigid, then shuddered.

"Fuck," he said, digging his fingers into her. He groaned when he came with her, pulling her up to put his lips on hers in a kiss so filled with passion it left her breathless.

They fell together and Ty rolled to his side, taking her with him, stroking her back and her hair.

Her eyelids felt heavy and if they weren't laying on the pool table in her bar she could fall asleep just like this.

"Damn," he said. "This is an uncomfortable bed."

She laughed, and they climbed off, got dressed, and drove to her place, where they undressed again and got into bed.

Jenna loved the possessive way Ty always drew her against him, wrapping his arms around her as they slept.

"Thank you for the best birthday I've ever had," he said as he kissed her.

She smiled and wriggled against him. "You're welcome."

The words hovered on the tip of her tongue, the words she'd

never said to a man before. But she couldn't say them, because he hadn't said them to her and she didn't know how he felt.

Coward.

Yeah, she sure was.

But she still wasn't sure if what she felt was real, or just a moment of passion.

So she let them go unsaid, and drifted off to sleep.

TWENTY-FIVE

TY HAD THE PLAN ALL WORKED OUT. AFTER TODAY'S afternoon game—which they'd won, thankfully—he told Jenna he had a surprise for her. He loved the excitement he'd heard in her voice.

He hoped she was as excited as he was about this. It would be a new beginning for both of them. He was nervous as hell, had never contemplated doing anything like this with any woman, but Jenna wasn't just any woman.

She was *the* woman. He knew it, he felt it, and he'd never been more sure about anything in his life. She was worth the risk.

She'd come to his game, and knowing she was there had meant everything to him. After all, this was the woman who'd hated sports and had vowed to never get involved with a guy who played them. If she could take the risk and change her way of thinking, then so could he.

He swallowed past the nervous lump in his throat and hoped to God he didn't screw this up.

He gave her the address of the place. He was parked out front, waiting for her when she drove up. She got out, wearing a dress, tights, and those sexy black boots with the spiky heels that never failed to make his dick hard. She buttoned her coat and ran toward him to give him a kiss.

"What is this surprise?" she asked, looking at the building.

"You'll see." He'd gotten the code from the real estate manager so he could show it to Jenna without the guy bugging him while he talked to her.

He unlocked the keypad and opened the door, turning on the lights and letting her in.

"It used to be a combination bar/restaurant," he explained as she walked in. "It closed about six months ago. It fits your parameters for space and location."

She gave him a quizzical look. "I don't understand."

"You could rip out the current bar here," he said, leading her inside. "Put the stage you talked about in the center here. There's already a great kitchen. Come on, I'll show you."

She grabbed his wrist. "Wait. What are you talking about?"

"Your music club."

"What music club?"

"The one you want to open. The second Riley's. If you don't like this one, I've got two others lined up to show you."

"You've got . . . You went looking for locations for a club?"

He grinned and shoved his hands in his coat pocket. "Yeah. Isn't this space great? I have to admit this one's my favorite, but the others aren't bad. Wait till you see the kitchen. And there's plenty of electrical."

Her smile died. "No."

"What?"

"No."

"You don't like this place? That's okay. We can go look at the others."

"I mean no. To all of it."

His stomach tightened. "Why?"

"I don't want any of this, Ty. If I'd wanted a club, I'd go looking for locations on my own."

Irritation spiked. "Okay. You don't want my help."

"I don't want to do this at all. Quit pushing me."

"Right. Because God forbid you should move forward with your life."

She lifted her chin. "What the hell is that supposed to mean?"

"Exactly what I said. I was trying to help, to show you some great places so you could take that step forward, take a shot at having what you really wanted."

"That's a lot of presumption on your part."

"Is it? We've talked about this for months. You know this is what you really want."

"If it's what I really want, and that's a big if, I'll do it on my own. I don't need you to help me. I don't need you for any of this."

He'd been wrong. About her, about everything. All this time he'd spent trying to help Jenna, trying to coax her into finding her own happiness, and she was throwing it back in his face. All the plans he'd made, assuming . . .

That's what he got for assuming she felt the same way he did.

"You know what, Jenna? You're right. You don't need me. You don't need anyone. You never did."

She lifted her chin. "You're right. I don't need you or anyone else trying to push me into something I'm not ready for. I'm tired of everyone nudging me, trying to force me into this. Just stop it. I like my life the way it is, so leave it alone."

Tears glistened in her eyes and the fear was so evident there he wanted to hold her, but he was angrier at her than he was sorry for her.

"That is such bullshit. You hate your life the way it is, you hate being stuck behind that bar, but you're too damned afraid to do anything to change it. You were afraid to go out with me, afraid to fall in love with me. Well you know what? I was afraid, too. You've met my parents. You know that story and you know how their marriage failed. The last goddamn thing I ever wanted was to fall in love. But you know what? I did anyway. I fell in love with you."

Her eyes widened, but he refused to acknowledge it. "And you know what happens when you fall in love with someone? You want to help that person. You want that person to grow. You want what's best for them.

"All you've done is keep me at arm's length the whole time we've known each other because you're afraid. Well I'm fucking tired of tiptoeing around your fear. So you win. I'm done."

He turned and walked toward the door and opened it. "The door will lock itself when you walk out."

He shut the door and walked away.

JENNA STOOD IN THE BUILDING AND STARED AT THE hanging wires, the dust and debris of what once was a thriving business, but now was nothing more than an empty shell.

That's how she felt inside as she heard Ty's car start up and drive away.

An empty shell. Destroyed like this building.

He loved her. He'd done all this for her, all this research and legwork and she'd caustically thrown it back in his face as if it had meant nothing to her.

He'd been so excited. This had been his surprise.

Then she'd let him walk away, because she was afraid. Afraid to take a shot at having the career she wanted, and afraid to reach out and grab the kind of love she'd always dreamed of.

She'd missed her chance.

She bit back the tears. She didn't deserve to fall apart. This aching misery she felt was all her doing.

Instead, she turned and walked out the door.

TY SLAMMED HIS STICK INTO THE PENALTY BOX.

Possible concussion his fucking ass. The defender had gotten in his way and he'd fought for the puck, slammed him up against the glass. They'd fought, just like a normal fight in a game. Punches had been thrown and his opponent had gone down like a falling bowling pin, even though Ty swore he hadn't hit him hard. The guy laid out on the ice had been milking it. This five-minute penalty was bullshit. Anger fueled him and he vowed he'd play tougher the next two periods.

He went into the locker room at the end of the first period, and after the typical pep talk, the coach called him aside.

"You got some issues we need to talk about, Anderson?"

"No. Just trying to win the game."

"You don't win the game by knocking out one of the opposing players and taking a five minute. Two penalties and it's only the first period?"

"Giving my all for the team, coach."

"All for the team? You're playing one-man vendetta out there. You have some bug up your ass. Pull it out and play like I know you can play, or I'll bench you. And if I have to do that in the biggest game of the season you aren't going to like the consequences."

The coach walked away. Ty dropped his chin to his chest and took a deep breath.

Shit. His head hadn't been in the game. He was pissed off and it was affecting his game play. He had to get it under control.

Eddie came in and sat next to him. "Look, man, I know you're under a lot of pressure. We all are. But whatever's going on in your head right now, whether it's the game or something else, it's affecting your game play at a time that's kinda critical for the team."

Ty didn't say anything. There was nothing to say. Eddie was right. He was letting the team down.

Victor laid his hand on Tyler's shoulder. "We are your friends. You have a problem, we're here to listen."

"That's true," Eddie said. "But if it's personal, leave it in the locker room and play hockey on the ice. You can't take it out on the other team because we need you to help us win the division. One more game and we're in."

Ty nodded. "I got this."

"Then let's go kick their asses," Victor said. "Only, don't kick their asses so much next time, yes?"

Tyler laughed. "Yeah. Understood."

Eddie stood. "All right then. Let's go win this game, and then we'll go out and get shitfaced after we win the division."

Ty stood and nodded to his friends. "Sounds like a plan."

JENNA TENDED BAR AND WATCHED THE ICE WIN THE division championship, wincing when Tyler got that five-minute penalty, knowing he was taking his anger and frustration at her out on another player.

But after that first period he'd come back and played clean and they kicked ass, scoring three goals and clinching the division. The bar had been packed solid and they'd served a ton of drinks and food. The celebration after the game win had been wild and crazy. Jenna had even brought out champagne for everyone in the bar, much to her customers' delight. Being busy kept her mind occupied so she didn't have to think about what an utter bitch she'd been yesterday.

After Ty had left she'd gone home and cried until her nose was stuffy and her eyes were swollen, then she'd washed her face and climbed into bed, but she hadn't been able to sleep. She'd ended up staying up all night, fighting the urge to go into the office and write some music—heart-tearing music about losing someone you loved.

In the end, she'd gone in and scribbled down the words because they were in her head—in her soul—dying to pour out of her. She knew she wouldn't rest until she wrote them down, until she picked up her guitar and sang some of the songs she'd written about heartbreak. Songs she'd written before she'd ever really been in love, before she'd ever lost someone she truly cared about. As the tears streamed down her face, she realized what a liar she'd been in her music, how her soul had never been in her work before, because now she could feel the words tear through her, could feel the agony of loss like never before. At that moment she honestly felt what it was like to hurt—and to have hurt someone.

Now all she wanted to do was sing and write, to hole up in her room and do nothing but put words to paper, melody to those words. But she was stuck at this goddamn bar, a prisoner of her own making.

A prisoner of her fear.

And lonely as hell.

She pulled her phone out of her pocket, grimacing as she looked at how late it was, yet knowing if the shoe was on the other foot, she'd drop everything to be there for her, no matter what time it was.

She dialed Tara's cell. Tara answered on the second ring.

"Jenna? What's wrong?"

"Nothing. Did I wake you?"

"Yeah. But it's okay. Is it Dad?"

"No, he's fine. I'm at work, but I need to talk to you. Can I come over? I know it's really late, so feel free to tell me no."

"Of course. Come on over. I'll put some coffee on."

"Thanks."

She told her assistant manager she was leaving and he could close up tonight. He assured he could handle it with no problem, since he closed on the nights she had off. She left and headed to Tara and Mick's house. They'd bought a new place in the country, so it took her about twenty minutes to get there. It was a gated community with huge houses on oversize lots.

Jenna pulled into the driveway and Tara was at the door, waiting for her. She'd thrown on yoga pants and a sweatshirt.

"Coffee's ready," she said, leading Jenna into the kitchen.

They took a seat at the table in the nook off the kitchen. Jenna stared into her coffee.

"What's wrong?"

She told Tara what happened with Ty, what he said to her before he walked out on her.

Tara sipped her coffee and nodded. "I understand all about running away from love. No one knows that better than me. I did my best to try to run away from it with Mick, and I almost lost him."

"It's not the same thing. Ty and I just don't see eye to eye. I think we just want different things."

Tara laughed. "Honey, I love you like a sister, but that's the biggest bunch of crap I've ever heard."

Jenna winced at Tara's brutal honesty. But that's what she'd come here for.

"I've never seen two people more in love with each other, or more stubborn. And I hate to see the two of you break up over fear."

"You mean my fear."

"Yes."

Her shoulders slumped. "I'm the queen of fear. I'm afraid of loving someone, afraid of taking a step to change my life, afraid of failing."

"Let me ask you a question." Tara poured another cup of coffee from the carafe on the table, added some cream and a dollop of sugar. "Is Ty's career as important a factor now as it was when you first started seeing him? If I recall, you were adamant about not getting involved with anyone in sports."

"Oh, yeah. That. Not at all."

Tara leaned back in her chair, cup in hand. "Why do you think that is?"

She thought about it for a few seconds before answering. "Likely because it was never a factor in the first place. It was a defense mechanism to keep men away, a good excuse. After all, what kind of men did I know other than men either involved with sports or who loved sports? If I made it a factor, I wouldn't have to fall in love."

"But Tyler took that factor out of the equation, didn't he?"

"Yeah. It didn't matter what he did for a living, because I saw beyond it."

"And you love sports."

Jenna laughed. "I do. You bitch, you knew that."

Tara gave her a knowing smile. "Of course I knew that."

"It's part of who I am, who I've always been. Oh, sure, I took dance classes, but that was to appease Mom. I've always loved sports. I loved playing basketball with Dad and Mick and Gavin out in the backyard. I love watching football and baseball and hockey."

"So what's the real problem?"

"The real problem is and has always been being tied to the bar. That's the hurdle I've been trying to overcome. And Tyler was the one who knew it, who spotted my frustration right off and has been trying to help me find a way to have it all. It was me who was too afraid to take a shot at having everything I ever wanted."

Tara didn't say anything.

She laid her head in her hands. "God, I've made such a huge mistake. I said such shitty things to him when all he did was try to help me. He offered me the moon and I threw it back in his face and told him to butt out of my life. What am I going to do?"

"Well," Tara said. "I can speak from experience and tell you it's never too late to get back what you love. But you're going to have to be willing to take some risks, Jenna, put yourself out there and be willing to fail."

She tried to take a sip of coffee, but her hands were shaking so she set the cup on the table.

"I love him. And you're right. It's time to stop hiding behind the safety of the familiar. It's time to stop being afraid."

She stood and pulled Tara into a hug. "Thank you for being here for me, for being my friend and my sister. I couldn't do this without you."

Tara drew away. "Yes, you could. That's what you need to realize. You can do this yourself. All you have to do is go for it and be willing to fail."

She left Tara's house, armed with the knowledge that everything she knew about her life was about to change.

TWENTY-SIX

THE FIRST STEP ON JENNA'S ROAD TO CHANGE WAS TO face her parents. She asked Gavin and Mick over, too, along with Tara and Liz for support.

"You're not going to tell us you're pregnant, are you? Gavin asked. "Because I really like Ty and I don't want to have to kick his ass over this."

Jenna laughed. "I'm not pregnant. And I kicked Tyler's ass enough. I don't think he needs any other family members doing it."

Her dad frowned. "What does that mean?"

"Nothing. I'll tell you all about that later. Right now there's something I need you all to know about me."

"Is she a lesbian?" Mick asked Tara. "Is this one of those coming out things where she's going to tell the whole family at once?"

Tara elbowed Mick in the ribs. "Would you just shut up?"

"Jenna isn't a lesbian," her mother said. "I'd have known about it years ago if that were the case."

Jenna rolled her eyes and waited for her family to finish talking about her. "And you all wonder why I never tell you anything."

"Go ahead, honey," her mother said. "We're behind you one hundred percent."

She sucked in a breath and let it out. "Okay. I'll be right back."

Gavin groaned. "I have a game in six hours, Jenna."

She ran outside and grabbed her guitar, then came in.

"A guitar?" Mick asked. "What's that for?"

"Shut. Up." Tara rolled her eyes at Mick.

Jenna got her guitar out of the case, then took a seat in the living room and began to play, figuring that would be better than an explanation. She sang one of the new songs she'd penned the other day, pouring her heart into the song about losing someone because you made a mistake, because you weren't honest with your feelings. She let her soul and her emotions come through, giving free range to her voice, uncaring what anyone thought at that point because she sang that song for all she had lost, for the pain she had cost someone she cared about. When she was finished, she looked up at the stunned faces of her family, and smiled, blinking away the tears.

"Sonofabitch," Mick finally said. "Where the hell did *that* voice come from?"

Her mother stood and ran over to her, clasped her hands around Jenna's face. "My darling girl. You have an amazing gift." She kissed her cheek. "And you asked for those singing lessons when you were a little girl. I just thought it was a passing fancy. I had no idea."

She saw the tears welling in her mother's eyes.

"I'm so sorry, Jenna. I didn't know. Why didn't you tell us?"

Jenna wiped the tears from her mom's cheeks. "It's okay, Mom."

"No, it's not. I'll never forgive myself for not giving you what you needed then."

"Oh, Mom. It's really okay." She hugged her mother.

Gavin came over, picked her up, and hugged her. "You're a super-star, Jen. Always knew you would be someday."

Her dad just sat there, tears streaming down his face.

"What song is that?" her mother asked.

"I wrote it."

"She writes a lot of music," Liz said.

She looked at her dad, who shook his head.

"Dad?"

"My baby. I had no idea." He broke down and sobbed. Jenna laid the guitar down and went to him and hugged him.

"Don't cry, Daddy."

"You sing like an angel. I'm so proud of you. But your mother is right. We should have paid more attention to you and what you needed. We didn't give you those singing lessons."

"She wanted singing lessons?" Gavin asked with a frown.

"Yes." Her mother swiped at the tears. "When she was younger."

"So you've had this inside you all these years and you never told anyone?" Mick asked.

Jenna shook her head.

"You are such a dumbass," Gavin said. "The only way you get what you want is to keep asking for it and keep pushing. You know how this family is. The loudest wins."

Jenna laughed. "Yeah, I realize that now."

"So what can we do to make sure your voice is heard?" her mother asked

She inhaled, let it out, and looked at her parents. "I want to open another Riley's bar. A music club where people can come in and sing. And I want to sing there."

Her dad cocked his head to the side. "Another bar?"

"Yes. I've done the feasibility study and we can afford it. But it means I wouldn't run the original Riley's anymore. I'd want to man-age the new bar."

"Do it," her mother said. "You belong in a place where you can use the talent that God gave you."

"How long have you been wanting to do this?" her dad asked her.

"Just . . . my whole life."

"Why didn't you ever say anything before now?"

"Because Riley's was your dream. And after your heart attack I had to make sure your dream stayed alive."

"Aww, my little girl." He made room on his chair for her to sit next to him, then tipped her chin with his fingers like he used to do when she was little. "Never live someone else's dream for them. It's not your job to chase my dream. I can do that. I'll admit I got a little lazy and complacent, hanging out here with your mom. And knowing you were holding things down at Riley's made it easier for me.

"I'm mad at you for not coming to us and telling us what you wanted to do, for wasting this amazing talent of yours for so long."

"It's not your fault. It's mine, for not speaking up sooner. I was afraid I'd fail, afraid I wasn't good enough."

Her mother snorted. "You are definitely good enough."

"She's good enough for a record contract if you ask me," Liz said.

"Maybe," Jenna said. "Maybe not. All I want right now is to have a club where musicians and singers can come and try out their stuff. That would fulfill my dream. Anything more than that . . . we'll see."

Her mother pulled her from the chair and took her hands. "All we've ever wanted for any of our children is to follow their dreams and be happy. We'd be delighted for you to open up another Riley's. We'll make it work."

It was like the world had opened for her, and all she could see was endless possibilities. She hugged and kissed them all.

"Thank you. You have no idea what your support means to me. But first I have to go find the man I love and see if I can repair the damage I caused. I'm afraid I might have lost him forever."

* * *

JENNA GOT LIZ TO GET HER TICKETS TO THE FIRST
playoff game tonight. She could have gotten club seats, but she
wanted to be in the front row, right where the action was. She wanted
Tyler to know she was there supporting him.

"These seats are freakin' cold, you know," Liz said. "We could be
in a heated club house, with all the food and drink we want for free."

"Bitch, bitch, bitch," Jenna said. "You're the one who got us seats
here before, if you recall."

"Yeah, yeah. There was a method to my madness for that game.
But now? It's just fucking cold down here."

"You are so high maintenance. It's a wonder my brother puts up
with you."

"The things I do for love. And your brother adores me from the
tips of my expertly painted toenails to the top of my gorgeous natural red hair."

"Don't make me gag."

Liz laughed. "I never much liked the thought of having to deal
with family. After all, I did my best to get the hell away from my
own. But you Rileys? You're all right."

"You love me and you know it."

"I do. I totally do."

The door opened and the players started filing out. Jenna froze,
not sure whether to turn and look for Ty or not. In fact, the thought
of slinking down in her seat sounded appealing.

Liz elbowed her. "Your coward days are over, sweet pea. Time to
woman-up and let your man know you're here for him."

She was right. She turned to face the players, and when Ty came
out, he spotted her right off.

And frowned, then turned away and walked up the stairs toward
the bench.

What had she expected, a dazzling smile and two thumbs-up? She was here to support him, not the other way around, so she clapped and yelled for the team when they took the ice for warm-ups.

At the face-off, Jenna tensed and didn't let go the entire time. The game was intense, a knuckle biter as the Ice and Denver went at it as if this was the last game either team was going to play. There were plenty of penalties, only this time Ty wasn't involved. He stayed clean, though he did plenty of bumping. When he crashed up against the glass right in front of her, she wanted to leap up and smack the guy who'd thrown him there. But Ty concentrated on advancing the puck, and when he scored, she screamed until she was hoarse.

The Ice were up two goals by the end of the second period, and Jenna's jaw hurt from clenching it. Defense had kicked ass so far, keeping Denver scoreless and their shots on goal unremarkable.

Ty had paid her no attention, hadn't once glanced her way through the entire game. Not that she expected him to. She wanted him concentrating on the game and not thinking about her. She wanted the Ice to win.

And when they did, shutting out Denver, she and Liz hugged and cheered along with everyone else in the packed arena. They waited until the crowds thinned, then went to wait on Ty outside the locker room.

"He's so mad at me," Jenna said, chewing on a fingernail. "I don't know if he'll even talk to me."

"You have to open the dialogue door somewhere. This is where you start."

The media kept them awhile, so Jenna paced back and forth, distracting herself by talking to a few of the wives and girlfriends of the players. Renee had texted her and asked her to give Eddie a big congratulatory hug for her since she was working at the bar tonight and couldn't be at the game. The two of them had recently become exclusive, and Jenna was happy for both of them. They made a cute couple. So when Eddie came out of the locker room, she congratulated him and gave him Renee's hug.

"I'm headed over to the bar now," Eddie said with a wide grin. "Hope Malcolm's got those steaks fired up."

She laughed. "You know he will. And the first round for you guys is on me. I've already let my assistant manager know."

Eddie kissed her cheek. "You're awesome, Jenna."

Eddie took off once Victor came out, and the trail of players coming through the door only made her more nervous, especially when she didn't see Ty.

"He snuck out another way. He's avoiding me."

Liz rolled her eyes. "There is no other way. He didn't sneak out. See? Here he is now."

Oh, shit. He walked out the door and suddenly she had no idea what she was going to say. Fortunately, Liz got to him first, throwing her arms around him and hugging him.

"It's a damn good thing you won tonight," Liz told him. "I've got potential product endorsement deals on the line, so the further you go in the playoffs, the more deals and more money I can get for you."

"Yeah, it's the only thing on my mind when I take the ice," he said.

"I'm sure it is." She winked, then said, "Well, I've got to talk to the big boss for a few minutes, so if you two will excuse me."

Liz made a discreet exit, leaving her alone with Ty, who leveled an expressionless stare her way.

It was her play.

"Great game tonight."

"Thanks. Surprised to see you here."

"Really? I don't know why. I wanted to support you and the team."

"Uh-huh."

"And . . . I wanted a few minutes alone with you so we could talk."

"I think we said it all the other night, Jenna. Not much to talk about. I'm tired after the game tonight."

"I understand. We both said a lot of things the other night, but we need to talk. I need to tell you a few things."

He laughed, the sarcasm clear. "There's more than what you already said?"

"I deserved that. But it's not what you think."

"Okay. Spill it."

"Not here. Come with me."

"I don't think that's a good idea."

She laid a hand on his arm. "Ty, please. I know you don't owe me anything. Not after the way I acted the other night. But if you'll just give me an hour . . ."

She hoped and prayed he wouldn't judge her on the last words she'd said to him the other night, that he'd give her a chance.

"Fine. You've got an hour. I've got to grab my gear in the locker room and meet with my coach for a few minutes. I'll meet you at your place when I'm done."

"Okay. Thanks."

She left and found Liz, who was chatting with the Ice owner, so she stayed in the background until she finished up.

"How did it go?" Liz asked as they made their way to the parking lot.

"He's still angry with me. I can tell. But he did agree to give me an hour."

"That's because he loves you."

Her heart squeezed. "Does he? His voice was so flat. No emotion in it at all."

They got into the car and buckled their seatbelts and Liz drove off in her usual crazy manner, but gave Jenna a quick glance. "Honey, you hurt him and men don't take that well. They shove their emotions deep inside where you can't hurt them again. In many ways they're a lot like women, though they'd deny that."

Jenna's lips curved. "Maybe you're right."

"I am right. They like to pretend they're tough and impervious to pain. Physically that might be true, but emotionally they can be hurt just like we can. Especially by someone they care about."

"I hurt him. I know that. I have to fix it."

Liz squeezed her hand. "Then go do that and win back your man. I need him in top shape for the playoffs."

Liz dropped her off and she hurried to get ready, nervous as hell about what was going to happen.

When Ty pulled up in front of the condo, she ran outside.

He got out of the car, but she already had her keys in her hand.

He frowned. "What's up?"

"We need to take a drive."

"Why?"

"Because I need to show you something."

"Jenna, I don't have time for this."

What he meant was he didn't want to go. She had to convince him. This was make it or break it for her. "Make time. Please. It won't take long."

He shrugged. "Fine."

He got into her car and she drove off. The silence was unnerving, but she knew idle conversation would be useless, so she used the time to prepare what she was going to say to him when they got there. She played it over and over in her head and by the time she pulled in front of the building, she thought she had it ready.

"What the fuck is this?"

What she couldn't plan for was Ty's response.

She got out of the car and keyed in the code she'd gotten from the real estate manager she'd called yesterday. Just as Ty had done, she'd asked for privacy to look over the building, telling him she was Ty's business partner and she wanted another look at the place. Okay, she lied, but it worked. She went inside, assuming he'd be curious enough to follow. If he wasn't, if he stayed in the car, her plan to make this all up to him would be ruined.

And she didn't have a Plan B. She probably should have come up with a Plan B.

She walked into the space and stood in the center, smiling as plans began to formulate. She'd made notes, started to set up floor plans, but none of it would make sense without Ty.

"Why did you bring me here?"

She turned to face him, her heart pounding so hard all she could hear was her own blood rushing in her ears. She took a deep breath to calm herself down, and prepared to face the music.

She took a step toward him, and stopped. "You were right. I like this place. It's an ideal location, the square footage is perfect, and the price is in the range I can afford. You have a good eye for real estate. I like your vision of what the club could look like."

He didn't answer. He wasn't going to make this easy for her. She didn't deserve for it to be easy. Not after the terrible things she'd said to him, how she'd thrown his surprise back in his face.

"I'd like to put the stage over on this side, though. With the windows on the other side, it'll let more light in the summer, and open up these walls to put a patio outside."

Still no reply. His hands were jammed so far into his coat pockets she was surprised he hadn't torn a hole in them.

"But I don't want to do this alone." She shuddered in her next breath, squeezing back the tears that threatened to fall. "I always thought I was tough and independent, that I could do everything alone. Turns out I'm not as tough as I'd like to think I am, and since I met you, being alone sucks."

She waited, her legs shaking so hard she was afraid she was going to crumple to the ground.

"You don't have to do it alone," he finally said. "You didn't have to do it alone. You were never alone and haven't been since we met. Not once."

The tears slipped out and ran down her cheeks. She nodded, taking another step toward him. "I know. I know that now. But I was afraid."

"Yeah, I know."

"I sang in front of my parents and my brothers."

He took a step toward her, a single step that made hope sing inside her.

"How did that go?"

"They loved my voice. I told them I wanted to open another Riley's—a music club—and that I didn't want to manage the sports bar anymore."

"What did they say?"

"They said I should have told them about my dreams years ago. You were right. All I had to do was muster up a little courage."

"There's nothing you can't do if you have a little faith in yourself."

"I'm scared, Ty. You were right. I'm afraid to fail."

He stopped in front of her. "It's okay to be afraid to fail. Everyone is, and if they say they aren't they're full of shit. But just because you're afraid doesn't mean you shouldn't try."

She laid her hands on his chest, and the reassuring beat of his heart gave her the courage she needed. "I never wanted a hockey player, but by God I fell in love with one, and I'm not about to let him go no matter how afraid I am of love."

He used his thumb to swipe at the tears on her cheek. "I'm afraid too, babe, and not much of anything scares me. Well, one thing does scare me."

She sniffled. "Yeah? What's that?"

"The thought of living without you."

She sobbed and fell into his arms. He pulled her against him and held her, kissed her hair and rubbed her back as she cried.

"I love you, Jenna."

That only made her cry harder. "I love you, too. I'm so sorry." She pulled back so he could see her face. "I'm sorry for everything I said. I want you to push me when I need it. I want you by my side, and no, I don't ever want to do this alone. I need you in my life, every step of the way. Without you I would never have gotten this far, would have never had the courage to go to that club and sing. I owe every step I've taken to you because you pushed me past the fear. God, I love you for that. And I hope you'll forgive me."

He kissed the tears on her cheeks, then brushed his lips across hers. "That's what love is all about, babe. Forgiveness. I watched my parents make a lot of mistakes in their marriage, and I'm bound and determined to never make the same mistakes in mine."

Her eyes widened. "What?"

"When I brought you here that first night, my intention was to show you the space, and if you liked it I was going to tell you I had put money down on it. I was going to buy it."

"What?" she asked again.

"I want to marry you, Jenna. And marriage means a partnership. A partnership means we take the good and the bad. I'm going to push you to be the best singer you can be, to chase your dreams. And you're going to push me to be the best hockey player I can be. Sometimes we're going to fight, but we're never going to give up on each other."

She put her fingers to her lips. "You're proposing to me."

"Yeah. I didn't buy you a ring, because in a partnership you should have what you want and I'm not presumptuous like that. We'll pick one out together."

Because he knew her. He really knew her.

"Just a wedding band would be nice. One of those pretty, slim ones with the diamonds."

"Whatever you want. But does that mean you say yes?"

She nodded, unable to stop the flow of tears. "Yes. Oh, hell yes. I love you. Of course I'll marry you. But are you sure you want to put up with me?"

He laughed. "'Til death do us part. And believe me when I tell you this, Jenna. When I walked out on you before, I was hurt and angry and needed some space, but I never had any intention of letting you go. I'm not my parents and I don't give up that easily. I'm in this forever."

She nodded. "So am I. I'll fight for you—for us—no matter what. We Rileys never give up."

Tyler had no idea love could feel like this—this overwhelming urge to protect, to want someone so badly they could hurt you. But he also knew he never had any intention of walking away from Jenna. If she hadn't come to him, he would have gone to her in a few days and told her he wasn't giving up on her.

He'd never give up on her.

Now all he wanted to do was show her how much he loved her.

"Do you have some tissues in that purse?" he asked as he held her while she finished crying.

She dug them out, blew her nose, and laughed. "I don't make the prettiest picture of a woman you wanted to propose to, do I? My nose is red and runny and my eyes probably look like something out of a horror movie."

He looked at her face. She was beautiful. "You're right. I should reconsider."

She punched his arm. "Smart-ass. You're going to be waking up to bedhead and this face for the rest of your life."

"This was not in the disclosure agreement."

"And you are not funny."

"Yes, I am." He drew her against him and kissed her. "That's one of the reasons you love me."

She threaded her arms around inside his coat and snuggled against him. "You're right. You make me laugh."

"Is that all I do for you?"

"No. You do a lot of things for me."

He looked around at the space, already envisioning the future, what this place would look like when it was fixed up. "You know, now that you've decided this is the place for you, we should officially christen it."

She tilted her head back to look at him. "In what way?"

"You know what way." He shrugged his coat off and laid it on top of the bar. "I've always wanted to have you on top of the bar."

"One of these days we're going to have to do it in the bed."

He turned to her and held out his hand. "What fun would that be?"

She followed him to the bar. "You're right. We'll do it in the bed when we're old and our bones are creaky."

He laughed. "I doubt that."

"What? That we'll ever be old and creaky?"

He pulled her coat off and slid his hands down her arms. "No, that we'll be doing it in the bed then, either."

When he kissed her, she sighed against his lips.

Yeah, he knew the feeling.

It was fucking perfect again, because she was back in his arms again. He moved his hands over her body, roaming all over as if he hadn't felt her against him in years rather than days.

He'd missed her. Being without her left a void in his life, an emptiness he never wanted to feel again.

Torn between wanting to linger and wanting to be inside her, he pressed his lips to her neck and inhaled her scent, then dragged his tongue across her throat, loving her shuddering response. She clutched his shoulders and fell against him, limp as he pulled down her loose sweater and pressed kisses to her collarbone and the swell of her breasts.

He scooped her up in his arms and sat her on top of the old bar.

"When we get this place fixed up," he said as he pulled off her shoes and socks, "I'm going to put you on the shiny new bar and make love to you again. And on the stage, too."

She smiled down at him, brushed his hair away from his eyes. He undid the clasp on her jeans and pulled them off her hips, drew them down her legs, then swept his hands up, loving the silkiness of her skin. His hands were scarred and rough, so different from her buttery soft body. But she didn't seem to mind his hands, especially when he palmed her sex through her panties.

She gasped and arched against him, clutching his coat in her fingers when he rubbed her pussy back and forth, using the barrier of the silk to tease her. She was wet, her musky sweet scent making his dick throb.

He pulled her legs to the edge of the bar and pressed his nose against her panties, drowning in her fragrance. He drew her panties aside and licked her, and she moaned, leaning her palms down on the bar for support as she thrust her pussy against his face.

One of the things he loved most about Jenna was her pure joy in lovemaking. She had no inhibitions, and she loved to come. And he loved giving her an orgasm, loved seeing her face when she let go.

He swiped his tongue over her clit, toying with the piercing before enveloping the bud between his lips and sucking on it. He palmed his cock, massaging it and giving it a squeeze as he slid his tongue between Jenna's plump pussy lips. Her salty sweet flavor made his cock tighten. Just the thought of sliding between those soft lips of hers making him want to unzip his pants and thrust inside her.

He lapped her pussy and clit up and down until she squirmed

against him, until he knew she was ready to come. Then he applied pressure to her clit and she let go, crying out with wild abandon and shoving her pussy against his face. He brought her down easy, kissing her thighs and belly before climbing up onto one of the old chairs and unzipping his pants.

He slid her panties down her legs and shoved them in his pocket, then went for a condom. She stilled his hand.

"No. No condoms anymore. It's just you and me, now and forever."

"You sure?"

"Yes. I want to feel you in me."

His cock quivered at the thought of feeling her silky wetness rounding him. That one night had been heaven. "I want that. I want you, just you, wrapped around my cock."

"Make love to me."

He pulled her off the bar and onto his lap. She straddled him and he watched his cock disappear into her pussy. She planted her feet on either side of the slats of the chair and rose up, then down on him.

"Oh, babe, you feel so good." He tangled his fingers in her hair and brought her mouth to his for a deep, penetrating kiss. He slid his tongue inside and fucked her mouth with it the same way he fucked her pussy, with long, deliberate strokes.

She whimpered against his mouth, held on to his shoulders, and lifted, then slid down, grinding against his cock in a way that made him groan.

His balls were on fire, quivering in anticipation of erupting inside her.

Buried deep like this, he pulled back, looked into the beautiful blue depths of her eyes, watched her lids partially close as her pussy clenched around his cock, all that wet heat surrounding him.

And when she quickened the pace, rocking back and forth and grinding against him, he was going to lose it.

"Come for me, Jenna," he whispered, licking her earlobe as he held on to her butt and pulled her tighter against him, grinding himself along her clit.

"Oh, God, yes, that's going to make me come so hard," she said.

When she dug her fingernails into his shoulders, he knew she was ready, and he thrust deep, holding her there while she fell apart. He felt her, felt her walls convulse around him as she came. She bucked against him in a wild frenzy as her climax tore her apart.

He couldn't hold back as the roaring freight train of his orgasm slammed into him. He jettisoned his come inside her, emptying everything he had and holding her tight while he poured over and over until there was nothing left.

Christ, that had been intense. It had always been that way with Jenna, and now that he held her again, it was as if the world had turned right side up again, and everything that had been wrong had been corrected. Something hadn't been right ever since that night he'd walked out on her. He'd pushed it all to the back of his mind because he'd had to concentrate on playing hockey, but his first thought had always been Jenna.

Work would always be work, but his first priority would always be the woman he loved, the woman he intended to make a life with. And now that he held her again, now that he could breathe in that unique scent that made her who she was, he realized he'd never be whole without her. That's what love was. He'd spent his whole adult life wondering what love was about, and now he knew. He'd never chased it, never wanted it, but it had found him anyway.

He lifted her off him and set her on the bar.

"Your coat," she said.

"Is fine. I want to look at you. Your body is flush and pink and beautiful."

He traced his tongue between her sex and hip.

She giggled. "What are you doing?"

"I think right here would be a perfect spot."

"For what?"

"Your next tattoo. I can envision a script pattern."

"Of?"

"My name, of course. Right near my favorite spot of your body."

She was quiet for a few seconds, then said, "Done."

He lifted his head. "Yeah?"

"Of course, as long as you get *Jenna* tattooed on your arm."

"You got it. Make an appointment with your tattoo guy next week. I want your name on me."

"Really? You'd do that?"

He stood. "I'm going to marry you, Jenna. I wasn't kidding about the forever part."

She leaned forward, threw her arms around him, and kissed him, then searched his face. "But ink really is forever."

"And so am I."

Jenna sighed as she looked down at Ty, reading the truth on his face.

This was all real. Him, the new club, her new life.

Facing her fears had given her some of the greatest gifts, the most important one this amazing man.

She'd put all her dreams on hold for so long. But now, thanks to Ty, his love, and a lot of courage, all her dreams were coming true.

COLE RILEY HAD BUILT HIS REPUTATION ON BEING tough, especially on the football field. He didn't yield, and when he had the ball in his hands, there was only one thing on his mind—the end zone. He was hard-headed and single-minded, and he liked to win.

Same thing with women—once he had a target in mind, he went for it until he scored.

So even though this was a target-rich environment, and more than half the sexy women at the party tonight were giving him the once-over, he hadn't hooked up with anyone in the few hours he'd been here.

Which was unusual for him. He liked the ladies. The ladies liked him. No ego on his part, he just enjoyed women. He loved being around them. They were sweet, fun to be with, they smelled great, and they made him feel good. There was nothing bad about that. In return, he showed them a good time, spent money on them, and never lied to them or tried to be anything other than who he was.

Women liked honest men. His mother would slap him sideways if he ever lied to a woman. He might be a little on the wild side, but he wasn't dishonest. He never promised a woman anything he wasn't willing to deliver.

Which meant he steered clear of women looking to hook a husband. He gravitated toward the party girls, like the hot redhead and the statuesque brunette who'd been hovering near his radar all night. Those were the women who wanted to have the same kind of no-strings-attached fun he did.

So why did his focus keep drifting to the cool blonde sitting all by herself at a table in the corner? She wasn't his type at all. She wasn't wearing a skin-tight spandex dress that showed off a lot of tits and ass. She wore a simple, short-sleeved dress that went to her knees, though she did have killer legs—legs he'd like to see a lot more of. She just wasn't showing off her assets.

She was beautiful, sure, with a face that would stop traffic. And the way she was dressed screamed money and high society. Maybe she was related to the team owner. But he hadn't seen anyone come within ten feet of the table in the past two hours. She was no wall-flower, but she wasn't giving off vibes that said "Come talk to me."

Wasn't his problem. He didn't know her and he intended to have fun tonight. Team parties were always a blast, and media free. He could hang out with his new teammates, down a few drinks, chill with the ladies, and just have a good time.

There were plenty of women here to have the kind of fun he was looking for. The blonde wasn't the right type. He could tell from the rigid set to her shoulders and the stick-up-her-ass way she sat that she wasn't a partier. She surveyed the room and gave off definite "keep the fuck away from me" signals, which was likely why no one approached her.

Still, he hated seeing anyone sitting alone. He went up to the bar and nudged Grant Cassidy, the Traders quarterback.

Grant turned, then nodded. "Hey, Riley. What's up?"

"Do you have any idea who that blonde is sitting by herself over in the corner?"

Grant followed the motion of Cole's head, then frowned. "No. Who is she?"

"No idea. I figured you know everyone on the team. Is she related to the owner?"

Grant shook his head. "Ted Miller's daughter is a brunette. And she isn't here tonight. I have no idea who the blonde is. She looks mean."

Cole laughed. "That's what I thought, too."

He should ignore her and concentrate on the hot brunette or the sexy redhead. But for some reason the lonely blonde in the corner kept grabbing his attention and wouldn't let go.

Maybe it was because she kept looking at him. Not in the way that other women looked at him—the take-me-home-with-you-tonight look. Her look was different. Cool and assessing, an occasional brief glance and then she'd look away.

He wasn't a game player. Maybe she was.

This was bullshit. He pushed off the bar and headed her way. She could throw off all the stay-away signals she wanted, but he was curious now. Someone that beautiful was alone for a reason.

He stopped at her table and her gaze lifted, slowly studying him. She didn't smile, but she didn't frown, either.

"You here alone?" he asked.

"Yes, I am."

Southern accent. It fit her. She was all peaches-and-cream complexion, full lips, and the prettiest eyes . . . like whiskey.

He slid his hand out. "I'm Cole Riley, wide receiver with the Traders."

She slipped her hand in his and finally gave him a smile, the kind of smile that made a man glad to be a man.

"Hello, Cole. I'm Savannah Brooks. Won't you sit down?"

Bingo.

LORD HAVE MERCY, BUT COLE RILEY'S PHOTOS AND videos did not do the man justice.

In person he made a woman go weak in the knees. Savannah was glad she was sitting down, because now she understood the mystique she'd read about in the tabloids and all the articles about him as a lady-killer.

She certainly felt the heart palpitations when he slid his very large hand in hers and graced her with one look of his drop-dead-sexy gray blue eyes. When he looked at you it was as if everyone else in the room fell away, and you were the only woman on earth. Which she knew wasn't true, because she'd studied him all night long, and there were at least twenty women focused on him like they were starving and he was meat.

He wasn't meaty at all. He was perfect and absolutely delicious. About six-foot one, two hundred and fifteen pounds of sex on a stick would be her guess.

If she were out scouting for a man, which she most certainly wasn't, she'd pick him out of a crowd. He stood out, with his inky black hair and gorgeous, well-toned muscled body, even if he did wear his hair a little long and shaggy. There was a certain presence to him. Arrogance, maybe, though she was surprised after reading his file that he wasn't standing on top of the bar or involved in a brawl or wrapped around two or three women in a dark corner.

Maybe the media had blown his off-the-field antics out of proportion. Maybe his reputation was more hype than anything.

"So, Savannah Brooks. Why are you sitting here all alone?"

"I'm observing."

He cocked a brow, his defenses obviously up as he bent forward, perched on the edge of the chair like he was ready to take flight. "You're not a reporter, are you?"

She smiled at him. "No. I'm definitely not a reporter."

He relaxed and leaned back against the chair, stretching his long legs out in front of him. "Okay, then."

"You don't like reporters."

"Nope."

"And why is that?"

"They lie."

"About you."

"All the damn time."

"What kind of lies have they told about you?"

"I don't want to talk about me. Let's talk about you. You have a beautiful southern accent, Savannah. Where are you from?"

Not at all what she'd read about him. That he was an egomaniac, that every conversation centered around him, his stats, his prowess in the bedroom, that he hit on women as a second career, pressuring them to go home with him.

Maybe the media did lie.

"I'm originally from Atlanta."

"But you don't live there now."

"No."

He smiled when she didn't offer any more information. He had an amazing, off-kilter smile that made her stomach flutter. She had to stop being such a girl about him. He might be flirting but she was here on business.

"Do you want me to guess?"

"Not at all. I live in Los Angeles."

"You don't look like the L.A. type."

She arched a brow. "There's an L.A. type?"

"Yeah. And you're not it. You're a Georgia peach. All southern re-fined, laid-back beauty. Not fast paced, get famous and noticed L.A."

"I have many clients in Los Angeles. That's why I live out there."

"But you travel—for your job? Is that why you're gone a lot?"

He listened. A good quality. "Yes."

"And what do you do for a living, Savannah?"

"I'm a consultant."

"Broad concept. What kind of consultant?"

"An image consultant."

"What does an image consultant do?"

"I assist clients who need help either boosting their image or changing it."

"That must be an interesting job."

"I love my work. To have a positive impact on people's lives is very rewarding."

He grinned. "Good for you."

"And what about your job, Cole?"

"I've played football since I was a kid. To be able to do this for a living? It's a dream come true. I'm very grateful."

He was poised, confident and polite. Why didn't he come across like this in interviews? Why was he portrayed in such a negative light? There was more to Cole Riley than what she'd read about in his file.

"Would you like a drink, Savannah?"

"No, I'm fine with the sparkling water, thank you."

"Okay. You still haven't told me what you're doing at this shindig."

"I'm meeting a new client."

His eyes widened. "Yeah? About to redo someone's image?"

"As a matter of fact, I am."

"Huh. I wonder who screwed up and needs a makeover." He looked around the room, studying all the players in attendance. "Couldn't be our star quarterback. He eats, drinks and pisses charm."

She resisted the laugh. It wouldn't be appropriate.

He looked at her, then around the room again, zeroing in on a group of players clustered in the middle of the room. "It's Moose Clements, isn't it? That guy couldn't give a decent interview if you gave him a personality implant. Or maybe Kenny Lawton, the Traders other wide receiver. You want to talk about attitude issues? That guy has serious problems. He's your new client, isn't he?"

She stood, smoothed out her dress. "Unfortunately, it's time for me to go. It was very nice meeting you, Cole."

"You're leaving?"

"I'm afraid so."

He grabbed her hand. "Wait."

She paused.

"I want to see you again."

"Oh, you will." She smiled as she walked out of the room. This was going to be very interesting.

COLE WATCHED SAVANNAH WALK AWAY, STRUCK BY HER elegant beauty. Definitely no stick up her ass. She walked with a slight sway to her hips—nothing obvious or attention grabbing about her, but she was all woman.

And dammit, he'd just stood there like a tongue-tied teenager and let her get away.

He should have gotten her number, or asked her out. Instead, he'd acted brain dead.

That wasn't his style. He moved to go after her, but a hand on his arm stopped him. He turned to see his agent, Elizabeth Darnell, looking up at him.

He frowned. "Liz. What are you doing here?"

"We need to talk."

He frowned and looked at the door. "Not now."

"Definitely now. Did you forget the meeting we agreed to?"

He might have forgotten, or maybe ignored Liz's edict that they had some important business to talk about tonight. Since he'd signed with her a few months ago, there'd been a lot of orders. He didn't like being given orders.

"Come on, Liz. We're at a party."

"You have plenty of time to party. And we had an agreement when I signed you," she said, giving him that steely eyed gaze. "Remember?"

"Yeah, yeah. I remember."

"Good. Then let's go."

"We're leaving?"

"Just across the hall. It's too noisy in here. When we're finished you can get back to the party."

Hopefully it wouldn't take long. Maybe Savannah was still around somewhere and he could hook up with her again.

Elizabeth led him to a room across the hall. It was a small meeting room with rows of tables.

"Have a seat."

"I'd rather stand."

She gave him the look, the one that meant she was going to argue until she won. He was just as stubborn, but time was important right now, so he grabbed a chair, spun it around and straddled it.

"What did I do now?"

"Tonight? Nothing so far. But I want to talk about your attitude."

He rolled his eyes. "That's what you wanted to meet about tonight? We've already had this discussion."

"I know. And we're going to talk about it again. The hometown crowd likes a winner. They also like someone who isn't constantly in the tabloids for an overindulgence of partying, for treading on his fellow players like they're the shit beneath his Nikes, for running up more speeding tickets than the national debt and for throwing very expensive paparazzi cameras into a fountain. And if that wasn't bad enough, you followed it up with a punch to the guy's jaw."

"Hey, he shoved the fucking camera in my face. Not just close to my face, but *in* my face. What was I supposed to do—say 'Cheese' and smile for him?"

"Yes. That's exactly what you were supposed to do. Or turn around and walk away. You need to learn to control your temper and be taught how to behave in public. You need some lessons on how to interact with the media."

Cole snorted. "I think I know how to handle myself just fine."

Liz tapped her foot, though how she managed to stay upright on those five-inch heels was beyond him.

"And if you recall, when I agreed to take you on as a client—mainly because no other agent wanted to be within five miles of you—and I managed to somehow get you signed with St. Louis, you agreed to do anything I asked of you."

He thought that meant the slightly painful salary cut he had to take. At least Liz was savvy enough to put performance bonuses in the contract. He'd show them he wasn't washed up. He was still an ass kicker and this season would prove it. "I did what you asked, didn't I?"

"Oh, the salary cut was just the beginning, Cole. Your image is toast. You know it, I know it, and Coach Tallarino knows it. If the coach wasn't such a good friend of your cousin Mick—and if he didn't owe me a few dozen favors, I guarantee you wouldn't have this job."

Cole wasn't buying it. He'd been signed because he had talent and plenty of it. Agents liked to make threats to keep their players in line. He knew how this game was played.

"The clock is ticking. It's only a matter of time before no one will touch you, no matter how good you are on the field. You're a PR nightmare."

He stood and faced Liz, doing exactly what she said he wasn't capable of. He took a deep breath and tried to keep his temper under control. "I'm a damn good wide receiver."

"That might be true, but until you stop the nonsense off the field and prove to the coach, your team, the media, and the general public that you've grown up and your bad-boy days are over, it doesn't matter if you score ten touchdowns a game. Reputation is everything in football."

He blew out a sigh. Why couldn't his stats be enough? What difference did it make what he did during his off hours? So he liked to party a little. So what? His bad rep was the media's fault anyway. He was thirty years old and still at the top of his game. After six years in the NFL, he'd damn well earned the right to relax and enjoy life.

But yeah. PR. He understood. And if he had to toe the line for a while until he got in the good graces of the fans and the coach, that's what he'd do.

"What do you want me to do?"

"I'm bringing in someone to help you."

He frowned "Who?"

The door opened and Savannah walked in. Relieved to see her, Cole grinned, glad he hadn't lost the opportunity to spend more time with her.

"Hey. I was wondering where you'd wandered off to," he said.

"You two know each other?" Liz asked.

"Yeah. We met earlier." Cole turned to Liz and frowned. "You know Savannah?"

Liz's lips lifted. "As a matter of fact I do. And you're going to get to know her a lot better. Savannah is your new image consultant."

He pivoted and looked at Savannah, who gave him a serene smile.

"*My* image consultant? What the fuck?"